BEYOND
fragile
BOUNDARIES

Jill Tipping

First published in Great Britain in 2012
by Kavanagh Tipping Publishing,
www.jilltipping.co.uk

ISBN: 978-1-906546-12-0

for Valerie

JULY 2002

His eyes were bloodshot and bulbous with rage; a fine layer of sweat covered his top lip – more to do with alcohol than the heat of the day. Stepping into the room, he stood just inches away from the young man. They were of equal height but the young one had not been drinking. Despite this advantage, he was intimidated, backing away with his hands held up defensively.

'You don't understand,' he protested.

'Oh, trust me, I understand perfectly! Who the hell do you think you are, strutting around the place half-naked, flexing your muscles? You like having women falling at your feet, don't you? It's a challenge, isn't it? Something to laugh about with your mates in the pub. Everything about you smacks of cheap bravado. You're nothing, do you hear? You really are *just a pretty face*!' He paused, noticing the young man begin to bristle and sensing strong fists beginning to clench. He knew he was no physical match for this young pup. He turned on his heel and made for the door. As he did so, he threw a last comment over his shoulder: 'I should have finished you off in that alley.'

Three months earlier ...

She switched off the engine and left the radio playing. Radio 4's PM was just coming to an end as she listened, without really hearing, Eddie Mair's final words for that day. She allowed her mind to drift, the heat in the car enveloping her like a soft blanket; an immense, heavy tiredness suddenly swept over her; she felt sad, disappointed, depressed. She found herself staring at the sleek, silver bonnet of the executive car she had coveted for so long. Well here she was, sitting in it, the new car smell still there, filling her nostrils, as if to push confirmation of her success further into her subconscious. She'd done it. But yet ...

Moments passed as she continued to stare ahead with unseeing eyes, then reality kicked in and she gave her head a little shake. How ridiculous! She had almost everything she had ever wanted: great business, two amazing kids, a wonderful home, a wardrobe full of smart clothes. At thirty seven years old, Carla Trelawny knew what success felt like: she lived it on a daily basis. She also knew what this creeping feeling of darkness was: it was cold, stark, unabridged loneliness – simple as that. With a sigh, she grabbed her Gucci handbag from the passenger seat, withdrew the keys from the ignition and wearily climbed out of the car. As she walked towards the front door, even the satisfying 'bleep' of the automatic car lock could not raise her spirits, for she was remembering what used to be: a strong pair of arms on the other side of that door waiting to welcome her home; his big, capable hands taking her coat, pouring her a drink. The lack of those arms made her ache inside. At times, she could see him coming up the hallway towards her, tea towel thrown casually over one shoulder, smiling eyes, the look that only two people in love share, a touch, the brush of a kiss with the promise of a noisy, family dinner ahead; the smell of stew on the hob; the radio burbling away to no one on the window ledge; the Times crossword lying on the table, half completed; work boots untidily abandoned by the back door: normal, everyday stuff – how she missed it.

She opened the door and stepped into the empty hall. Her throat tightened with a now familiar contraction and she crumpled, allowing herself, just once more, to sit on the stairs and wail like a small child, to just keep repeating his name, over and over, to let her eyes stream and her nose run, smudging and blotching her carefully applied makeup. Gareth: her beautiful, wholesome, perfect soul mate of a husband, her best friend – gone. There one minute. Gone the next. How could that be? So vital, and then suddenly so very cold and still. It had been eighteen months since he had been hit by a car while out on a Sunday morning cycle ride, and killed instantly, but the unfairness strangled her as she allowed wave upon wave of helpless despair to wash over her and consume her, body and soul.

A snuffling, scratching sound brought her slowly back into her life. After a few shuddering, last ditch sobs, she got up and kicked off her shoes like a bad tempered little girl, then padded off into the kitchen to greet the ever faithful, ever there and ever wet-nosed Banjo. Using his instinctive emotional intelligence, he looked up lovingly into Carla's tear-stained face and wagged his tail ferociously, indicating his support and faithfulness.

'Hello, boy. You're always there for me, aren't you? How's your day been, poochy? Time for a bit of loving?' Sitting down, she took his floppy, Springer spaniel ears in her hands and rubbed and scratched them, just how he liked it. 'Come on, boy, let's get some tea.' Taking tinned meat and biscuits out of the cupboard, she began to prepare Banjo's food, finding the normal, mundane task extremely soothing, as though her busy hands kept her mind from betraying her with sad thoughts.

Putting his dish on the floor, she checked her watch. 'Shit! Late!' With renewed energy she shot up the stairs, two at a time, and into her bedroom. Her mind flitted over the fact that it was now always as she had left it: no discarded clothes on the chair; no books and papers scattered over the floor. She smiled. I used to find that so irritating, she thought to herself. What I would give to see it now!

Quickly shedding her navy blue jacket, cream shift dress and tights, she pulled out a pair of jogging pants and one of Gareth's old sweatshirts, not caring that it was huge on her; it brought her a measure of comfort. Snug walking socks followed. There was something about changing from office clothes into cosy gear that she loved, and today was no exception. Her spirits started to lift a bit. A good sobbing session was very cathartic, she decided, as she looked at herself in the mirror and then looked more closely at her blotchy face. What a mess! Dashing into the bathroom, she applied cleanser, removed what was left of the day's make up and splashed her face with cold water. Re-checking it in the mirror she felt better; an English rose complexion and good bone structure were reflected back at her and she bared her slightly crooked teeth in a smile before giving herself an appreciative nod. 'You'll do.'

Grabbing the washing basket, she hurried back down the stairs, picked out the dark coloured clothes and pushed them into the ever-ready, gaping mouth of the washing machine. Quickly adding detergent and conditioner, she switched on the machine and turned to Banjo, who was sitting watching her from his bed by the kitchen radiator. 'Come on, let's go and get the boys, Banjo. Where's your lead?'

He jumped up and sped past her to the back door to stand staring at her pink-spotted wellies. He knew the routine.

She walked the short distance to her mother's house, feeling washed out but much more calm and they spent some time chatting while her boys, Stefan and Bryn, finished watching a Mr Bean video – one of their favourites and bought especially for them by their grandmother. Not only had Carla's mum been her rock during the past months, but loosing Carla's dad a few years earlier to a sudden heart attack had also given her some experience of acute grief.

'You're coping with everything really well, Carla,' she said, 'but I'm worried that you're working too hard.'

'But, Mum, I need it right now. And anyway, you know I love it and I've always worked long hours. That's how I got where I am.'

'I know, darling, but don't wear yourself out. You need time to allow the natural grief process to happen. You have to let it out.'

Carla threw back her head and laughed, open mouthed, at the complete irony. Ten year old Stefan looked up and scowled at his mother's outburst.

'Mum, if you had seen me an hour ago you would know you don't need to worry about that.' She continued to giggle and felt slightly light headed.

Her mother smiled at her daughter's laughing face and joined in. 'Well, that's good then. Why are we laughing?'

By this time, both women had tears in their eyes and were laughing in a manner bordering on hysteria. Bryn came up to Carla and leaned against her, concerned that the two most important people in his life, were, in fact, losing the plot. Carla stopped laughing and put her arm round him with a sigh, drawing him close to give him a cuddle.

On the way home with the boys and the ever bouncing Banjo, Carla thought about what her mother had said. Was she working too hard? Was that a covert way of saying that she was neglecting the boys? She hadn't really thought about that side of things. They talked about Gareth all the time: over evening meals, on walks in the park with Banjo at the weekends, on the way to school in the car; but was she doing enough for Stefan and Bryn?

She thought about her friends, and whose opinion on the subject she would trust. There was Verity, her long term friend from school, of course. Now what would she say? Carla could easily imagine it: *Carla you really should put the boys first. After all, they're only eight and ten – old enough to understand what's happened but not old enough to work out how to deal with their emotions. You should be there after school at the very least. Get some help at work so you can go part time.*

Hmmmm. Perhaps she wouldn't speak to Verity. As lovely as she was, she was also the epitome of mother earth: perfect mother, perfect house, perfect garden; she took her two kids to school (walking with the school walking bus, of course) and was back at the school gates at three thirty to collect them. Jo went to ballet classes and played the piano beautifully; Stuart went to art class and was shaping up to be a pretty good chess player. Stefan and Bryn, on the other hand, liked Mr Bean, climbing trees and getting muddy on the rugby pitch on Sunday mornings. Not so very accomplished! No, she wouldn't speak to Verity.

Back at home, after the boys had had their baths and she had read them a story before kissing them goodnight, she ate a bowl of cornflakes and poured herself a glass of wine. I know who I want to speak to, she thought, and checked her watch. Yes, she thought, picking up the phone, she should be home by now.

'Trudes! It's me!' she announced when the phone at the other end was answered.

'Carla, Carla, Carla! Darrrrling! How are you?'

'Oh, you know – surviving. Fancy popping round for a quick glass or six?'

'Darling, I'd love to, but I have a guest later.' Trudy lowered her voice conspiratorially. 'You know what I mean.'

'Oh, really? Damn! Who is it?'

'This one is called Georgio, if I remember correctly. He's been here a few times before. Great arse! Tight as steel, luvvy, I can tell you! Worth every penny!'

'Georgio the gigolo! Now I've heard it all. How much?'

'Seventy five quid. Does everything: licky, licky, fucky, fucky, the lot. Then what I really like about him, dear heart, is that he pisses off and leaves me alone to go to sleep. Brilliant! Like all the others.'

'Trudy, you are truly unbelievable! How do you do it?'

'Listen darling: I have a cleaner and a gardener; I have someone to service my car, someone to paint my house, and someone who cooks when I have dinner parties. So why shouldn't I have someone to satisfy my sexual urges? It makes perfect sense to me. Anyway, enough about me, tell me about you. Big G – and let me tell you, darling, he certainly is big – is due at nine thirty, so plenty of time for us to chat. How are you doing? Still wailing round the house like Miss Haversham?'

'Pretty much, to be honest. I did it again today: sat on the stairs and howled like a mad person.'

'Good. That's exactly what you should do. The reason that you're coping well, darling, is because you do allow yourself these moments. It has to be done. My god, you've suffered a tremendous loss! You deserve some feeling-sorry-for-myself time.'

'Mum thinks I'm working too much.'

'Well, that's bollocks for a start!'

'I'm wondering if it's her way of saying that she feels I'm neglecting the boys.'

'Also bollocks!'

'Maybe, but it's got me thinking that, well, they're missing a father figure – a male presence around the house.'

'Hire one in, then! Hang on, I'll have a look in Yellow Pages for 'Rent-a-Daddy' and we'll see what we come up with.'

'Oh Trudy! Really!' Carla laughed and sighed. 'I don't know, maybe she's right, but it's difficult providing what they need and having to be both parents now. Gareth was always home by four so he was there for them; now, Mum picks them up and what with my dad not being around anymore ….'

'They have male influences at the rugby club, don't they?'

'Yes, but just for a few hours a week on a Sunday. Adam and Craig are their coaches and they're great lads, but they're only in their late teens or early twenties themselves.'

'Does that matter? They're still males of the species. Why not rent one of them? As I said, I rent people when I want things done. I have the money, they have the skills. Voila! Everyone is happy.'

'Hmmm!'

'Oops, darling, must dash! I've just remembered I've got to pop to the shop for some chilled wine. It's Friday tomorrow, though. How do you fancy fish and chips at your place with the boys? My treat.'

'All right, my lovely. See you at six? I'll get home early. Ciao.'

'Ciao babe, and chin up – we'll make a plan. I'll bring my notepad. Mwah.' And she was gone.

Off to drink wine with a lover she hardly knows, thought Carla, who does, however, have 'buns of steel'! Nevertheless, maybe Trudy was right: not about the gigolo, that wasn't her style, but she could certainly be a bit more creative when it came to providing male company for the boys. A bath and a good book was the recipe for the rest of the evening, though.

*   *   *   *   *

'Adam! It's six thirty! You're gonna be late, love!'
Silence.
'Adam!'
'What? Okay Mum. I'm up.'
Turning away from the bottom of the stairs and making her way back into the kitchen, Joyce shook her head and smiled to herself. She wondered how many other mums across the country were, at this moment, bellowing up the stairs to sleepy teenagers. That was his last call, though: if he was late for work that was his look out; she was an advocate of learning from your own mistakes.

True to form, she heard the bathroom door close and the bolt slide noisily across. Adam was the only one in the house who ever bolted the door. He had done it since he was tall enough to reach. Funny lad.

Familiar noises of the shower being turned on and the water groaning in the pipes reached her ears as she sat down at the kitchen table, cradled her early morning cup of tea in her hands and looked out into the small back garden. The shed windows stared silently back at her, as they had for the past twenty years. She sighed. Somehow she felt older than her fifty two years. Hard physical work as a cleaner had put callouses on her palms and reddened her hands, but it went deeper than that. Fifty two! Over half a hundred, she thought. When did that happen? She felt constantly tired these days – world weary. That was it: world weary.

Aimlessly she turned the pages of the celebrity gossip magazine that was sharing the table with her. Beautiful faces smiled out at her with impossibly white teeth. The slim, tanned limbs of perfect people – royalty, pop stars, actors, business tycoons – covered every page. They're not real though, she told herself and closed the magazine, pushing it away in disgust. If she could have seen her face, at that moment, she would have seen bitterness, regret and a sense of a loss written all over it. For a full minute she stared listlessly at the floor with unfocused eyes, until the flushing of the upstairs toilet jolted her back into the moment and she automatically tutted as she noticed the crumbs and a piece of stray pasta on the tiled floor next to the cupboard plinths. Standing up, she bent down, picked up the pasta and with a hand supporting her aching back, shuffled over to the swing bin. Looking round the kitchen she sighed again: it had been like this for twenty five years now. How she would love a new kitchen with granite tops and posh new tiles, lights under the wall units and shiny stainless steel taps – like Mrs Trelawny's kitchen. Now that was a kitchen to behold and a joy to clean – her favourite job of the week.

Her thoughts strayed to Carla Trelawny: how sad to lose your husband at such a young age. And those poor little boys! No dad to take them to football matches or teach them how to fish. Terrible business. Gareth Trelawny had been a wonderful man: caring, strong, always cracking jokes. She had thought him amazing – and so sexy too! She smiled secretly to herself, remembering how she had fantasised about him. It felt naughty – disloyal – but wonderful. Gareth had been Joyce's imaginary lover in the moments that she had privately to herself. It was his face she had pictured as Tom pounded away for his weekly release. You couldn't call it making love, thought Joyce with a mental shrug. She was not sure that Tom had ever actually 'made love' to her. It had been that way for years. He just fucked.

She could hear him, still snoring upstairs. Thirty seven years they had been married, but had they ever really been lovers, or even childhood sweethearts? Hardly. After falling pregnant at nineteen, a quick trip to the registry office, a weekend in Brighton and then the toil of looking after a baby in a one bedroom flat in Margate had been her lot. She sat back down heavily and folded her arms across her chest. Thinking back, the children had been her life from very early on. Jacqueline and Simon had been everything to her, and with only two years between them she had been flat out. Whilst her friends were giggling about their latest sexual encounters, she had been experiencing sore breasts, sleepless nights and never ending trips to the laundrette.

She knew she wasn't being entirely fair to Tom, though. There had been happy times with him and she really couldn't complain, could she? She thought back to how good he was with the kids: strict, but steady – a good father. He was five years older than her and he had taken responsibility for getting a teenager pregnant – had 'done the right thing by her', as they said in those days.

Then there was her youngest, upstairs now, getting ready for work: her beautiful boy, Adam – her illicit secret, born from an agonisingly precious and all-too-brief passion eighteen years before.

Sighing, she started to prepare his lunch of peanut butter and salad cream sandwiches – not something she would choose, but he liked them. As usual he had not left himself enough time to make them himself, as his dad said he should. She cut them in half and packed them into an old ice cream container, washed out and kept specifically for the purpose. She then wedged the tub into the grey rucksack he kept by the back door. Next, she put the kettle on and set the table for Adam's breakfast. She enjoyed these times with him. As a teenager he wasn't overly communicative at that time of the morning, but she was content to just watch him as he ate his breakfast. Over the past four years she had watched him develop from a gawky, spotty youth into a stunning boy with features that melded together to give him the appearance of a man five years his senior. She knew she must make the most of these early mornings with her son because, before long, he would be snapped up by some lucky girl somewhere.

* * * * *

'Thanks, everyone, for all coming in early today; I appreciate it. Jonathan has kindly offered to pop out for coffees so are we all up for lattes this morning?' Carla scanned the faces of her account managing team, all seated around the boardroom table and all nodding, except Barry.

'Oh, Jonathan love, can you get me a green tea? Thanks, hon.'

Carla smiled to herself. So very Barry. 'Good,' she said to bring attention back to her. 'Getting straight on to the meeting then – you have your agendas in front of you – the main thing I want to discuss today is the new Triton account. This is a big one and we need to shine. It's the type of account I want us to be working on all the time, so let's pull out all the stops and be amazing. Yes?'

Bright, young faces grinned at Carla from around the room and she could not help stealing a few seconds to simply breathe in the atmosphere they created. How she loved them! They were dynamic, fun and at times exhausting, but she relished working with them. Not only were they good at what they did, but their energy made her feel alive and provided her with the distraction she needed to keep her from dwelling on the loss of her husband. That was all very well for her, she suddenly thought, but what about her two young sons.

All that morning, Trudy's words rattled incessantly around Carla's head: Rent-a-Daddy. Very funny – or was it? Maybe she should think about bringing someone in who could kick a ball around the garden with the boys, watch rubbish TV with them that she just considered a wall of noise, and teach them how to stand up for themselves. But who? She looked around the office as she pondered. Barry? Well, lovely as he was, she was not sure he even liked children; as a young, gay man, his pastimes seemed to be a bit on the risqué side. Her PA, Jonathan, was married with two children of his own; besides, he spent every work day catering to her every wish, so he was unlikely to want to spend his off time in her presence. She looked down at her desk and the Triton file that looked longingly back at her. Oh, well! Time to get on with work. She had put the thought out there. Something would turn up.

* * * * *

Little sympathy was coming Adam's way on Sunday morning as he slumped into a chair at the kitchen table, heavily hungover. A win the previous afternoon, which had put his rugby team at the top of their league, had culminated in a night out with his friends and too much celebrating. God, how he hated himself for it right now.

His father glanced over the top of the *Mail on Sunday*. 'Well, you're a bloody idiot, aren't you, son?'

'Pretty much, Dad. Thanks for that!'

His father huffed and went back to his newspaper. Stomach churning, Adam tried to distract himself by looking at the football results on the back page but his eyes wouldn't focus, so he sat with his elbows on the table and his aching head in his hands.

'Here you are, love,' said Joyce, placing two Aspirin, a pint of water and two pieces of lightly buttered toast in front of him.

Adam looked up at her gratefully and gave a weak smile. 'Thanks, Mum.'

At eighteen, the world was pretty much his oyster. He was fit, popular, had a ready smile and was not one for taking life too seriously, although he was aware that eventually he would have to make some decisions about what he was going to do in the future. He was working, temporarily, at a local farm and with the spring weather he was enjoying it: he liked being outside and he liked the physicality of the job; using his body to earn a wage suited him. But the farm had only ever been intended as a stopgap, and he had recently been thinking about possibly looking for something else quite soon.

Not this morning, however. Adam's most pressing problem as he cycled to the rugby club for the weekly coaching session, was keeping his breakfast down, which he realised he was not going to be able to do. After noisily leaving the contents of his stomach behind a hedge on the road side, he arrived at the club pale, shaking and slightly late.

'All right, mate? You look like shite!' commented Craig, his fellow coach who was already setting up, placing cones out in a shape ready for the first training session.

Adam waved him away and wordlessly made his way to the clubhouse. He walked into the first set of doors and then, feeling the bile start to rise in his throat, burst through the second set and bumped straight into Stefan's mother, Carla Trelawny, who was coming out with steaming cups of coffee in both hands.

'Oh, no! You clumsy oaf!' She stepped back, coffee all down the front of her Barbour jacket and on the floor.

'Oh god, sorry Carla! Can't stop! Gonna throw up!' He clasped a hand over his mouth and ran full pelt into the gents.

'Oh for god's sake!' Carla put the cups down and went back to the kitchen to get some paper towels.

Having dabbed inadequately at her jacket and cleaned up the floor, she was emerging from the kitchen with fresh coffees as Adam was coming out of the toilets.

'Sorry, Carla. You okay?'

'Yes. What's the matter? Are you okay yourself?'

'I think so. Self-inflicted I'm afraid.'

Carla raised her eyebrows and tutted. 'Idiot!' she smirked. 'Getting that plastered? Something I would never do!' Her smile broadened and she winked conspiratorially at him before turning away and going through the now open door.

A current of energy shot through Adam and his heart raced. He stood staring after Carla. What just happened? He watched her go down the steps, cross the tarmac, walk on to the pitch and over to the other mums. He just watched. He wasn't sure why. He just did.

'Stefan! You need to communicate! I want to hear you calling for the ball more. In fact, I want to hear all of you shouting out more, okay? Right, huddle!

Gather round! Come on boys, run in! Quickly! Quickly!' yelled Adam.

Sipping her coffee, Carla watched sympathetically as Adam then made a dash into the bushes to, yet again, she assumed, heave up into the shrubbery whatever was left in his stomach. Luckily, the boys didn't seem to notice. She thought that all Adam had probably wanted to do that morning was to stay home and spend most of the day under his duvet; she appreciated the fact that, despite feeling like hell, he had made the effort and was out there giving his all.

Observing him return to the pitch, she realised he was a stunning looking boy: tall, broad shouldered, with thick, sandy blonde hair and a weather beaten tan that made his startling blue eyes stand out even more. She was shocked to recognise pure animal lust rising up in her – something she had not imagined she would ever feel again. Yet, why not? In that moment, the awareness that she was a free agent and that her life had not ended at thirty seven was hitting home forcefully. She knew she was not interested in Trudy's game of gigolo hunting: it couldn't be just sex for Carla. She wanted the chase, that first look when eyes lock, the tease – no words but an exquisite promise of things to come. Tongues sparring. Undoing shirt buttons. The feeling of warm, male flesh under her fingers and the sound of a husky groan as skin touches skin. The act of giving and receiving pleasure.

Her eyes had followed him and she was momentarily horrified at the realisation that the object of her erotic fantasy was Adam Barnes – her friend Joyce's son! Good god, he was only eighteen. What was she thinking?

With training over, Adam was looking forward to handing back his band of ten year olds to their respective parents and spending the rest of the day nursing his hangover. He did think he should first apologise again to Carla, though. 'Hi,' he said, sheepishly waving, 'I hope you didn't get burnt earlier. I'm really sorry about bumping into you.'

Carla laughed and Adam drew in a sharp breath. What was it about this woman that was making him feel whatever it was he was feeling? He couldn't put a name to it, but he liked it. She had laughing eyes, a gorgeous mouth – he couldn't take his eyes off her face. Suddenly, he felt like a grubby little boy and uncomfortably dropped his gaze.

'Don't worry about it, Adam,' she was saying. 'The way you're feeling it's great that you came out to coach the boys, at all, and from the look of you, I'd say you're suffering enough.'

He looked back at her, reassured. 'Do I look that bad?'

'I'm afraid so. Nothing that a hot bath and Sunday lunch won't cure, though.'

'Is that an invitation?' He flashed a mischievous grin and was rewarded with a blush from Carla.

'Cheeky! I'm sure your mum is far better at cooking a roast than I am, anyway.' Carla looked around for her sons. 'Stefan! Bryn!' she called. 'We're off now. Come and say goodbye to Adam.'

'See you Carla. Bye, champ.' With a ruffle of Stefan's hair, Adam jogged off to help Craig put the equipment into his car, while Carla began the journey home to the time of the week she now hated the most – Sunday afternoons without Gareth.

* * * * *

Despite feeling exhausted and dehydrated, Adam could not sleep that night. His mind was full of images as he lay in the darkness: Carla's laughing face; the way her eyes creased at the corners and her nose wrinkled; the way she had looked away, blushing. He was experiencing new emotions: desire that was not purely physical, as it always had been up until then. It was flowing through him and he was disturbed to feel the start of an erection, which did not last because his thoughts turned – of their own accord it seemed, because he had not chosen to think about it – to the first time he had experienced an upheaval of emotion in connection with sex: the time he had lost his virginity at the age of fourteen. It had not been a good experience.

His mother had decided to raise some much needed cash by renting out the spare room, which had formerly been his older brother Simon's room. Simon and their sister Jacqueline had both left home when Adam was just a toddler. The age gap between them was so wide that his mum always said it was like having two separate families, and Adam had certainly always felt like an only child.

So there he'd been, a lanky, spotty bag of testosterone, when his mother had opened up their home to two sixteen year old French students for two weeks. From the moment she arrived, long limbed, olive skinned Monique, with her short dark hair, huge brown eyes and accented English, had held him transfixed. The way she moved and glanced at him out of the corner of her eye had soon had him in torment, causing him sleepless nights filled with frustrations he had not experienced before.

The other student, Veronique, was a brazen, flirtatious tease who had constantly whispered he knew not what into his ear in her singsong French language. Although she was not an ugly girl, she was the complete opposite of Monique and he had felt somewhat repelled by her as she both terrified and confused him.

He had come home, one afternoon, from his friend Josh's house after they had been talking all morning about sexy Monique and describing in detail what they would like to do to her. The day was muggy, the still air thick and cloying, and he had been hot under the collar in more ways than one. The house had been quiet as he splashed cold water on his face at the kitchen sink. His mum was at Mrs Trelawny's on a Friday, doing her cleaning, and his dad would not be home until after six. A soft giggle had reached his ears from the girls' room and he could hear them chatting away in their native tongue. A door upstairs had opened. A floorboard had creaked at the top of the stairs, immediately after which another fit of giggles had erupted from the girls. Scampering of feet had been followed by the slamming of the bedroom door. All was then quiet.

He had stiffened, his breathing shallow and his heart beating faster than normal. He had moved towards the stairs, drawn there as if by some magnet.

Like a cat burglar, he had started to climb, feeling like a predator stalking its prey, except for the feeling in his pants. Nearing the top, he had heard soft, sweet words from Monique.

'Adam, that is you, yes?'

His pulse had quickened. 'Yes.'

'Come see what we have for you, Adam.'

'Why?'

'Come. You will want to see, and we want to show you.'

Licking his lips and wiping his clammy hands down the sides of his shorts, he had felt awkward, unsure, frightened but incredibly aroused as he stood motionless at the top of the stairs, his imagination running riot and his erection straining and painful. This was the moment he and his friends had often talked about, but these girls were sixteen – they would be experienced. And French! It had felt dangerous in so many ways. For one thing, his mum would be livid if she knew what was happening and he had half hoped she would walk through the front door and shout out, 'I'm home!' Then he would dash to the bathroom, throw water on his face to calm himself and run down to greet her, have a glass of squash, talk about normal things and forget about what was going on behind that door.

But there had been no call up the stairs, no sound except the whispers on the other side of that door.

'Adam!' Monique's voice was pulling at him. 'Come, let us show you something you will like. And you can touch it.'

He had to do it. This was the moment. With shaking hands he had slowly turned the door handle and even more slowly pushed it open and stepped inside. The room had been dim as the girls had closed the curtains, and for a minute Adam had not been able to see clearly. As his eyes had adjusted to the light he had seen Monique standing between the beds, one of which was on either side of the room. She had been partially blocking his view of Veronique, who seemed to be half lying, half sitting on the bed, propped up on one elbow; only able to see her face and shoulders, he noticed that she was only wearing her bra.

'Shut the door, Adam.'

The door had clicked as he pushed it to, and his fate had been sealed.

'Adam,' Monique had continued, her voice caressing his name and driving him even more to distraction, 'have you ever touched a girl?'

He had touched Stacey Bradley's breast through her sweatshirt once, during a frenzied snogging session behind his dad's shed, but he didn't think that counted. 'No.' The word had come out in a husky whisper, not sounding like his own voice. He was sweating and his T-shirt clung to him. He felt dizzy and disoriented, totally out of his depth, but he had wanted to go on, ready to step into the unknown.

Monique had taken a step towards him, lifted her face to his, put her hand at the back of his neck and pulled his head down. He had closed his eyes as his lips met hers and he had gasped as her tongue quickly darted out of her mouth and found its way into his. She tasted like lemon sherbet. He had put his arms around her but she had pulled away and smiled up at him. He was at least five inches taller than her and he had gazed for what seemed like an eternity into her large brown eyes as she smiled up at him through her eyelashes. Holding his gaze, she had slowly lifted her daisy covered T-shirt with one hand and guided his hand beneath her clothing with the other. 'Touch me,' she had whispered.

He had hesitated, feeling as if he would explode at any moment, but then he had felt her skin, soft and silky, warm and slightly tacky with the heat of the day.

'Touch me high up, Adam,' she had murmured.

As his fingers had traced their way up her body, she had closed her eyes and slightly tipped back her head. Spurred on by what he thought was desire in her face, he had moved his hand higher, his eyes widening as he reached a small round breast with a hard nipple that softly brushed his palm.

That was the moment when things had taken a different turn to the magic he had expected. Monique had laughed softly at him and pulled away, her clothing dropping back down to veil further pleasure. She had stepped aside and turned towards Veronique, whom he had forgotten was in the room.

Although wearing a bra covering her ample breasts, Veronique's shorts and knickers had been round her ankles as she lay back on the bed, feet together, knees apart. In the gloom, he could see that she had one arm behind her head and was looking directly at him with a strange expression on her face. Shock had shot through him as he realised that she was touching herself through a thick mat of dark pubic hair, moving her fingers up and down; he had been able to hear the soft squelch of her wetness. He didn't like Veronique, at all, and had been tempted to turn and run, but seeing her so openly on show, performing such wanton acts, had been mesmerising.

The smell of sex had been strong in the room as Monique moved back to stand in front of him, her mouth slightly open, her lips moist. Once again, she had brought her face up to meet his and he had tasted her lips, felt her hot breath on his mouth, but all too soon she had pulled away.

'Would you like to touch me again?'

'Yes,' he had croaked.

'But first, Veronique wants to see how big you are, Adam.' Monique had reached out, touched him through his shorts, stroking and tracing his shape through the material. He had gasped and thrown his head back, screwing his eyes tight. 'Take off your clothes. I want to see you,' she had continued, her voice sweetly seductive.

He would have done anything for her at that moment – anything – and had promptly shed his T-shirt, discarding it on to her bed. Watching her face all the time, taking encouragement from her gaze, he had then unzipped his shorts, popped open the top button and eased them over his stiff erection, which was poking comically through the gap in his boxers. Monique had looked down and drawn in her breath, circled her finger round the tip and spread the bead of fluid around the end. Adam had thought he would pass out. He had never felt anything like this before and had reached out to touch her, but she had moved away.

'You want to touch me, don't you Adam?'

He had nodded, dumb with desire and breathing deeply to control the urge building inside him.

'You will take these off, Adam?' She had indicated his boxers.

He had obliged, and stood there, naked, proud and erect in front of them both, not knowing what to do next, but needing release from the blood pumping through him.

'If you want to touch me again, Adam, you must put this in Veronique.' She had drawn a slim finger along the length of his shaft and his knees had nearly buckled.

What? No! This was not how it was meant to be. He did not want Veronique.

'Then you can touch me,' Monique had said, 'I will let you touch me anywhere, Adam.'

He had looked over at Veronique, who was then openly masturbating and by the look on her face getting quite close. He had walked over to the bed, not really knowing what to do but assuming he was just supposed to get on with it. He did not like this girl and was disgusted by the smell of her sex, but, keeping his mind on the promise that was 'Monique', he had pulled off Veronique's shorts and knickers and knelt between her legs as she moved her hand out of the away. He had been able to feel the stickiness of her fingers on his left buttock when she had put her hands on his hips.

By then, Monique had also taken her clothes off and was standing naked beside them. Adam watched as she had turned and pulled the desk chair to her and sat down, legs apart, close to his face. His penis, butting against Veronique's thighs, and the feel of her hot skin on his erection, had combined to create an excitement that he could hardly contain.

'In me, Adam,' she had huskily murmured.

With his eyes firmly fixed on Monique, with her petit, olive skinned body and her neat little triangle, he had allowed Veronique to guide him inside her. As he had entered and taken his first push into the body of a woman, his mind had exploded, he forgot how to breathe, his seed shot out and he had grunted loudly, arching his back as he pushed in again and then once more, fully emptying himself and losing all sense of time and reason. A moment had passed before he realised he was still propped up over Veronique, and she was glaring up at him, her mouth a thin line.

'No! No! More Adam! More! I want more!' she had shouted, looking ready to punch him.

Monique had started to laugh. Curled up on the chair with her head thrown back, she had pointed at him and emitted witch-like laughter.

His pleasure had soon turned to the acute pain and hurt of shame, and he had instantly pulled out of Veronique, who then saw fit to slap him round the face. He had not understood: what was supposed to have happened that didn't? What had he done wrong?

Monique had still been laughing, pulling her clothes back on at the same time, when, without a word, he had swept up his clothes and made for the door, still hearing her laughter as he ran into the bathroom and slammed the door behind him, locking it and throwing his clothes on the floor before sinking down on to cold tiles next to the old bath. There, he had silently begun to sob.

It was like thinking about a completely different person, he now realised with a wry smile into the darkness of his room. How things had changed since then. It was true, he had kept away from girls for quite a while after that, just focussing on his rugby and his male friends; but soon the pain and embarrassment had faded and since then there had been quite a few encounters of a much more successful nature.

Adam sighed and rolled over, rearranged his pillow and drifted off into a dreamless sleep.

*   *   *   *   *

There was always order at the Stanford house: a place for everything and everything in its place. As he reached for the stainless steel kettle for his regular early morning cuppa, Paul looked around the perfectly appointed kitchen: Verity's pride and joy. She spent most of her time in it making tasty meals, helping the children with their homework, preparing endless costumes for school plays, drinking coffee with her friends and being the great mum that she was. She came top of his list when it came to her mothering skills. His two children, Jo and Stuart, even had their own pin-board, on which was neatly compiled their latest achievements, invitations to parties, memorable photos and their own calendar of events. Paul found it difficult to keep up with all the activities that his wife and two children were involved with and whilst waiting for the kettle to boil he used the time to glance over the board and see what they would be getting up to that day. It was Monday and the day ahead looked busy, as always: ballet for Jo and chess club for Stuart that evening. That morning, Verity was going into school to listen to other people's children read and the children needed to take cakes in for a charity event that lunchtime.

Their schedule was more hectic than his own, he thought, not for the first time. He spent most of his day hunched over a drawing board and Mac screen, designing mainly shop fronts and offices. He worked in the city and a daily commute into London Victoria had been a regular part of his life for nigh on ten years. He liked to be at his desk by eight, so that, technically, he would be able to leave by four and be home to enjoy more time with the children; but it never happened: he rarely made it home before seven thirty, so time with Jo and Stuart was brief during the work week, as it was with his wife, Verity.

He sipped the hot, strong tea and revisited the problem that had been bugging him for some months now: his marriage. The thought caused a heavy sigh to escape his lips as his eyes roamed the kitchen. Every night that kitchen had to be 'put to bed', as Verity termed it, and she would not stop until everything was tidied, scrubbed, polished and prepared for the following day. He was often asleep by then, always mindful of his five o'clock alarm call, and had long ago given up trying to get her to come to bed with him; that part of their marriage had dwindled to nothing. The shy, sexy, nymph-like creature he had met and married twelve years before was now a single-minded, cold fish – well, with him anyway. When had things changed? Why had they changed? Was it something he had done, or had they simply drifted apart, only connecting through the children? He did not know why he was even thinking about it since he no longer cared – not now that there was someone else.

Instantly, that someone replaced thoughts of all else, as she did most of the time. He was not having an affair. Oh, no! He wanted far more than just an affair. The rush of adrenaline that thoughts of her produced sent him spiralling into the fantasy relationship with her that he craved. When would it happen? How long could he wait before possessing her? He would wistfully look out for her when in the town on Saturdays with the family, hoping, just hoping, that she might be there at the same time. He 'casually' drove past her house, just in case he was able to catch a glimpse of her. A hundred times a day, he would look at her number on his phone, thinking about ringing her, but what would he say: 'Hi Carla, just phoning to ....' Phoning to *what*? He hadn't felt like this in years – like a teenager all over again – unsure and excited all at the same time.

Checking his watch, he saw that it was time to start the walk to the train station. He rinsed out his mug, dried it and put it away in the cupboard with all of the other matching mugs. He disposed of the teabag in the recycling tub and wiped the kitchen counter, taking care to rinse the cloth out and then fold it neatly over the tap spout, suddenly raising his eyebrows at his own behaviour, irritably realising how well *trained* he was. From the fridge, he automatically collected the lunch he knew would have been prepared for him by his wife the night before and stacked with two other lunch boxes. Moments later, he silently left for the day.

Verity glanced at her two impeccably dressed children dutifully eating their cereal. It was eight o'clock, almost time for the school day to begin, and it was Monday, her favourite day of the week. Her pulse quickened and she felt her cheeks flush with excitement as she thought about the morning ahead. She enjoyed the time she spent helping the less able children to improve their reading, but it was more than that: her hour's visit meant that she could spend the whole time in the presence of Mr Goodban, who was twenty six, new to the school and taught class three in this, his first permanent post.

Although most of the mothers thought him 'dreamy', no one knew about Verity's infatuation with Mr. Goodban, or Terry, as she liked to privately think of him. Whatever her fantasies were, she kept them to herself, not wanting to tarnish the 'perfect mother' mantle that she wore so proudly and so well. But, of course, she also saw young Mr Goodban – Terry – as very dreamy indeed. He had reddish-brown hair, fair, freckled skin and wasn't particularly tall or handsome; but broad shoulders, a tightly trimmed beard, soft, brown, attentive eyes and a shy, bashful smile all combined to have a magical effect on women. So today, tucked away in the reading corner at the back of the classroom, Verity would make sure, as she always did, that she positioned herself so that she could surreptitiously watch him. Even better would be if they enjoyed a short tea break together, which was something that happened infrequently but was a definite high point for Verity. They never talked about anything personal but his attention on her was enough.

She took a deep breath and pushed back her chair. 'Okay, my lovelies, off you go and brush your teeth. Jo, you need to get your ballet bag.'

'Okay, Mum,' Jo replied, skipping off into the hall.

Stuart looked at his mother through dark, tired eyes. At eleven years old, he was already studious – serious, like his dad – with an artistic streak that consistently amazed his parents.

'You looked tired, sweetheart. Are you okay?'

He nodded but Verity was not convinced. She didn't miss much when it came to her two children. 'Come on. What's up?'

'Oh, nothing. I just couldn't sleep last night.'

'Why not?'

'I was just thinking about stuff.'

'So you had a "busy brain"? It kept putting thoughts into your head?'

Stuart considered this for a moment. 'I think so. Every time I closed my eyes I started to worry that you or Dad might die – like Stefan's dad.' He shrugged. 'It just worries me, that's all.'

'Oh, sweetheart!' Verity moved round to his chair and crouched beside him. Looking up into his doleful face, she stroked his forehead, moving his fringe out of his eyes. 'You mustn't worry about that. Nothing is going to happen to us. We're solid, we are!'

As the word 'solid' came out of her mouth, Verity felt like a complete fraud: she knew her marriage was rocky, to say the least, but she smiled reassuringly at her son, hoping that the doubt in her heart would not show through.

Stuart pulled away from his mother's caress. 'Okay,' he sighed with a wan smile and sauntered away to follow his younger sister.

Verity watched him go. He was so like his father, it was frightening.

*   *   *   *   *

'Hi Joyce! '

'Hello, Carla love, you're home nice and early. I'm almost done here. Are you okay for me to carry on? I'm just going to put the bins out for tomorrow.'

'Lord, yes! Don't let me stop you! And by the way, thank you for all you do; it makes a huge difference to my day, coming home to a sparkling clean house.' Carla grinned happily at Joyce who returned the look with affection.

'My pleasure, Carla. Fancy a cuppa?'

'Sounds good. I've got a while before picking the boys up from Mum's, so you finish what you're doing and I'll put the kettle on.'

After filling the kettle, Carla stood at the kitchen window and watched Joyce preparing the bins for the following day's collection. She had known Joyce for many years and she realised how privileged she was to have such a trustworthy person to clean and tend to her house while she was out at work – good cleaners were so hard to come by. Joyce was so much more than that though: she often ran errands for Carla, taking her work suits to the cleaners, returning library books and, on occasion, picking the boys up from school if her mum was not available. Carla thought of her as an absolute treasure and part of the family.

The kettle came to the boil and obligingly clicked off. Carla took two mugs out of the cupboard and popped in her favourite, hard water tea bags – ideal for the water in the chalky county of Kent. Carla was very particular about her tea – builders' tea – so strong you could stand your spoon up in it. Kicking off her shoes, she sat at the breakfast bar and breathed in the fresh, clean smell that greeted her every Monday and Friday after Joyce's visit.

Joyce came back in with Banjo who had been supervising the wheelie bin exercise. 'There! All done!' she smiled.

'There you go, Joyce. Take the weight off your feet. I've left you to put your own sugar in.'

'Thanks, love. So, how have you been?'

'Really good, actually,' Carla lied, opening up her eyes so wide that Joyce could immediately see that that was not the case at all.

'Your voice is saying one thing but your face is saying another,' she observed. 'How are you coping? Work okay?'

'Work is the one thing that I don't worry about, to be honest. I know I'm good at what I do; my client and staff retention is testament to that. I've got a great team and although the hours are long and jam-packed, I think that work has been my saviour over the past year and a half. You know,' she mused, 'I cannot believe that Gareth has been gone for eighteen months. It seems like only yesterday that he was here; I keep expecting to turn over in bed and see him there, and it's still such a shock when he's not.' Carla's eyes began to moisten and there was a catch in her voice.

Joyce gently put her hand on Carla's arm. 'I know love, and you've been very strong in my book. I'm not sure I could have coped with being a widow the way you have, when my kids were small, and I didn't even work; I was just at home all the time. So how you keep a business going at the same time is beyond me.' Joyce smiled encouragingly at Carla, who sniffed as her eyes smiled back over her mug of tea.

Although she was a very private person who rarely talked about her feelings to people outside her immediate circle of family and friends, Carla found herself wanting to open up to the older woman who cared for her home while she was out earning the money; it felt right. 'Joyce, I'm really worried about the boys,' she confided. 'They seem to have become quite introverted and I don't feel I can give enough of myself to them. I'm just not a big enough person to be mum, dad and provider. I don't know how to be a single parent. How do you give your children the start they need in life when there is only one of you?'

Joyce felt Carla's pain as only another mother could. 'It's not an easy journey, Carla. Being a parent in normal circumstances isn't, but when you've been through what you have it's even more difficult. But listen, knowing that is half the battle and the other half is accepting that you *are* only one person and there will be times that you feel inadequate.' Joyce's face softened as she continued. 'Your boys don't see you that way though, Carla. You're their mum and they love you for what you are, not what you feel you should be for them. Does that make sense?'

'Are you, in fact, saying that I cannot be all things to them so I should stop trying to be superwoman?'

Joyce laughed. 'That would be a start! Have you talked to the boys about it?'

'Not directly. I don't want to pile my own worries on to them. I try to get them to talk about Gareth as much as possible, and it's as though I'm trying to retain his male influence for them. But I'm not sure how much good that can do: they're so young, and they'll forget. Besides, I want them to look to the future, not keep dwelling on the past.'

'You're tying yourself in knots, love.'

Carla smiled. She had not really spoken about her greatest fear in this way; it was emotionally draining, but it felt good and right to get it out. 'I know,' she conceded. 'But, you know, Gareth was just so masculine – such a bloke – and such a role model for those two boys. They were different when they were with him: more outgoing and daring; just normal, carefree boys doing what boys do. In fact, at times, it used to wind me up because together they were like three boys together, mucking about, doing boy stuff. Now, Stefan and Bryn just sit in front of the TV or computer, as if they've forgotten how to be boys. It's ... I don't know ... lethargy! Everything is too much bother, like someone has come along and drained all of their boyish energy out of them.'

Carla put her head in her hands, feeling the threat of tears and embarrassed to find she could not stop them; her chest heaved with the release of pent up worry and behind her hands she allowed her face to pucker up in distress.

'There you go, love.' Joyce discreetly wedged a piece of kitchen roll in between her hands and Carla accepted, gratefully, with a noisy blow of the nose.

'I don't know what to do,' she whimpered like a lost and helpless child herself.

'Well now, let's see. You've been on your own for quite a while now, so don't panic when I say this, but have you thought about getting out and about a bit and maybe dating?' Joyce laughed as Carla looked at her, aghast. 'I'm just asking the question, Carla love. Don't look so horrified.' She patted her arm and bravely continued. 'You're only in your thirties. There's a lot of life out there for living, you know. And I just thought that if you had someone else in your life you would be able to share the bringing up of the boys – if he was the right person, of course. It's just a thought Carla – just a thought.' Joyce worried that she had gone too far so she sat back and waited.

Carla, meanwhile, was actually shocked – not because of what Joyce had suggested, but because she had been thinking the same herself. So many thoughts were now rushing through her head: maybe it was time to move on; maybe she should stop picturing Gareth around them and start looking for some real, male flesh and blood to share their lives. It wasn't that easy, though, was it? It wasn't just a case of finding someone to go out with and have some fun; it was making sure that person was the right one to be involved in her sons' lives, too. That was the *real* issue. And besides: how to begin? She turned bewildered eyes to Joyce. 'How do you start dating?' she asked. 'No one has asked me out, so far, so why should they start now?'

'It's definitely a tricky one,' Joyce sighed, 'and I'm no expert, but you could start by taking down your "closed" sign.'

'My "closed" sign?'

'Yes. Maybe you're giving the impression that you're not available. Men can sense when a woman doesn't want to be approached and no one likes rejection, so they stay away. You could start by doing something like taking a class or joining a club or something.'

Carla groaned. 'What, like county cross stitch or something?' she laughed. 'Not really me, is it Joyce?'

Joyce joined in with a resigned giggle. 'You could try one of those dating agencies.'

Carla rolled her eyes to the ceiling. 'Er ... maybe not, Joyce. I'm not sure I like the sound of that, at all. I actually do think you have a point, though. It's time to get on with my life, which doesn't mean I love Gareth any less, but I have to face the fact that he's not here and he's never going to be.' She slapped the table, as if to make the point to herself as much as anyone, and put on a brave smile for Joyce. 'Tell you what: I'll start going out with Trudy. She's an expert at snagging a man!'

Both women laughed, and the subject was closed. Carla would have to find her own way through that particular conundrum. They fell into an easy silence, for a moment, and Carla gazed out of the window, taking in the wooden fence panel that had blown down again at the far end of the large garden and really needed replacing. The pond also needed clearing out and although she managed to keep the grass cut she was struggling with maintaining the rest of the garden, especially as the mild spring weather was progressing; the shrubs were about to start exploding and the weeds would soon be taking over.

'Joyce,' she said, 'I've been meaning to ask you: do you know of someone I could hire to come and keep the garden under control – someone trustworthy, like you? I could do with some general work around the house, as well: the decking needs a coat of sealant and I noticed, the other day, that the guttering at the front needs attention – there's a blockage somewhere.'

Joyce thought for a moment. 'Tell you what: I'll ask our Adam to come round and see what he can do. He's pretty handy and he could do with the extra money to get his car back on the road.'

Carla felt her cheeks begin to burn, remembering her momentary lustful thoughts about him at the rugby club the past weekend, but she dismissed the embarrassment as soon as it came. Adam was trustworthy and the boys knew him. Ideal. 'That would be great, Joyce. Ask him to pop round or give me a call if he's interested.'

When she later waved Joyce off as she drove out of the driveway and back home to her husband and grown up son, she realised that, in a way, she envied Joyce her complete family unit. That was what Carla had imagined her family would always be: a complete unit. Well, it was up to her to do something about it, she thought, as she went back into the house and closed the door.

*   *   *   *   *

Trudy put the phone down and sat looking around the room, dumbstruck. Did that conversation actually happen? She found her voice and laughed out loud to herself, clapping her hands together in glee. 'Oh! My! God!' she said with acute emphasis, to nobody. Carla Trelawny had just suggested they go out clubbing! She might have to pinch herself! She was flabbergasted and perhaps a little concerned about Carla's rationale for making such a suggestion, but she did not dwell on it.

Trudy was a good time girl who seemed to enjoy nothing more than a night out, a few drinks, some crazy, girly dances followed by who knew what at the end of the evening. To the outside world, she was a carefree, bubbly, raucous character who was always upbeat and enjoying herself; many people were envious of her exciting lifestyle. Carla was not one of them. There was a secret side to Trudy that only Carla really knew: the person who longed for security, love and depth in her life. An inability to have children had created a massive void in her that she filled with a fast moving life of executive parties, nights away in expensive hotels (business, of course), designer clothes, cocktails and gigolos. But Carla was the one Trudy turned to when she was lost in misery, drowning her sorrows in the gin bottle and making drunken phone calls full of maudlin wailings and sorrow.

Since Gareth's death, however, Trudy liked to think she had gone some way in redressing the balance by returning the support so freely given by Carla on so many occasions over the years. She had done her best to be a springboard for her, always there with an upbeat solution to Carla's low moments. Carla said she loved her for it, and Trudy felt privileged to be there for her childhood friend in her hour of need. Still, she was not so sure about a night out in a club with Carla. It was not something she had ever expected to be sharing with her.

Regardless, the date had been set for a week the following Friday. That gave Trudy ten days to think about how to introduce her friend to the right type of entertainment. She did feel that what Carla needed was a good old fashioned 'shag' – a bit of 'rust removal'. Trudy did not advocate celibacy under any circumstances, and eighteen months without sex was incomprehensible to her. In fact, her voracious appetite for sex had been one of the reasons that her last marriage had ended: her husband, Marcel, had been twenty years her senior and unable to keep up with her, which had resulted in Trudy looking elsewhere. When Marcel had come home, one day, to find his naked wife straddling the young guy who worked at the local petrol station, he felt it was time to call it a day.

Trudy had been totally philosophical about the whole thing and said that from then on she would not be giving her attention to just one man, but would be spreading her talents around and enjoying life. Carla had laughed at that comment and raised her eyebrows in disbelief; but, if that was Trudy's plan for the short term, so be it!

Trudy thought long and hard about her night out with Carla and came to the conclusion that it was not a frenzied clubbing session that Carla needed. It would be better for her to just get used to spending time with men in a dating situation again, so, just a night out that included male company would fit the bill.

She flicked through the numbers in her phone. Justin, who ran the bar at the Pig and Whistle, was a nice guy – not her type at all, but that was nothing to go by. Then there was Roger Dexter, a salesman from the garage where she had bought her latest car; he was recently separated and had two children. Oh, wait a minute – halitosis – no good. Ah! Steven Bishop, the policeman with the sexy smile and a truncheon to match! Yes. He owed her a favour for getting him out of trouble with a clinging ex-girlfriend. That had turned out to be a night to remember!

It had happened one Saturday evening the previous autumn, she recalled. She had been out with friends having a few after-work drinks in the wine bar near the cathedral, when she spotted a tall, well- built man having an intense discussion with a woman in the corner by the ladies' toilets. The woman had obviously been drinking and was just about to cause a scene. The guy was attractive in a Ross Kemp sort of way, with a number one haircut and strong features. He looked as though he worked out and she could see under his jacket that he was wearing the white shirt and black tie sported by the local police force.

Since she was not lacking in self-confidence and he had a certain raw quality about him, which she found alluring, she had walked up to the girl, been all sisterly and talked her into leaving the guy alone because he just wasn't worth the aggro. Then she had waited outside with the jilted girl, listened intently to her tale of woe until the taxi she'd ordered turned up, put her into it and left her to it. Job done.

Steven Bishop had been so grateful that he had bought Trudy a drink, then another, then dinner; he had remained so grateful that he then allowed Trudy to take him home with her and had gifted her with a night of athletic passion it would take her a long time to forget. Yes, Steven Bishop would be perfect if he was still available, and there was only one way to find out. With a naughty smirk she pressed his number.

*   *   *   *   *

Adam cycled home deep in thought. Work that day had dragged and although it wasn't a bad place to work, he was bored, bored, bored. He needed to move on with his life and was thinking about talking to his best friend, Mel, about it, when they went swimming later. She had a habit of speaking unvarnished truth, which was one of the reasons he liked spending time with her. His male friends thought it odd that his best pal was a girl and none of them seemed to believe that they had a platonic relationship; but they did, apart from a drunken snog at the rugby club last Christmas, during which, unbeknownst to Mel, Adam had thrust and gyrated a little too much and though he had covered it well, he had, in fact, almost lost control. His shame had been excruciating, he remembered, and he'd felt like a fourteen year old again, in the bedroom with two French girls. Mel had not laughed: her face had shown disappointment, which was almost as bad. Neither of them had spoken of it since; it was just something that happened and they had left it in the past, or so Adam thought.

He hopped off his bike and pushed it up the path beside the house he shared with his parents. Kicking open the old gate at the rear, he wheeled the bike into the shed at the bottom of the garden and, in passing, glanced through the shed window. Everything looked so familiar: his mother at the kitchen sink; life going by in its everyday way. And here he was, after a mundane day on the farm, putting his bike away in the shed in the garden of the house he had lived in all his life. It really wasn't good enough. There had to be more to life than this mediocre normality that was beginning to suffocate him; something needed to happen.

Except for Mel and a few of his rugby mates, his friends from school had scattered. He had had no interest in keeping in touch with them as all their lives seemed to be heading in different directions from his. But now he stood imagining them living exciting lives at university or travelling in Australia, or some such faraway place. The restless desire for change was surging through him and he was no longer content to just let life pull him along.

Pushing open the back door, he was greeted with the smell of sausages sizzling in the pan. 'Smells good, Mum,' he said giving her a peck on the cheek as she carried on scrubbing carrots at the sink.

'Good day, love?' she asked, noticing he seemed deep in thought.

'Mmm. Same old,' he muttered absently while leaning on the kitchen table looking at the back page of the daily paper. Always football! he thought, turning the pages to find the one of rugby that was normally all the space given to his favourite sport. He sighed in irritation at the eight pages of football stories and massive, close up pictures of screeching players with open mouths and blazing eyes, eventually reaching the single column on the Zurich Premiership title race and a bit about preparation for England's summer tour.

'What's up love?' his mother asked, turning to look directly at him.

'What? Oh, nothing. That's the problem, Mum: nothing's up! Nothing's happening! I'm bored!'

Joyce dried her hands on the tea towel and hugged her son from behind. 'You're only eighteen, luvvy. Something will turn up that will change things, you'll see. Oh, by the way, I spoke to Mrs Trelawny today. She needs someone to help her with outside stuff around the house – you know, gardening, bit of fencing, painting, that sort of thing. Interested? It would be extra money for you.'

Adam stared at her, his mouth dropping open without him realising.

'Adam! Close your mouth, you look a bit gormless.'

Snapping his jaws shut, he pulled himself together and processed the information his mother had just passed on to him. 'Well, I'll think about it,' he said carefully. 'I'm not sure when I'll fit it in, though. I do already work, remember.'

'I doubt she's after a full time handyman, just someone to do a few hours a week. Give her a call

and ask her - her number's in my book in the hall –
or she said to pop round, if you are interested.' Joyce
busied herself at the stove. 'Dinner will be ready in
fifteen minutes,' she announced over her shoulder as
she switched the gas on under the saucepan of sliced
carrots. 'Go and tell your dad.'

Adam went in search of his father and could
hear him in the bathroom having his daily shower
and shave. 'Dinner in fifteen, Dad!' he called up the
stairs, looking at himself in the mirror over the
telephone table as he stood there, and ignoring his
mother's address book. As a rugby mum, Carla's
number had already been in his own address book
for some time.

*   *   *   *   *

The pool was crowded that night, and the fast lane
had three other swimmers in it when Mel and Adam
arrived. Even so, Mel was taking the opportunity to
practise all the strokes. She was a strong swimmer
and still made appearances for the local swimming
club, even though it wasn't always possible to fit in
training sessions like she used to because she was an
assistant manager at a care home, which meant that
she worked shifts.

She had the well-developed shoulders of a
swimmer and at five foot eight she was not someone
Adam would want to pitch himself against in a
physical fight. He enjoyed the play fights they often
had though; it was good to feel a woman's body
close to his without having all of the usual urges. He

46

would always win – but only just. She occasionally went out on dates, which she usually told him about afterwards, but there didn't seem to be anyone particularly special to her. Adam was just glad they stayed mates and she seemed happy with that too. As he pushed off from the side and stretched out in the cool, blue water, he felt content for the moment; a good swim and a couple of drinks with Mel always cheered him up.

Sixty four lengths later, he stopped, breathing heavily from the exertion, and turned to stand at the end of the lane to watch Mel complete a length of butterfly. With strong shoulders rising up out of the water, she was a sight to behold and drew the attention of all those in the pool who were not head down swimming themselves. When she reached Adam, she stood up straight away and started chatting as she peeled off her goggles.

'You finished?' she asked.

'How do you do that?' he laughed.

'Do what?'

'Do a length of 'fly and then just start talking as though it was just a stroll up the road.'

'Easy, babe. Have you seen how crap I am at rugby though?' She grinned, putting her goggles back in place and diving straight back under water to do another couple of lengths before finishing her session for the night.

Adam shook his head in amazement, heaved his strong body out of the pool in one swift movement, much to the admiration of the nearby female pool attendant, and made for the changing rooms and a hot shower.

'Do you want a packet of crisps as well?' Adam called over to Mel in the sports centre bar.

'Yes, just plain, please.'

Adam brought over their drinks: a pint of lager for him, an orange juice and lemonade for Mel. After a while, chitchatting about this and that, they got on to the subject of work.

'I've got to be honest, I'm pretty fed up with it at the moment,' confessed Adam.

'Really? I though you liked being outdoors?'

'Oh, I don't know what I want at the moment. I'm just fed up with the status quo. I want something to happen.'

Mel leaned forward and put her hand on Adam's forearm. She liked to touch him; he felt strong and warm. 'Don't give me all that "I'm fed up" bullshit!' she said intently. 'If something in your life is not how you want it, there's only one person who can change it. And guess what, babe: it's you! Change it! Simple as that!'

Adam was taken aback by the sudden fire in Mel's eyes and the intensity of her expression.

'Get my drift?' she said, staring at him to accentuate her point. 'God, Adam, you're young, strong, clever and popular. I know dozens of guys who would give their right arm to be you.'

'You do?' Adam was shocked.

'Yes, you plonker! Time to wake up and smell the coffee!'

Adam blinked and leaned slightly back from her. Time to 'smell the coffee'? What had got into her? All of a sudden, she'd gone all dominant and forthright, unlike the Mel he had known for years. Never mind smelling the coffee; more like time to steer the conversation away from all this fearsome passion. 'Okay, I get the picture. Thanks, I think,' he grinned, relieved to see her physically relax and draw back into her chair. 'Have you seen Pogo's tattoo?' he asked, thinking this was safer ground.

'Yes, it's an unholy mess, if you ask me.'

'Really? I was thinking of getting one. Not like Pogo's, though: just one of those tribal looking ones to start with.' He pulled up his shirt sleeve, baring the top of his muscular arm. 'Here,' he pointed.

Mel sighed and tipped her head to one side. 'Don't Adam. Don't get a tattoo.'

'Why not?' He was finding her very puzzling.

'Because …' Mel hesitated, 'because you're beautiful and perfect as you are. Why would you want to spoil that?'

Adam stared at her, lost for words and unsure how to take such extravagant compliments from Mel; it wasn't how they talked to each other. Her words hung in the air between them.

'Let's go,' said Mel tersely, embarrassed and annoyed with herself for going too far. 'I've got an early start in the morning.'

They were both quiet on the way home, lost in their own thoughts and emotions as something between them began to shift.

*   *   *   *   *

When her mobile rang, Carla was just packing her shopping at the checkout in Tesco. It was a number she did not recognise; nevertheless, she propped the phone against her shoulder and answered it. 'Hello?'

'Hi Carla. It's Adam ... Adam Barnes.'

'Adam! Is everything all right?' Her thoughts went immediately to Stefan rather than the work Adam might do for her.

'Yes. Mum asked me to get in touch because you may need some help in the garden and stuff?'

'Oh, of course! Sorry Adam, I wasn't thinking. I thought you were calling about Stefan. Anyway, are you interested in earning some extra cash?'

Adam laughed. 'Always Carla!'

He sounded so mature on the phone and it unnerved Carla slightly. It was the way he used her name. She liked it.

'Good! I'm at the supermarket checkout so I can't talk now. Could you pop round to the house later?'

'Okay, I'll come round after training tonight. It'll be after nine though. Is that okay?'

'Perfect. The boys will be in bed.' Damn! Why did she say that? It sounded as though she wanted to see him alone. What a prize idiot! 'They'll get excited if they see you and I'll never get them to bed,' she said, recovering quickly. 'Time to pay, so I must go. See you later. Bye Adam.' She felt hot and flustered and smiled apologetically at the checkout girl who was sitting enjoying a momentary breather while Carla collected herself.

After packing away the shopping, that evening and having hot chocolate with the boys, she ran their baths and then they all played 'I spy', lying on Stefan's bed. Bryn had his own bedroom but after

50

Gareth died he had taken to sleeping in Stefan's room, so Carla had suggested they share for a while, until either of them got fed up. It still seemed to suit them both and Carla saw no point in forcing a change.

By nine thirty she had removed her makeup and changed into soft, grey sweatpants and top. Chopin was playing softly in the background, the lights were low, the room warm and comfortable, and she was propped up on the sofa with her notebook on her knees, busy working out a new client proposal that she had not had time to complete that day. She looked at her watch. Maybe Adam wasn't coming round after all. Even as the thought hung there, there was a tapping sound on the lounge window. Banjo shot up from his position at her feet and gave a snuffled bark. 'Shh, it's okay boy,' she reassured him, closing her notebook and dumping it on the coffee table before padding barefoot over to the door, where she could see Adam in silhouette against the street lighting. Banjo was close at heel as she opened it and grinned at Adam. 'Come in,' she beckoned.

Adam looked around as he followed her through to the kitchen. 'Great house, Carla. My mother often says how much she likes working here.'

She turned to look at his young face as he sat down on one of the stools. He was flushed from rugby training and he had an impressive bruise forming under his right eye. Carla could not help noticing how his club T-shirt fitted snugly around his upper arms and allowed herself a momentary fantasy of arms like that encircling her in a naked embrace. 'Thanks, Adam,' she said, smiling to herself at the difference in content of her thoughts and her words. 'Your mum is a complete gem. I'm not sure what I would do without her really.'

'Yeah, she's good, my mum,' he smiled.

Carla just kept on looking at him, feasting her eyes on him and enjoying his masculine presence in her kitchen.

'So,' he said eventually, 'what sort of things do you need a hand with?'

Carla realised she was staring and pulled herself together, hoping she hadn't made the poor boy uncomfortable. 'First things first,' she said. 'How about a beer?'

'Yeah, I'll go for that. Thanks.'

And so Carla and Adam's friendship began.

* * * * *

Trudy had it all arranged: they would start with drinks at the Walnut Tree, then go for a meal at Giovanni's and finish up with coffee at her house.

She lived in the centre of town, just behind the cathedral, in a beautiful cottage which she owned outright, a fact she took pleasure in sharing with her many friends. After she and Marcel had divorced she had wanted something to make her feel better; a house purchase had done the trick.

During working hours she ran a recruitment agency on the outskirts of London – London clientele without London rates, she often told people. Although not the outright owner, she had bought heavily into the company and so was a substantial shareholder. She had been in recruitment all her working life and loved the chase and tension of sealing the deals with big clients. She shared business ambitions with Carla and they spent hours discussing sales techniques, marketing ploys and staffing issues. Once a month, the two friends had attended business women's seminars in the capital and Trudy, much to Carla's amusement, had often got up to mischief on their nights out afterwards. These trips, however, had come to an abrupt halt when Gareth had been killed and Carla's world had temporarily ceased to turn.

Trudy was attracted to the bad boys, so Gareth had not been her type but he was perfect for her best friend. She vividly remembered the phone-call from Verity that Sunday: she had still been in bed, recovering from a late night of drinking and passionate sex games with Pierce, who had been part of her life for a few months then. She had sleepily reached across him to pick up the receiver.

'Trudy, you have to come quick! Gareth's been knocked off his bike. He's in hospital. We need to go to Carla.'

'Fuck! Where are they?'

'Margate Hospital. We're on our way there now. See you when you get there.'

Trudy had pulled on a track suit, left the slumbering Pierce to his own devices and jumped into her BMW to drive the ten miles to the hospital. When she got there she had been taken straight through to a room where Carla was standing with Verity's arms round her, obviously in complete and utter distress. No words had been needed for Trudy to know he was dead. She had just gone to them and added her arms to Verity's, holding Carla. It was the only thing she could have done.

From that day, Trudy and Carla's friendship had strengthened and deepened, and though Trudy would never have wished it to come about that way, it had: she had been there for Carla in the bleak, black moments of grief, holding her hand as she had screamed out in bitterness at the unfairness of life. It was the two of them against the world now.

Lately, she had been concerned about Stefan and Bryn. To her inexperienced eyes they had withdrawn and seemed to only find solace in each other. She thought Carla was, maybe, trying too hard to make things normal for them, rather than helping them to come to terms with the fact that their lives would never be the same again; that they now had a different life, without a daddy. Trudy felt that that had to be fully accepted by all of them, Carla included, before they could really get their lives back.

But what did she know? She was barren. No babies had, or ever would, come from her womb. She had been a disappointment to the men she married and to her parents, who had died without ever knowing the joy of a grandchild. Trudy knew her demons well.

Nevertheless, she also knew how to have fun and she was going to enjoy double-dating with Carla, especially since it was to be blind dates for both of them: Steven had jumped at the chance of a bit of fun and had promised to provide the fourth member of the party – another policeman.

She had called Carla earlier to make sure she was ready and still good to go. Carla had sounded falsely enthusiastic, which Trudy thought odd, since it was more usual for Carla to express her true feelings about things, but then she decided she was analysing too much; it was only a night out, after all, and no big deal.

At six thirty she was in the kitchen preparing a pre-date G and T for herself and Carla. She heard Carla knock at the door and scurried through the sitting room to the on-street front door to let her in. Carla had made a real effort and looked divine, which pleased Trudy and allayed her former doubts about Carla's commitment to the evening. Her shimmering, silver shift dress and black satin sandals with matching handbag looked just right for the occasion. Carla was certainly stylish. 'Good lord! Look at you!' she gushed.

Carla gave a theatrical twirl and Trudy nodded approvingly. 'Come in the kitchen. G and T?'

'Yes please, it'll calm the nerves,' Carla said, accepting the glass filled with lots of gin and crushed ice but not much tonic. 'I got a taxi, so no driving to worry about tonight,' she added with a naughty look.

'You're looking pretty flushed, honey,' Trudy remarked. 'You been on the bevy already?'

'Certainly not! How dare you!' Carla playfully slapped Trudy on the backside.

'Well, girlie, something has tickled your fancy tonight. Who's got the boys? Your mum?'

'No, not tonight, I got a babysitter.' Carla looked away as she said this.

Trudy picked up something from Carla's seemingly innocent reply. 'Oh yes? Who's that then?'

'Just a guy from the rugby club.'

'A guy!'

'Don't panic, he's their rugby coach. Right about now they're in their element kicking a ball around the back garden.'

'Oh, I see.' And she *was* seeing something, even though she was not sure what it was. Who was this rugby coach? Something was not quite as it innocently seemed, but now was not the time to probe. 'Cheers, girlfriend,' she said with a wink.

'Back at ya,' replied Carla, grinning from ear to ear; it was going to be an interesting night.

Adam had spent the day leading up to that night at Carla's house, clearing the pond and replacing the broken fence panel. He wasn't sure there was enough work to warrant the one day a week she had requested but she was paying him half as much again as he was getting for farm work, so he had cut his time there to four days to allow Fridays at Carla's.

The first Friday had been mainly clearing gutters and mowing the two large lawns at the front and the back of the house. He had been gone by the time Carla arrived home at seven that night, but this particular Friday he was still there when she returned, mid-afternoon, to collect the boys from school and get home early – to get ready for her night out, he assumed.

She had called him a few days previously to ask him if he would stay on and babysit after work on Friday. He was happy to because he rarely went out on Friday nights prior to Saturday matches during the season, especially at this time of the year when things were so tight in the league and all the clubs were fighting for promotion or against relegation. His team was in the top three so things

56

could go either way, and since it was his first year playing men's rugby as opposed to youth, he was anxious to make a good impression.

It had been a warm spring day and he had thoroughly enjoyed himself. Clearing out the pond had been a messy job but it had been something different from the usual and he liked the feeling of being appreciated: when Carla arrived home she had clasped her hands together and squealed with delight to see the work he'd done, which included jet washing the decking – something she hadn't expressly asked him to do so she was tickled pink. He liked to see her excited and happy after looking pretty miserable for so long, for obvious reasons.

'So where are you off to tonight then?' he asked as they shared a cup of tea on the fresh, clean deck. The sun was on its way down but it was still warm and there was little breeze in the shelter of the garden.

'I'm going on a blind date, apparently.'

'Really!' Adam felt a stab of something. Was it jealousy?

'Yes, my friend Trudy has decided that I need to spend more time with men, so she's arranged a couple – not both for me, of course!' Carla giggled self-consciously. 'It's just to make up a foursome. Anyway, it will be a bit of a change: I haven't been out on a date for what seems like a hundred years.'

Adam smiled weakly and went back to sipping his tea, watching Carla as she drank hers and looked around her newly tidied garden with smiling pleasure. Yep – there it was: he was feeling green-eyed with jealousy. Whoever this guy was tonight he was a lucky bastard, he thought. And feeling unable to deal with the thoughts burning inside him, he got up and took his cup back into the kitchen, not liking this turn of events at all.

Carla stayed outside, enjoying the peace and tranquillity of the moment. The boys were watching TV and were excited that Adam was going to be giving them their tea and seeing them to bed. It was a rare treat.

Adam went to wash his hands and caught sight of himself in the mirror over the basin in the downstairs toilet. He was filthy dirty and his hair was matted; he also badly needed a shave, as always after a day's labour. In preparation for an evening of babysitting indoors, however, he had brought clean clothes and wash bag in his kitbag. 'Is it all right if I catch a shower before you go and leave me in charge?' he called to Carla through the kitchen window.

'Of course. Use the one off my bedroom; it's less cluttered and the shower works better. Which reminds me – that's another job for you at some stage – the boys' shower head needs adjusting.'

Carla smiled as Adam tipped her a salute and disappeared from view. She was relaxing for the first time in what seemed like years, and even getting her life back: she was going out; her boys seemed happy with the presence of the very sexy, albeit very youthful (she reminded herself) Adam, and her business was going well. Her hard work was paying off and the month end figures she had just been provided with by Jonathan showed a hundred percent increase on last year's already impressive profit margins. Now that she was the sole bread winner she felt huge pressure to make her business a success but had not imagined things could go as well as they had this past year, and her bank balance reflected it.

Gareth had not had much life insurance – it was something they had just never got round to thinking much about. It had been enough to pay off the mortgage and provide a more reliable car, but the rest of the income was down to her – not that it fazed her; she had always been the main wage earner. Gareth had never had any serious career ambitions and had, in fact, been in his element as a stay at home dad before the boys started school, forging a deep bond with his sons – one of the reasons she worried so much about them now. When they started school he took on part time work to supplement their income, doing maintenance for local residents and businesses, but he was always there for them at the end of the school day.

She could now hear them being boisterous in the lounge, which made her heart sing. At least they were happy tonight.

Upstairs, Adam stood in Carla's bedroom – not a good place to be in his present state of mind. It was tidy and very feminine, smelt of her perfume and the bed was neatly made with a silver coloured dress laid across it, reminding him that she was going out with a man that night. There was no reason why she shouldn't, but he had to admit to himself that he did not like it and quickly passed through to the en-suite bathroom, pushing his thoughts away. He focused on his shower and tried not to look at Carla's toiletries as he stripped and stepped under the power shower. The water, cascading over his tired muscles, soothed his irritation and he remembered Mel's words: if something isn't right, change it, and he realised that one of the things he needed to change was his love life. He needed a girlfriend. He hadn't been bothered before, finding girls a pleasant distraction from work and rugby, but not looking for anything more. Now, though he had no idea who it might be, he really needed someone to take his mind off the woman whose shower he was currently occupying.

Downstairs, a short time later, Carla looked at her watch and realised that if she was to get to Trudy's by six thirty, she did not have too much time to get ready. Her shower had not been running for some time now, and though Adam had yet to make an appearance downstairs she thought it would be safe to venture up. Even so, she climbed the stairs with slight trepidation. 'All done, Adam?' she called.

'Yes, I won't be a minute – just finishing shaving. Come in, I'm decent.'

When she went into her room she immediately saw that the door to the en-suite was open and he was standing in front of the mirror wrapped only in a towel. She caught his reflected grin.

'I expect you need to come in here,' he said.

'Er … no … no problem … take as long as you need. I'll … er … I'll just wait downstairs.'

'No, really Carla, it's fine, I've finished. I'll go and get dressed in the spare room.' Quickly rinsing his razor and putting everything back in his wash-bag, he turned to face her.

She was standing in the middle of the room looking shaken.

'You okay?' he asked.

'Yes, of course. I'm just not used to seeing all this semi-nakedness in my bathroom,' she grinned, taking the tension out of the situation and allowing her eyes another moment to take in the view. He was breathtaking. She forgot how young he was and wanted to reach out and run her hands over the fine covering of hair on his chest and trailing down towards the area covered by the towel. She resisted and dragged her eyes back to his face. Lightly tanned and clean shaven, his piercing blue eyes were accentuated and, at that moment, fixed directly on hers. For what seemed like minutes, but was probably only seconds, their eyes stayed locked, until Adam broke away and walked past her towards door. She wanted to call him back. She wanted to run her hands down his strong arms, drown in his blue eyes and kiss his beautiful, sensual mouth. This was no boy, but a fully-fledged male, and he knew it!

As he walked out into the hall and across to the spare room, Adam noticed that he had goosebumps and his nipples were hard and erect. There was chemistry between him and Carla. He was not imagining it. He had seen in her eyes that she felt it too: there was something between them that kept coming back each time they saw each other. He imagined turning back into the room, taking her in his arms and kissing her delicious mouth, the way it could only happen in a film because she was probably twice his age and way out of his league. And she was about to go out on a date. His mouth twisted at the thought that any sexual tension she may have felt just now would probably be unleashed on the lucky sod who was her partner for the evening. He couldn't bear thinking about it and quickly got dressed, packed up his kitbag and went downstairs to his noisy young charges.

*　*　*　*　*

The wine bar was crowded and buzzing, as were most places in the city on a Friday evening, and it was favoured by people in the mood for a sociable night out. Carla's stomach was churning with a mixture of apprehension and excitement, something she had not felt for a very long time.

'There they are!' announced Trudy, leading the way through the throng of early evening drinkers and glancing back at Carla to make sure she was following. Together they squeezed through to the back of the room, to an open space near a wide inglenook fireplace.

Things look promising, so far, thought Carla, seeing their dates for the evening. She was not sure which was which but both had that solid, dependable look about them. The one on the left, leaning against the brick wall of the fireplace, had close-cropped hair and smiling eyes. That must be Steven, she thought, when he straightened up at the sight of Trudy making her way towards them. His companion, dark haired and wearing spectacles, had a more serious look and regarded Trudy with interest.

'Hi, guys! Great to see you!' Trudy enthused, kissing Steven on both cheeks and smiling her winning smile at his friend.

'All right, Trudy? Good to see you again. How's the dripping tap?'

She laughed. 'My god, you've got a good memory! All fixed thanks to Brian the plumber,' she said with a wink.

'Trudy this is Trevor,' said Steven with a smile.

Trevor took Trudy's hand and put it to his lips. 'A pleasure to meet you, Trudy,' he said with great emphasis on the word 'pleasure'.

Carla wondered whether he knew of Steven and Trudy's previous encounter.

'Oh, how very genteel, Trevor! Pleasure to meet you too.'

To Carla's surprise, Trudy was blushing.

'Guys, please meet my very best friend, Carla.'

Carla stepped forward and shyly shook hands with both of them; you could tell a lot from a handshake. Trevor's was warm but slightly limp, whereas, Steven's was firm, his palms callused, and he looked directly into her eyes, almost in an interrogatory fashion, as if he were looking straight through her and reading her deepest thoughts. It crossed Carla's mind that he may well use this technique to get those he had arrested to confess, which made her feel uncomfortable. She gave herself a mental shake and scolded herself for being so dramatic while turning slightly away from his intrusive stare to glance towards Trevor and then back again. 'Very nice to meet you both,' she smiled graciously even as doubt began seeping into her mind. Perhaps she was not ready for this, she thought, involuntarily dropping back a pace and distancing herself from the group.

Steven burst her solitary bubble by suggesting she might like to help him get the drinks in – his treat of course. Carla politely agreed and they made their way to the bar to wait for the next available bartender. The crowd was making it impossible for her to keep her distance as Steven leaned against the bar and turned to look at her. She could smell his after shave and see the stubble starting to grow on his chin. His T-shirt was tight fighting –a bit *too* tight fitting – and tattoos were peeping out from under the sleeves. She was shocked to find herself wondering what he looked like naked, but then his masculinity was pretty overpowering and she couldn't help but imagine him 'in the act' as it were.

She was also quite shocked by her own inability to find something to talk about. Communication, in all sorts of ways, was her job and she was good at it because it came naturally to her, making it one of her main strengths. Nevertheless, she was now tongue-tied and could not understand why. She just kept smiling at Steven in what she hoped was a reassuring way.

'You okay?' he enquired. 'I suppose this is all quite difficult for you.'

Carla looked at him in surprise. 'No, er … I mean, yes, I'm fine, thanks. Why do you ask?'

'Trudy's filled me on what's happened to you. I'm just making sure you're okay because you seem a bit uptight.'

Carla sighed and visibly relaxed. 'Is it that obvious?'

'I'm afraid so,' laughed Steven. 'And please call me Steve,' he added, giving her arm a quick caress – not an unpleasant sensation, she found. 'If it's any consolation,' he continued, 'Trev is going through a bit of a bad time, too, at the moment – messy divorce and issues getting access to his kids.'

'Oh, I'm sorry to hear that. How is he coping?'

'He seems to be heading for a breakdown at the moment. In fact, I could use your help tonight, keeping him off the booze.'

Carla glanced over at Trevor, who was leaning towards Trudy and watching her intently as she chatted on in her energetic fashion. Steve called her attention back to the matter in hand.

'What would you like?'

'Gin and tonic, please; Trudy will have the same.' She thought it best to stick to gin after the mammoth drink Trudy had supplied.

After re-joining the other two, they all chatted inconsequentially until it was time to go to Giovanni's. The table was booked for eight and since Carla was beginning to feel the effects of the alcohol, she was looking forward to having something to eat.

The evening was going at a much slower pace for Adam. Stefan and Bryn had kept him occupied with constant demands for his attention and after tea he had ended up taking them to the park for a rugby ball throwing and kicking session, getting home just before it got dark. They had taken a while to settle but both boys were pretty much asleep by the time nine o'clock came.

Left to his own devices, Adam was restless. The television was on but nothing was capturing his interest; he tried the newspaper, to no avail – he couldn't concentrate – and finally returned to staring at the TV screen and glancing at the digital clock on the video player every few minutes, which was pretty pointless as he had no idea when to expect Carla home.

Not realising he had dozed off he was suddenly jerked awake some time later by the sound of a car. The light thrown from the headlights swept across the room through the un-drawn curtains and he shot up, rubbing the sleep from his eyes and realising that his heart was beating faster as he waited for Carla to come through the door. He took a deep breath, waiting for the sound of her key in the lock. Instead, there was a quiet knock, which he found odd and hurried to open the door. Carla was not alone. She stood grinning at him, supported by a man he had not seen before.

'In you go then,' encouraged Steve as he guided her through the door and into the hall. Carla started to giggle and Adam ushered them both through to the lounge and shut the door so as not to wake the boys.

'Thanks lad. You okay to get home?'

The hair on the back of Adam's neck stood up. Lad? Home? Who was this guy that he thought he had the authority to dismiss him from Carla's home?

'Er… what's your name?'

'Steve, and you're Adam I take it?' He held out his hand for Adam to shake, which he did.

'Yes. I'm Carla's friend.'

'Is that right? I thought you were the babysitter! Anyway, you can get going and I'll make sure she gets to bed.'

Alarm bells were going off in Adam's head. This was tricky. 'No, you don't understand: I'm staying the night. I'm all set up in the spare room.'

Steve's expression suddenly changed from affable to territorial. 'You can get going, mate. I'll see she's okay. Do you need money for a taxi?'

Adam felt panic rise in his chest. This man was big, powerful and more than twice his age. He looked over to where Carla was half lying, half sitting on the sofa, obviously unaware of the sparring that was going on. He did a rapid mental assessment of the situation: he hadn't planned to stay –the idea had occurred to him on the spur of the moment – but his kitbag in Carla's spare room would confirm his statement if necessary; if he squared up to this guy he could end up getting pasted over the wall and dumped outside on the drive – not an option he wanted to consider; if he didn't stand up to him and just meekly made his way home, what might the consequences be for Carla, alone with this guy? That settled it. 'Look,' he said, summoning all the courage he could muster, 'Carla is obviously pretty drunk and she's my friend –I've known her for a long time – so I'm not going anywhere. I'll look after her and the kids, and I think it's probably best if you go and maybe give her a call in the morning when she's sober and can make her own decisions.'

Steve's face twisted into an unattractive sneer. 'So you're going to have a go at giving her one, are you?'

Adam had never punched anyone in anger before and the sound of his knuckles hitting the bone was not one he relished, although it was one he would remember for a long time. Steve's head flipped back and he smashed into a picture on the wall, dislodging it and sending it crashing to the floor. Knowing that this was the moment when things could go terribly wrong, Adam simply walked away, out of reach of Steve, who was clearly shocked by the attack. Adam knew he had overstepped the mark and was immediately ashamed of his action, but he had been pushed to the limit: a whole evening of worrying about what Carla was doing and who she was with had made him tense and edgy.

Carla had sat up at the sound of the altercation and was now trying to get up on to unsteady feet. A moment followed when they all stood still and silent, no one knowing quite what to do next. Adam's knuckles were throbbing but the adrenaline rush was keeping the pain at bay. Steve looked at Carla, who was staring wide eyed at both of them, her alcohol befuddled brain trying to take it all in. Why had Adam done that? Should she be cross? As far as she was concerned, the evening was ruined and any relationship with Steve was hanging in the balance; beyond that, she did not know what to think. 'Steve … I …' she stammered, not knowing what to say either.

'Save it, Carla!' he said, making for the door. 'I don't need this fucking crap. Give me a ring sometime when you've got your Rottweiler back on his leash!' With a final sneer of contempt at Adam, he opened the door, made his way up the hall and out through the front door, closing it firmly as he went, while Carla and Adam stood in silence. Steve backed his car out of the drive and drove away into the night, and still they stood there.

'Adam, what the hell just happened?' Carla eventually asked, having sobered up to some extent as a result of events.

Adam sat on the sofa and put his head in his hands. A multitude of emotions swarmed through him: he felt drained of energy and immensely tired, although anger still coursed around his veins; but most of all he felt foolish – eighteen years old, out of control and foolish. 'I'm sorry Carla. I just lost it.'

'What made you hit him? I don't understand any of this.'

'He said something insulting.' Adam thought about the glib comment Steve had thrown at him. He would no more have taken advantage of Carla than fly to the moon. Yes, he had feelings for her – maybe just a crush – but his respect for her was huge and that guy had been totally out of line. There was no way he could tell Carla how he was feeling though, and why he had lashed out. She was a mature, professional woman who had brought two children into the world. He was an eighteen year old kid.

Carla came and sat beside him and took his sore hand in hers. 'Adam, talk to me.'

He looked into her eyes. She was definitely not at her best with glazed eyes and smudged makeup, but he thought she was lovely. He held her gaze for some moments and without thinking gently ran the back of his uninjured hand down her cheek, giving her a small, closed mouth smile. She returned it with an impish grin and if ever there was a time to kiss a girl, this was it. But Carla was not a girl.

'I'm going to get going,' he sighed heavily.

'Don't go.' The plea was hardly above a whisper.

He so wanted to just take her in his arms and kiss her sweet mouth. She was tilting her head to one side and gazing directly into his eyes. It was torture. He wanted to lay her back on the sofa, right then and there, and hold her close. But he didn't believe she was thinking clearly and Steve's comment was still resounding in his ears. He was stone cold sober and had to take charge before his resolve crumbled.

But then suddenly she sat back on the sofa, her mood changed. 'God, I feel like crap!' she declared, 'Why did I drink gin and then wine?'

Grateful for the lightening of the intensity, Adam took charge and jumped up purposefully. 'Right, I'll get you some water. Drink all of it and then go to bed. I'll camp down in the spare room to make sure you're okay.'

She nodded and rewarded him with a grateful sigh. 'Thanks, Ads.'

He basked in her use of his pet name and feeling a bit better about himself, went out into the kitchen to fetch her some water.

Later that night, lying in Carla's spare room, he ran through the events of the day, picturing the moment that she saw him wearing just a towel and acknowledging that it had been his little test to see if he could evoke a reaction from her – and he could: he had seen that she was aroused. The fight with the 'boyfriend' had been the low point of the evening, by far, but her request for him to stay had pretty much negated that. He was excited, terrified, and there was no one he could talk to about all this. His friends would egg him on with chants of 'MILF' which disgusted him; Mel would give him one of her you-need-to-be-careful looks, and his parents would go spare, his mother in particular; she would see her job at risk and her little boy being defiled by an older woman.

His parents had no idea about raw passion, he was sure. There did not seem to be anything but a resigned respect between them. That was not how he would ever want his life to be and, that night, in Carla Trelawny's spare bedroom, he made a pact with himself: from that moment on he was always going to set his sights high and he was never, ever going to settle for second best.

'I don't actually feel too bad,' thought Carla as she slowly opened her eyes the following morning , before she moved her head and the pain that shot through her felt like her brain had shattered into tiny shards. She groaned and turned over to look at the clock with sore, screwed up eyes. Nine thirty! What was happening? She never slept in that long, not since the boys had been born and broken nights and early mornings had left her incapable of sleeping late. The children would never normally have allowed it anyway, so what was going on? Then she remembered: Adam was still there and probably on the sofa watching Saturday kids TV with the boys. That was why they had not come in to wake her. Oh my god, she was going to have to face Adam. How very embarrassing!

Delaying that moment, and not wanting to move her head again, she lay back and made herself review the events of the previous evening. Dinner at Giovanni's with the policeman, Steve. He had been quite nice, but she seemed to remember feeling that he was consistently invading her space. He was just too close most of the evening and at one point she had delicately excused herself for an unnecessary visit to the ladies because he had surreptitiously placed his hand on her thigh and she had allowed it to remain there for far too long. By that time she was pretty much smashed and had thrown caution to the wind, yet something had been holding her back; there was something about this man that made her feel unsure. Maybe it was that he seemed overly anxious to get close to her. She did not understand the rush but at the same time had not been sure how to put the brakes on.

As the evening wore on and the wine had continued to flow, Steve appeared to become more attractive and Carla had allowed his hand to return to her leg and start to gently and seductively rub up and down the entire length of her thigh. The early evening view of Adam in his near nakedness had kick started her libido and she was getting turned on with the strong, manly touch of this stranger. When the time to go had come, Carla had clumsily waved goodbye to Trudy, who had spent most of the evening consoling Trevor, he having diminished into a sobbing heap in the corner as the drink took effect. Trudy had decided that he needed to go home with her and she would apply some of her 'special' therapy. So Carla, without thinking, had climbed into Steve's car and as she had sunk into the soft leather Land Rover seats and closed her eyes to stop the street lamps spinning in front of her, she had realised she had lost the ability to make rational decisions and was submitting to whatever was coming her way.

She hadn't objected when he had pulled the car up alongside the park away from the streetlamps; she had not pulled away when he undid his seatbelt and leant over to kiss her passionately on the mouth; in fact, her lips had parted and accepted his tongue as it invaded her mouth. His hot breath had been everywhere and she had felt stifled – trapped – but the drink had dulled her mind and she had not seemed to have any capacity to work out what to do. She had known that this was not what she wanted though, so she had pushed him back with a real effort to focus. 'I'd like to go home now, Steve,' she'd said, training her eyes on his face. Steve had obliged, although she couldn't remember what his reaction had been. Had he been angry, polite, kind? Had he thought she was inviting him back? Maybe she had given him that impression.

She painfully turned her aching head over toward the bedside table to look at her picture of Gareth. She felt wretched – and silly. 'Oh, Gareth, if only you had not gone out on your bike that day,' she whispered. 'If you'd gone a different route; if you'd left the house just thirty seconds later.' If, if, if!

Then she remembered what had happened when they had got home – Adam and Steve had fought! She still did not understand why. What had made Adam so angry? She had never seen him like that before; but then, she had never seen him playing rugby either – maybe he had more fire in him than she knew. The thought slightly excited her, and when she recalled their brief encounter on the sofa that excitement rose substantially. She could remember him touching her face and she had wanted him to kiss her. She had been disappointed when he hadn't. Her excitement was short-lived, however. How ridiculous, she thought, to get so drunk that she allowed herself to be in that position with such a young man! What an idiot! What was she thinking? Well, obviously, she wasn't, and she felt disgusted with herself, and ashamed. How was she going to face him?

There was a sudden tap on the door.

'Yes?' she called, pulling the duvet up around her. Fully expecting Adam to come in, she was relieved, or was it disappointed, to see Bryn's little face poke round the door.

'Mum, are you ever getting up? Adam has gone down to the shops to buy us comics and crisps. He says it's law that everyone under the age of twelve has to have comics and crisps on Saturday mornings.'

Despite the hammer in head and her churning stomach, Carla laughed out loud at Bryn's serious expression. 'Well,' she said, 'as it's law, thank goodness Adam was here to sort that out!'

'I know, Mum. Adam is the best. Can he come to stay every Friday?'

'I'm not sure about that, honey, but sometimes, perhaps. Would you run downstairs and pour me a glass of orange juice, ready for when I come down, please? I'm going to get in the shower now.'

Off he ran and Carla gingerly got out of bed, wondering as she did, was it her imagination, or did Bryn seem brighter, more energetic, just happier?

The shower felt wonderful on her tender skin; it caressed and relaxed her, made her feel human again. After shampoo and conditioner had been applied and duly rinsed, she stood with her eyes closed and her head back, allowing the water to cascade over face and body, and thought about the wakening of arousal she had experienced the previous day, allowing images to flow through her mind: Adam wrapped only in a towel; Steve's manly presence, strong hands and hot kiss; Adam's impossibly blue eyes, full of youth and inexperience, and his gentle touch on her cheek. He had an energy that ran right through her; she could feel it whenever they were together.

In response to the free-flowing pictures filling her mind, Carla slowly reached down and touched herself; she was so very hot and excited. Hugging herself with her left arm, she began to pleasure herself, moving her right hand slowly at first and then with increasing speed as the energy grew. Her orgasm hit in huge waves, her eyes screwed up tight and then opened wide as she gasped; her knees gave way so that she gradually slid down the tiles to sit panting on the ceramic floor, her mind still shockingly filled with the face that had come to her as her exquisite climax had taken control.

*   *   *   *   *

Verity looked around the kitchen, pleased that everything was in place, and swiftly walked through to the lounge, straightened and plumped up a few cushions and slid her finger along the top of the book case. Dusty! Quickly rushing out into the hall, she opened the cupboard under the stairs and returned to the book case with a duster to remove the offending specks. As she was shaking the duster outside the front door, Paul came up the driveway pushing his bike, having been out for a ride for no apparent reason, which he had taken to doing recently. She had no idea why but didn't think to question it – too many other things to think about.

'Paul, would you mind moving the bins out of sight into the garage?' she called.

'They're all right where they are, aren't they?'

'If they were, I wouldn't have just asked you to move them, would I?'

Paul shrugged as Verity gave him one of 'those' looks that meant the conversation was over and once more she had got her way. What did it matter, if it kept her happy? He was always on the lookout for a quiet life, and Verity's moods these days were very…. He wasn't sure how to describe them …. Tetchy! That was it: she was very tetchy. He couldn't imagine Carla ever being like that; he couldn't imagine her being anything but soft, feminine and loving, as she had always appeared to be to him. Much to his envy she had quite obviously adored Gareth, and it had always seemed natural for them to go out of their way to please each other. He and Verity, on the other hand, seemed to need to score points against one another more often than not. He had thought about talking to her about it to try and improve everyday life, but there never seemed to be the right time, and he really did not relish the backlash that was likely to meet his efforts – so he left it.

Life plodded on, relentlessly, day in and day out: work, children's activities, Sunday roast, cutting the lawn, washing the car and then back to work again. He wondered, as he compliantly pulled the wheelie bins through the side door of the garage, if everyone's home life was like this. Was it just part of life and you had to get on with it, or did everyone feel this persistent, nagging, depressing disappointment? He was thirty eight years old and felt sixty when he caught himself looking forward to retirement. He remembered in his youth telling his father off for always looking to retirement – wishing his life away. Pitiful: at age thirty eight he had become his father!

Still, the silver lining to his cloud on this particular day was that Carla and her kids were coming round for tea. Verity was good in that way, often inviting them round because, she said, Carla must find it difficult without Gareth on 'family' days. Paul had liked Gareth – what was there not to like? But he had also been jealous of him: he had a beautiful, sexy, successful wife; he had a great physique and was ridiculously fit. He had cycled, played squash, often gone out for the impromptu jog around the park and would turn up, tanned from working outside on one of his labouring or gardening jobs, wearing shorts that hung from his hips below taught stomach muscles; whereas, he himself was pale, hairless and his body was slack from sitting in the design office day after day. He should do something about it he supposed; otherwise, he couldn't really blame Verity for gazing at Gareth during summer barbecues in the garden when everyone used the big, inflatable swimming pool she had bought for the kids one year; Gareth, with his shoulder length hair and flashing smile, had been a handsome bastard. Paul sighed. Gareth was also very dead. That fact and Carla's grief had been the green light for him to try getting closer to the woman he had, up until then, only admired from afar.

Verity had unwittingly helped, during the first few months after Gareth's death, by frequently sending him round to do odd jobs and keep on top of the gardening for Carla. Normally, he would have objected to this going on for any length of time, but being in Carla's house with her had quickly become his favourite part of the weekend, and he had been a large part of her life during those first few months, quietly sharing her grief and holding her when she broke down and cried.

His genuine care for her had now warped, however, into secret fantasies: Carla naked on her smooth white bed; Carla lying beside him in the early dawn; Carla sitting astride him, her breasts swinging as she bucked up and down above him, satisfying her own longing. He had felt guilty, at first, when it was Carla in his mind as he made love to Verity; they were of a similar build and he imagined he was kissing Carla's full lips and stroking her breasts. He had still believed he loved Verity then, not realising that somewhere in between wedding bells, nappies, exhaustion and school dinners, something had died.

He sighed again and glanced round the tidy, ordered garage: bikes on their racks with relevant helmets attached; washing machine and tumble dryer standing side by side ready for duty; recycling bins – brown, green and blue. Everything in its place, so sickeningly clean, even in the garage! For a moment he felt a terrible rage erupt inside him. It was time he admitted that being married to Verity had slowly suffocated and emasculated him. Or was he to blame for letting it happen? He stood there, not sure with whom he was angrier – himself or Verity. He thought it best to just wait until he calmed down before going back into the house.

Some moments later, he walked back into the home that seemed to have become a prison.

'Oh, there you are,' said Verity. 'You took ages doing that – I thought you were never coming out of the garage. Anyway, I thought a film would be fun for the kids tonight? They still haven't seen *Monsters Inc.*, so would you pop down to the video store and get it?'

Verity planted a peck of a kiss on his cheek as though he were eleven years old, and with a shrug of resignation Paul picked up the car keys.

Hours later, the tea all eaten, the dishes all stacked in the dishwasher, the kitchen returned to spotless order and the four children all watching the film, Verity and Paul sat down with Carla in the kitchen, glasses of wine all round. Carla took a sip but then went over to the kettle to make herself a cup of tea.

'I'm off alcohol today,' she admitted with a grimace. 'I got a bit worse for wear last night.'

Verity expressed anxious surprise. 'Don't tell me you've taken to drinking on your own!'

'No. Actually, I went out on a date!'

Verity and Paul looked at her open mouthed – Verity delighted, Paul, not so much.

'Oh my gosh! How was it? And more to the point, *who* was it?' gasped Verity.

'His name is Steve. He's okay, but I'm not sure if I'll see him again.'

'Really, why's that?'

'Well, this will all seem very odd and random, but the guy who babysat for me – Adam, the boys' rugby coach – well, he punched Steve when he brought me home.'

Paul, rendered speechless by this new turn of events, was anything but calm. Steve? Adam? Who were these men suddenly getting involved in Carla's life? He could feel his face burning with indignation and hurt. He hoped the two women had not noticed, but he felt as though he was going to explode. He was fifteen years old again and had just discovered that the best looking girl in the school was not in love with him and was never likely to be. He was feeling very hot. He had to get out. Mumbling an excuse about checking the football scores, he left the room and stood in the hall trying to compose himself while hearing laughter coming from the kitchen, as Verity and Carla continued to discuss the unlikely events of the previous evening. He had to find out who these men were and check them out – for Carla's sake, of course.

He opened the front door and stood staring out across the garden to the road beyond, his jealousy brimming over and his mind in complete turmoil. He needed time to think – to make a plan. He had thought he had one, but things had not gone at all as he had expected, and his stomach lurched with humiliation as he remembered the last occasion he had gone to Carla's aid.

It had been late one evening that her electricity had suddenly switched itself off. She had sounded anxious on the phone, as small incidents like this often floored her, and he had been pleased to be able to come to the rescue. He had known it would just be the trip switch but he was not going to tell her that; he had jumped in his car and driven round to be her knight in shining armour. The sight of her when she opened the door had made him catch his breath: she had looked so young in a pair of pink cotton pyjamas and fluffy slippers, and not at all embarrassed in front of him, as if she was already seeing him as part of her life. Candlelight had given the house a romantic feel and he had been hesitant to do the job he came to do, wanting instead to enjoy his infatuation with this woman in the soft atmosphere.

Stefan and Bryn had been asleep in bed as Paul had quietly fiddled aimlessly around in the metre box, trying to make it look as though it was much more complex than the mere flick of a switch. She had been boiling a saucepan of water on the gas hob when he had gone back to the kitchen to tell her he would need another fuse and was just going to the car to get one. On his return he had found coffee waiting for him and Carla smiling at him over the top of her own coffee cup. Her large eyes had seemed inviting. She had remained silent, which had added to a certain tension in the room. Was she saying something to him with that look?

She had put her cup down. 'All sorted?' she had asked with a tight, bright smile.

He had been just two steps away from taking her in his arms. 'Yes, just need to fit the fuse and then all should be well. I'll just …' He had stopped – it was now or never. He had been hot with lust and uncertainty, could feel his excitement building and with the way she was looking at him through wide, sexy eyes, had thought she wanted him. In a single movement he had stepped up to her, cupped her head in his hands and brought his lips to her closed mouth. For those few seconds, he had been transported to another level, the like of which he had never before experienced. She had smelt of coffee and face cream. Exquisite.

Like the smashing of a mirror, the moment had been destroyed as quickly as it had begun: Carla had pushed at his chest and moved away from his grasp.

'Paul! No! What the hell are you doing?'

'Carla, please ...' He had gone to move towards her again and had been horrified to see her backing away, putting the breakfast bar between them. 'Carla, I want you so much ... please.'

'Paul, this is ridiculous! You're my best friend's husband, for god's sake!'

'So what? My marriage is a sham, Carla, you know that. It's you I want to be with. I only ever think about you.' He had continued to approach her, pleading as she had carried on backing away.

'Paul! Stop this! I'm not ready for any relationship. I don't want any man in my life. I'm just not ready. Paul, please!'

He had heard fear in her voice. That was not what he wanted! He wanted to comfort her and hold her close – not frighten her. He had held his hands up. 'Okay, Okay! I understand, and I'll wait, Carla. I didn't mean to push you. You just looked so lovely standing there.' Carla had just stood staring at him, and he had suddenly felt very weary and a complete fool. 'I'll finish up and get going.'

'Yes, I think that's best. And Paul? ' He had looked up expectantly. 'Let's not talk of this again; let's pretend it never happened, okay?' She had looked at him anxiously.

'But it did happen, Carla. There's something between us. We've become very close since Gareth died and I know you have feelings for me – you just haven't been able to let them out yet.'

Carla had just stood with her arms folded and not answered, which had seemed like an agreement to him.

Hadn't he been patient, waiting for the time when they could confess all to Verity and start their lives together? Looking out at the spring evening, remembering the touch of her full lips on his, he could not understand other men suddenly appearing in her life. Hadn't she said she was not ready for another relationship? Why hadn't she even looked at him when she told them about going on a date. He needed more information – he needed *her* – and he would not rest until he had both.

His fantasy had crossed a line from which there would be no turning back.

*   *   *   *   *

The match was never going to be easy. Adam's team had come up against their opponents several times and it had always been a bitter balance until the final whistle blew and today was no exception. In addition,

Adam had found it really difficult to concentrate and his team members had noticed that he was not particularly on form. Still, thirteen-fifteen was not a bad score and it gave them a bonus point. Even though they had been beaten, it had been close.

Mel had come along to watch as it was a home game and she waited patiently for him to come out of the changing room into the clubhouse for his post-match meal. She loved watching him come out. The club blazer, white shirt and striped tie really suited him and she revelled in his good looks. She looked up as he came through the door, flinging his kitbag down on to the pile to join his team mates and those who had stayed behind to console their team. He was completely unaware of the stir that he caused amongst the young girls as he engaged in friendly banter with other team supporters who were standing around drinking pints. When he spotted Mel she tingled with delight as he made straight for where she was sitting on a stool at the edge of the bar and they exchanged smiles. Jealous eyes turned her way.

'That was pretty crap, wasn't it?' he said resignedly.

'Pretty much' she agreed. 'Where was your head today?'

'Don't! I feel bad enough as it is,' he frowned and took a big gulp of the pint of coke that she had waiting for him.

'Where were you last night? Your mum said you didn't come home.'

'I stayed at Carla Trelawny's. I work for her on Fridays, now, and I stayed on to babysit her boys so that she could go out.'

Mel wasn't sure how she felt about that but she knew not to make a 'girlie' fuss. It wasn't how they were together. 'Oh, right,' she said in a manner that did not match the emotional turmoil she was feeling, 'she's the one whose husband was killed a while back, isn't she?'

'Yep.' Seeing something he couldn't quite understand in Mel's face, Adam was suddenly anxious to change the subject and picked up his coke. 'I'm off to get my grub. I'll see you in a minute.'

Mel was left alone with her thoughts. She didn't know Carla Trelawny very well but she had been the talk of the club when her husband had been so tragically killed in a road accident. They had had a collection and bought the boys some Lego to help them through it. She wasn't sure that Lego had been entirely appropriate but maybe it had taken their mind off things for a while. She felt uncomfortable about Adam spending time at her house: Carla was an attractive woman and she knew young men had fantasies about older more experienced women. Was it jealousy? She had known she was in love with Adam for some time and the feelings she was now experiencing were simply confirming it.

Adam had always been her mate. They had been close since the first year at secondary school when she had lived opposite the Barnes' house in the flat above the corner shop with her mother. Her parents were divorced and she had loved being with Adam and his family, spending most of her time over at their house, even if Adam wasn't there, and Joyce had treated her as one of her own, knowing that Mel's mother was an habitual gambler and Mel was left at home on her own for hours on end with very little food in the house. Joyce had filled a huge gap for Mel and provided her with the love and sustenance that she was badly in need of at that awkward age.

When she was sixteen, Mel had left and gone to live with her father in Dartford, where she got a job in a shoe shop. That hadn't lasted long and she was soon back, this time staying with the Barnes family for six months. During that time, she and Adam had become soul mates. It was obvious to her that he regarded her as a sister, but the feeling was far from mutual. His strong, muscular frame, engaging smile and pretty blue eyes had turned her head, as they would any girl of that age. Joyce could see this was happening but Adam had no idea and since unrequited feelings had not been something Mel was prepared to endure up close, she had got a live-in job at a local care home for adults with learning difficulties. Although she still had a bed at Adam's house, she rarely went back, knowing that the more she acted like a sister, the more Adam would treat her like one – and that was not her aim.

No one knew Adam like Mel; he trusted her implicitly and talked openly with her about anything on his mind. Their friendship had taken on a different dynamic the previous Christmas, however, at the rugby club party. Mel had been working in the kitchen serving the food to the members, who had really only come to drink, play ridiculous boy games and generally behave very immaturely, in her eyes. The bar had closed at midnight and the lads had started to make their way home or on to late night clubs in the city. Adam had been in high spirits, and though not actually drunk he hadn't been fully sober either when he'd come into the kitchen to help Mel finish the clearing up.

Afterwards, they'd left together through the back door. It had been pitch dark and ice had started to form on the concrete pathway. Mel had walked cautiously to avoid slipping but to no avail: one minute she'd been upright – the next she'd been lying on her back on the ground.

'Fuck!' she'd gasped as pain shot through her back and legs.

'Christ, you okay?'

She had felt foolish but also anxious because she had hit the ground with considerable force. Adam had been crouching beside her, peering into her face with concern as she'd gingerly got up. His breath had been hot on her face and smelt, not unpleasantly, of beer. He'd carefully helped her to her feet and continued to watch her closely as she'd stood still for a moment to let the shock wear off and check that all her limbs were in working order. As her eyes had grown accustomed to the dark and she could make out the features of his face, something had happened – whether it was the shock of the fall or the romantic feel of darkness, she wasn't sure, but she had leant forward and gently kissed his mouth, lingering for a few seconds before pulling back.

Her forwardness had shocked her and it seemed to have shocked Adam too. They'd both stood in complete silence not really knowing who was supposed to make the next move. Adam had then decided that he quite liked what had just happened. Taking the lead, he'd leaned in to kiss her in return, the passion had kicked in and he'd pinned her up against the clubhouse wall, pushed his tongue into her mouth and groaned as he felt her respond.

Mel, thrilled that the boy she loved so much had finally realised that she was a hot-blooded woman, had put her hands under Adam's jacket and run them across the chest she had watched develop from boyhood. She had felt his strong contours and his nipples standing proud; the desire for him to touch her in the same way had become so strong that she'd undone her coat toggles.

As his attention seemed to stay on the kiss, she had taken his hand from her waist and guided it to her breast inside her duffle coat. She had been aware of his sharp intake of breath as his hand enveloped her and, at first, he hadn't moved it, but then he'd started to caress and mould her. With excitement building and their kissing becoming more urgent, Adam had flattened Mel against the wall with his body even further. With her coat undone she had been able to feel his arousal through his jeans as he thrust himself against her. He had started to move up and down against her body, grinding himself into her and leaving her physically breathless. Aroused herself, she'd parted her legs to allow him better access. Though their clothing and the angle they were standing hadn't created the desired effect for Mel, she had let Adam continue.

Suddenly, following a series of frantic movements, Adam had pulled away and stood back panting. 'What the fuck are we doing?' he'd gasped.

Mel had been shocked and hurt. Wasn't it obvious?

'Mel, we're mates. We can't do this, I'm sorry, let's go home.'

And that had been it! Mel had been left frustrated and overwhelmed with desire, love, rejection and a hundred other emotions. They had not ever even discussed it and Mel felt that it hung between them like the elephant in the room that it was. There were not many nights, however, that she did not allow herself the luxury of a replay in her mind as she lay in her room at the care home. It wasn't romantic or very promising for the future, but it was all she had.

Now she had the presence of Carla Trelawny to cope with. She knew that Adam had been with a few girls, but none of them had been more than a one night stand. So why did she feel this was different? Why did she feel so threatened by the woman for whom Adam was working? It was less about Carla and more about Adam really – something in the way he had spoken about her and then dismissed the subject, as though there were something to hide. But she's at least twice his age! thought Mel. Did that make any difference though? Because there was something going on – she was sure of it.

* * * * *

Adam didn't dislike Sundays, he just felt at a bit of a loss as to what to do. Joyce always laid on a great Sunday spread and invariably there would be either his sister or brother around to enjoy the feast along with his nieces and nephews. Today, however, as he stood in the shower, he was feeling agitated – wrong, somehow. It was a peculiar feeling, as if he were living the wrong life. His mother, being a realist, would laugh, if he told her, raise her eyebrows and tell him he was a dreamer and a romantic. Mel, on the other hand, had once said that you could be anyone or do anything you wanted, as long as you believed in yourself. How did she know these things? he wondered, in passing, as he thought about how he loved nothing more than to sit with her in the garden or in a corner of the pub and dream up what they would do if they won the lottery. He always had grand ideas about setting up charities and businesses so that his money could do some good or make more of itself. Mel said she wouldn't tell anyone about the win because once they knew everyone would suddenly want to be your friend, even if they weren't in the first place.

Today, though, it wasn't money on Adam's mind, it was Carla: Carla with her soft dark hair, bewitching green eyes and sweet, sweet smile; the way her eyes sparkled when she laughed captivated him. Friday seemed such a long way away and he wondered what she was doing today. Sundays were family days and that must be tricky for her with the boys and no husband around. Maybe he should call her. But what would he say? And anyway, maybe Steve had called and was with her now; maybe they had already slept together and were starting a new relationship. That thought paralysed him. He had to know. 'Crikey!' he said aloud to himself. 'You're becoming obsessed!'

Nevertheless, over a breakfast of bacon and eggs, Adam decided he could not go the whole day without knowing if big, bad Steve was there or not; he would cycle past and see if his car was there.

90

The decision made, he grabbed his jacket, blew a kiss to his mum, manoeuvred his bike out of the shed and began the ride over to Carla's part of town. He had a car but it was in bits in a friend's garage needing a new sub-frame. He preferred his bike, in a way; although not so good in the middle of winter, it was definitely easier to park. He lived in a small terraced house with a long, narrow rear garden on a street which was bordered with terraced houses, like soldiers on parade, and was always lined with cars. Some people had created little parking areas on the tiny patch of ground at the front of their houses but most residents had to fight for a parking space.

Carla's house was detached and stood on its own plot of land up the hill towards the university. He hadn't asked her too much about her work, but he did know she owned a company that did marketing for other companies – that was how she had described it. Most of her clients, she said, were in London so she often went up there for meetings; sometimes she went further north and stayed overnight. Adam was a little in awe of the fact that she was the boss and had people working for her; it added to her charm, as far as he was concerned; it also put her even further out of his reach.

It was a fresh spring day and the sun was doing its best to warm the air and give everyone a taste of warm summer days to come. Adam was excited as he cycled through the city centre, but he also felt quite immature: what was he doing, snooping on Carla like this? And what would he do if he saw Steve's car outside? Knock on the door and demand to know what was going on? Ridiculous!

He still pedalled on though, slowing as he reached the end of Carla's road. Now what? Carla lived in a cul-de-sac – not the sort of place that you would be 'just passing by'.

As he sat thinking about this, one foot on the road to balance himself, movement caught his eye. Shading his eyes from the bright sunshine, he saw that it was Carla, fortunately walking away from him towards her home without having seen him. Either side of her walked her boys, both holding her hands – a little family, minus one. Adams' breath caught in his throat at the bitter-sweet sight and he knew exactly what to do.

He called to her as he came pedalling up behind her, and she looked round, a huge smile spreading across her face as she saw it was him.

'Adam! How lovely to see you. What are you doing out this way?'

He could have lied and made up a story about visiting a friend or dropping something off to someone, but he didn't. 'Well actually, I came out to see you guys!' There! He had said it.

Carla's smile did not dim; she did not look reproachful or suspicious; in fact, her smile widened. 'And we're very pleased to see you, Adam, aren't we boys?' They both nodded enthusiastically. 'So, join us for chocolate. We've just been to buy some.'

Pushing his bike alongside them, Adam told the boys about his disappointing match the previous day and invited them all to come and watch sometime, saying he was sure he would have played better had they been there.

Carla made tea for them and orange squash for the boys and they sat and devoured all the chocolate, even though the plan had been to save some for later.

'So what do you normally do on a Sunday?' Adam asked, as he was once more perched on a stool at the breakfast bar. Carla's eyes darkened and he regretted his question. 'Sorry, that was stupid of me. I didn't mean to be tactless.'

Carla leant over and put her hand on his arm. There was that electric shock again!

'Don't apologise, Adam, we're friends, right? And friends shouldn't have to tread on egg shells. Gareth died eighteen months ago and there's not a day goes by that I don't think of his smile, his voice and the way he used to tease me; his easy manner; his cooking!' She raised her eyes to the ceiling and shook her head, laughing and trying to lighten the mood. 'But Adam, Gareth is dead and the boys and I have had to accept that. But I tell you what: I've learned to enjoy each day and every hour of each day, because you never know when it is going to be your last.'

Adam watched her face as she spoke. There were tears in her eyes but she was on a roll and he didn't want to stop her. He held his breath as she continued.

'You get one life, Adam. Live it. Do what seems right. Listen to your instincts – your gut feelings. You're young and you've got your whole life in front of you – no ties, nothing to stop you doing or being whatever you want.' She opened her eyes wide. 'How exciting is that?'

Suddenly, he felt fourteen again. It wasn't that he didn't agree with her; it was that she was speaking to him as though he were a young boy ready to go into the world. Right now, he didn't want that. He wanted her to need him like she did the other night.... But she had been drunk then – not the real Carla who was strong, independent and powerful – not needy or weak. He should have realised that. Carla was magnificent. He could see her now in the board room, closing the deal. He could see her standing up to suits who thought that as a mere woman she wouldn't be able to fight them, and he could see her winning. Well, he realised, he was obviously attracted to strong women.

Carla was waiting for a reaction from him. In keeping with what she had just said, he decided to say exactly what he felt. 'That is very exciting, Carla. But do you know what's even more exciting, right now?'

'What's that?'

'You!'

She sat back and looked at him thoughtfully, her head tilted to one side. 'Well, thank you,' she said, smiling, 'but why do you say that?'

'You're so passionate about life. You're so … you're so … alive!' he enthused, no longer caring whether or not he was being tactful. She had given him permission to be real and honest, so that was what he was being.

Silence filled the room and they just looked at each other. If it had been the movies, one of them would have approached the other to instigate a sensual embrace. But this was reality, so they just sat and looked for what was probably only seconds but seemed to Adam like a lifetime.

Carla broke the silence. 'I think, after all that, we need more tea.' Her emotions were in turmoil at what was happening between the two of them. She was just about holding on to her decorum, but only because she managed to tear herself away from those blue eyes and do something normal – make the tea. Her thoughts scampered back and forth as she busied herself with kettle and tea bags. Common sense was telling her to put a stop to all this, but her heart was urging her on into the unknown. The Friday night moment on the sofa had re-ignited her passionate side. She felt sixteen again. It was delicious. But she was a mother. She wasn't Shirley Valentine. She had responsibilities. People relied on her both at home and at work, and she had a reputation that had to be kept intact for everyone's sake. But what had she just been preaching to Adam? One life … do what's instinctively right. What felt instinctively right to her, at that moment, was to walk over to this young man, take his face in her hands and gently kiss his adorable mouth. And why shouldn't she? He was free. She was free. But there was a massive wall standing between them, wasn't there? A wall that was nineteen years high. She had been older than he was now when he came kicking and screaming into the world. The depressing thought that she was more than twice his age and old enough to be his mother hit home as she poured boiling water over tea bags.

Adam had gone out into the garden to play swing ball with the boys and she watched him as he stood behind Bryn, helping him to angle the bat in the right way. Such a male thing to do: she would never think of teaching Bryn that. From her position to one side of the kitchen window she could see out without easily being seen and allowed herself a moment to enjoy looking at Adam. He was a strong, powerful figure, as tall as Gareth but broader, and he had an easy way about him which exuded confidence – unusual in one so young. His sandy coloured hair was thick and slightly unruly, and his tanned features gave him that irresistible look of carefree youth and physicality. Not something you often saw in an office environment.

She knew that Adam was not academically inclined: Joyce had said that he always struggled at school, been like a caged animal waiting for release back into the wild, and was just sixteen when he went off to work full time on the farm. She said she had worried about her beautiful, blue eyed boy who seemed to have no plans for the future, but she just trusted that he would find his way in the end. She described him as a free spirit and, right now, as Carla watched him playing and laughing with her boys, she knew exactly what Joyce meant. And it was alluring, to say the least. But how did she deal with this developing situation? She had brought this young man into her life; he was falling for her and she was in danger of reciprocating. Was it because she was lonely or did she really have feelings for him?

Since it wasn't something she could solve right away, she allowed herself to just watch and admire, and perhaps fantasise a little as she took the mugs of tea out into the garden and placed them on the picnic table. She dragged her eyes away from him as she wiped the dew from the deck chairs with a tea towel, then looked up to see him coming to join her. He grinned and sat down, stretching out his long legs, saying nothing. They achieved a companionable silence that Carla found both soothing and pleasant.

'Stay for lunch.' The words were more command than request. Adam nodded, once more locking her gaze and making her head spin.

'Love to.'

They returned to their silence as though much had been said between them. Both knew something was about to happen. Neither of them knew when or how, but there was a developing urge in both of them to see this through to its conclusion, whatever the consequences. Tomorrow she may feel differently, she thought, but sitting in her garden Carla was prepared to take the next step.

Joyce was changing the beds when she heard the phone ringing and almost didn't get to it on time.

'Hi, Mum. It's only me.'

'Oh, hello love. Is everything all right? Where are you?'

'I'm at Carla's finishing off a few bits from Friday. It looks like it's going to take a while so Carla's going to give me something to eat. I didn't want you to expect me home.'

Joyce felt a fleeting moment of worry for her son, but she let it go and was glad that he was taking his job with Carla so seriously.

'All right, love. See you when I see you. Simon and the kids are here for lunch so it's all going to be a bit manic here, anyway. 'Bye then, love.'

''Bye, Mum'

Adam replaced the phone in the charger and stood still for a moment in Carla's kitchen, feeling a mite guilty that he had told his mother a white lie, but he knew it was best that way. She wouldn't understand. How could she?

Carla looked up as he came back out into the garden. 'All okay?'

'Yes, she's fine. Simon's coming round later, anyway, so it will be busy enough for her without me being there.'

Carla nodded and patted the seat for him to sit back down. While the boys played, they talked about how they were getting on at rugby, and then moved on to Carla's future plans for expanding her business. Adam talked through his dilemma of feeling unsettled about his life and his realisation that he was ready to step out into a new career, if only he knew what. They laughed out loud at Stefan's impersonation of his little brother trying to hit the ball and Bryn chasing him round the garden, never quite able to catch his bigger, faster brother. The sound of her boys shrieking with laughter made Carla's heart sing; it had been missing over the past eighteen months. Banjo was joining in and even he sounded more excited than usual.

When Stefan came over and dragged Adam up to practise his rugby passes with him, Carla continued to watch and just enjoy it all. Her mum had been right: the boys definitely needed more male input in their lives. The truth was, so did Carla, but was this the right man? For a minute, her mind went into panic mode. There were three young men in her garden, right now, whom she had the capacity to hurt if she got things wrong. Maybe she should be far more careful: she was the mature one here, so she should make sure her relationship with Adam did not get too heated; otherwise, there could be dire consequences for all of them.

If she was completely honest with herself though, she wanted him. Even admitting that was terrifying but extraordinarily exciting and her heartbeat quickened. Despite all the reasons she should not get involved with him, she suspected she would be unlikely to resist.

Adam was thoroughly enjoying himself. His decision to cycle over to Carla's that day had been the right one; he felt proud that he had made the move and had not let fear and uncertainty stop him. Where things would go from here, he was not sure. His relative inexperience with women was a slight concern but he was getting a definite feeling that Carla was attracted to him. It was the breathy, spontaneous way she said things to him out of the blue: when she'd asked him to stay on Friday night and then again when she'd asked him to stay today, it was as though her heart was doing the talking, as opposed to her head.

After a lunch of soup, fresh crusty bread straight from the oven and strong cheddar cheese, they took the rugby ball and an excited Banjo up to the park to run off some energy. When the boys decided they wanted to play on the swings, Carla and Adam sat on a bench near the noisy play area; Banjo sat panting next to them. Adam gently took her hand and held it beside his thigh and she did not resist; her hand felt small and soft in his. Without looking at her, he plucked up the courage to talk about what was in his heart.

'What's happening?' he said, almost in a whisper.

'I don't know,' she answered in the same way.

He turned to look at her and it took all of his will power not to kiss her. Her mouth was closed and her eyes were wide with anticipation and uncertainty. 'I know I can't right now, but I so want to kiss you,' he said.

She gripped his hand tighter and she looked away, as if trying to avoid her emotions. 'I'm scared, Adam.'

He returned the squeeze of her hand, not sure how to react. Blood was pumping through his veins at an alarming rate and his own emotions were all over the place. So many things frightened him, too: his inexperience with women; rejection if he did things wrong; the disapproval of his family and Mel, if they knew. All of it paled into insignificance, however, when compared with the burning desire he currently felt for the woman beside him.

Carla's mouth had gone dry. Was this really happening? If she did not stop this now it could be a disaster. But she was on fire and there was no denying how much she wanted him. His hand was strong and warm, and she didn't ever want him to let go. He gently stroked her knuckles with his thumb and his touch sent a surge of desire through her, quickening her breath. She wanted more.

The moment came to an abrupt end as Banjo spotted another dog he wanted to investigate and shot off across the park, ignoring Carla's calls. Since the sun was starting to go down and there was a chill in the air, they decided they would just follow him and make their way home.

There was an extra car in the driveway when they arrived back at Carla's house. The silver Mercedes was parked haphazardly across the drive, blocking any other access. Carla laughed when she saw it. 'Trudy!' She ran up the path to greet her friend who was standing at the open door, having let herself in with her own key, which Carla had long ago entrusted to her.

'Hello, darling,' she said, a wicked grin on her face as she looked past Carla to fix her eyes firmly on Adam walking up with the boys. 'What have you been up to?'

Carla knew exactly what she was thinking and quickly introduced Adam, realising Trudy would not have any idea who he was. 'Oh, Trudy, this is Adam, Joyce's son. Adam this is my best friend, Trudy.'

'Well, hello Adam,' said Trudy with a full length appraisal.

'Very nice to meet you, Trudy.'

Carla looked at Adam, whose face was registering some discomfort. Perhaps he thought Trudy might take a bite out of him! She could be a bit overwhelming at times. 'Come on. Let's have hot chocolate,' she suggested, as she ushered everyone indoors.

With the boys in front of the TV and hot chocolate consumed, Adam decided it was definitely time to remove himself and leave the women to their girlie chat; there was an awkward atmosphere and he could guess what the subject was going to be.

'Thanks for a lovely day, Adam.' Carla threw him a smile laced with mild relief as she saw him to the door; she was feeling the tension too.

He looked down at her and smiled back. 'It's been good, hasn't it?' Then he bent his head and kissed her softly on the mouth, lingering for a few seconds. He saw her eyes close and as he pulled away she stood for a split second before opening them and smiling up at him. There was no need for words; he simply touched her cheek.

Two minutes later he was cycling down the road in the fading light, his heart full and his face beaming.

Meantime, Carla had returned to the kitchen to face Trudy's inevitable inquisition. She grinned as the expected curiosity erupted.

'Is *he* the babysitter?'

Carla nodded, still grinning from ear to ear.

'And is my intuition failing me here, or is there something going on?'

At this, Carla's smile faded and she sighed as she hoisted herself back on to a stool. 'God, Trude, I don't know .... Yes, if I want it – but what? How far do I let it go? There's just so much at stake here, and you know what? You're the only person I can talk to about it.'

'Well, what's happened, so far?' Trudy raised an eyebrow.

'Not much, but at the same time, so much. I'm both excited and terrified. He's so very, very young!'

'Listen girl, you're not exactly drawing your pension yourself. Hell, what's the problem? He likes you – obvious to my eyes. You like him – even more obvious. You're both adults … just! So, get on with it! Have some fun and stop thinking about consequences all the time.'

Doubt clouded Carla's face. 'But what about his mum and all his friends? And my mum?'

'What about them?'

Trudy's question hung in the air for a moment.

'I take your point: why should I arrange my life according to what others might think? Nevertheless, there *are* consequences that I *do* have to consider.'

Trudy rolled her eyes at that, before continuing along her own line of thought. 'He's a real looker, Carla, and he seems mature for his age, as well. How old is he? Early twenties?'

Carla burst out laughing. 'I wish! Try eighteen!'

'Holy cow, Carla! I see what you mean!' Trudy gave one of her crooked frowns. 'But it's still time you had a bit of fun, even if it is with someone of such tender years.'

Carla wasn't sure, and the more she thought about it, the more she worried about the effect their encounter, however it turned out, might have on those close to both of them; her sense of responsibility also included Adam.

Later that night, after Trudy had left and the boys had gone to bed, she put on some music, sat down with a magazine and tried to take her mind off her quandary. Leafing through pages like an automaton, however, she soon realised that she wasn't even coming close to taking in what was on them, and smiled ruefully to herself. How could it be otherwise? She was having her own real life drama, let alone reading about anybody else's.

Magazine forgotten, she gave herself up to the thoughts crowding all else from her mind: it was time to be the adult and do the sensible, responsible thing, which was putting a stop to any romantic entanglement with Adam. And if she was going to do that, she had to do it sooner rather than later, before Adam got really hurt. The decision made, she was pleased with herself and felt some relief that she was mature enough not to disregard her responsibilities in favour of her desires. At the same time, fooling herself was not one of her character flaws, and she could not ignore one persistent thought: could she remain mature and not lose her resolve the moment she next set eyes on him? Well, she would just have to be strong.

She turned her thoughts to the work week ahead, testing her ability to banish Adam from her mind. Her diary, she remembered, was packed: apart from everything else, the Triton case was now well underway and she had a client feedback meeting, for which she needed to prepare a presentation; she also had to be in London for meetings on Friday. She was glad of the distraction business provided; it would help her to keep her feelings in check.

Adam, on the other hand, could not stop thinking about Carla. His young heart was full to the brim with the promise of what could be. That Tuesday, though, he took time off from his daydreaming to go out for a few beers with the boys from the club. It was his friend Josh's twentieth birthday and the night promised to be fun. They planned to start off at *The Archer* and then go off for an Indian in the city centre.

The pub was busy for a Tuesday and there were a lot of people there that Adam knew. Josh's sister, Becky – two years Josh's junior – had joined them with one of her friends and Adam was well aware that she had a crush on him. He thought she looked very sweet with her hair in plaits, wearing tight fitting jeans and a figure-hugging top. Unsurprisingly, both she and her friend managed to corner him, fluttering eyelashes and constantly touching his arm as they vied and sparred for his attention. Usually, Adam would have been flattered and may well have made his choice and walked one of the girls home, so he was amazed by just how disinterested he was: they seemed like little girls to him and he wanted only to disengage from their attention. Finally, he managed to extricate himself by going over to the television in the corner to watch some of the mid-week football match.

'I think you're in there, mate,' said Josh, coming over to him with another beer and taking a draught of his own pint.

'What do you mean?'

'Becky's mate – she's got the hots for you, you lucky bastard. I've been trying my hand there for weeks. No joy. You walk in and she's putty, mate. I don't know how you do it.'

Adam snorted, suddenly realising he just did not want to be there in the pub or talking to Josh; and he certainly didn't want to be pressured into taking things further with Becky's friend. He downed his pint quickly while hiding his dissatisfaction, and went back to the bar to buy the next round.

Five pints later, he found himself with Becky's friend, Ruby – or was is Rosie? Adam neither knew nor cared – he wasn't really thinking straight. What he did know was that he was helping her out of her jeans as she lay on the back seat of Josh's car, her soft, yielding body ready to relieve his frustration.

His excitement was intense and he felt the physical need to release the pressure. Her thighs felt warm and soft as he hurriedly unzipped his jeans and pushed them down to just below his buttocks. She gasped as he pushed her legs apart. Fumbling for the packet he habitually kept in his pocket for times such as these, he ripped it open with his teeth and half kneeling up, rolled the condom on.

She pulled his head down to hers and kissed him. He felt her tongue work its way into his mouth and he obliged; she tasted of spiced rum and cigarettes. She was moaning and groaning in a way that struck him, in passing, as false, as he pushed her legs open wider and guided himself inside her, giving a thrust that made her shout out and push against his chest. 'Careful!' he heard her say as he slowly started to build his rhythm. The cramped space in the car was not helping, but soon the familiar building sensation began to take over and blood hammered in his ears. His thoughts were not for the girl beneath him and somewhere inside he felt disgust for what he was doing, but he could not stop. Then the moment came: he threw back his head, eyes tight shut and breath rasping as the climax blasted everything else from his mind.

The pulsation subsided and he looked down at Ruby – or Rosie – and she was smiling triumphantly – like the cat who stole the cream, Adam thought – while he was feeling a little sorry that he had used her, but not much – she had wanted it. He just hoped she wasn't expecting him to hang around with her all night, because that wasn't going to happen. He withdrew from her, removed the used condom and pulled up his jeans, after which he got out of the car to give her room to get her clothes back on.

Back in the pub, he left her and went into the gents to throw the condom down the toilet. He shut the cubicle door and sat on the seat, putting his head in his hands. He was relieved of sexual tension but he felt wretched. Had he just been unfaithful to Carla? How would she react if she knew what he had done? Would she understand, or would she be disgusted and hurt by his lack of self- control? He had no idea; Carla was uncharted territory. She was the path to the unknown, and if that night's activities had shown him anything, it was that, more than ever, she was the journey he wanted to take. He was no longer prepared to settle for second best.

*   *   *   *   *

The next three weeks came and went, life unfolding pretty much as usual. Adam's Fridays at Carla's house were busy, but she was not there on any of them, meetings in London having kept her away. She left notes for him with detailed lists of what needed to be done and thanking him for his work the previous week. Adam spent each week looking forward to Friday and was crestfallen each time he realised he was not going to see her. Rugby training had also finished for the season so he didn't see the boys either. But at least he was in her house, amongst her things, doing what she had asked. He liked that.

The weather was still and balmy for late May, and the garden was heady with the scent of honeysuckle when Adam arrived in T-shirt and shorts for his day's work on the fourth Friday since seeing her. He found the usual note on the breakfast bar but this time his heart skipped a beat: Carla would be back around one o'clock, it said. As his mother now only worked mornings at the house, he drew a deep breath and felt the butterflies of anticipation rise in his stomach: he would be alone with Carla.

The work on the list was all out in the garden. Keeping the grass under control at this time of year was a never ending chore and, today, he would also be creosoting the back fence. Remembering to hydrate for the work ahead, he filled a pint glass full of filter water, drank it down in one go and then went outside, whistling, to begin his day's work.

As the morning sped by and the weather grew hotter, Adam discarded his T-shirt. He was careful not to burn but liked the feel of the sun on his back as he worked. Over the past weeks he had gained a deep tan as he did most years. He had raised a few eyebrows from the women at work on the farm as he stripped off, and they wolf whistled and laughed; harmless flirting he enjoyed.

Carla arrived home feeling good about the weekend. She had worked hard, put in long hours and was due some relaxation. She would pick the boys up from school herself, today, and she was looking forward to spending a little extra time with them. She would treat them to fish and chips and a trip to the cinema that evening, she decided. She smiled when she saw Adam's bicycle in the driveway. She felt she had pretty much got her feelings under control; it was certainly easier when she kept her distance. Not that she had been avoiding him: her workload had meant she was just not about very much. In a calm, mature way, she was now looking forward to seeing him and establishing their relationship on a level at which they both felt comfortable.

Then she saw him.

Putting her bag down on the breakfast bar, she just stood mesmerised. He was moving some stones from the pond area over to where they had bonfires on chilly autumn nights, and he was wearing nothing but a pair of shorts and workmen's boots. 'Damn!' thought Carla, as all of her resolve rapidly drained away. She continued to observe him: he was muscular, tanned, capable, semi-naked – and in her garden. Gathering herself together she took a deep breath. 'Hello you!' she called out of the window.

He smiled a killer smile and waved back. 'Hi! How are you?'

'I'm fine,' she replied. 'Don't let me stop you. I'm just going to get changed and then I'll fix us a drink.'

He waved in agreement and carried on working.

As she ran up the stairs, Carla tried to get her emotions under control. It's just because he's standing there in the garden with virtually nothing on, she told herself – purely a physical reaction.

She looked out of her bedroom window, knowing it was not a wise thing to do. There he was – Adonis! It was an overused term. Nevertheless, an Adonis was in her garden!

She quickly showered and pulled on shorts and a T-shirt, feeling a little embarrassed by her pale legs compared to Adam's bronzed body. She scolded herself for thinking about that body again but still stole a little look out of the window. Not seeing him anywhere, she assumed he must have come into the kitchen for a drink, and she left her bedroom to go down and join him.

She stopped short. He was there, at the top of the stairs. She was shocked and almost paralysed with uncertainty. What to do? His cornflower blue eyes were fixed on her, the light from the landing window and his deep tan combining to set them ablaze. She felt her stomach roll with desire. Silence stood between them, thick with promise, as they both stopped, each transfixed by the sight of the other.

Carla could see lust in Adam's burning gaze and she no longer had any doubt whatsoever about what she was going to do. She knew what he wanted, and she knew exactly how to give it. For herself, she wanted to feel those strong arms around her and that beautiful, young body pressing against hers. She wanted to feel Adam inside her – but that would have to wait. First, she wanted to show him pleasure that he may not have experienced before. She wanted to see his face at the pitch of passion. Knowing she must make the first move because he was hesitant and probably fearful of rejection, she took a step. He did not move a muscle as, barefoot, she moved slowly towards him. She was aware of his sharp intake of breath as she took his hand and leaned back slightly to run her eyes all over his body.

Adam did not want to interrupt whatever Carla had in mind for him. This was the moment he had dreamt about; it was happening, right now. Even though she was only touching his hand he could feel his skin burning as she looked at him; it was deliciously sensual. Then she reached up to his shoulder and brushed his arm from shoulder to elbow with the back of her fingernails. He thought he would expire. She continued to look at him for what seemed like an eternity, neither of them speaking. Then she gently tugged him into her bedroom. It smelt of her. She was everywhere. He could feel his addiction to this woman begin, and he welcomed it. She stopped in the middle of the room, took her hand from his and moved behind him, indicating that he should stand still by placing her hands for a second on both of his upper arms. He stood motionless, blood pumping.

Cool hands on his shoulder blades moved to trace the contours of his muscles all the way down his back. Having reached the base of his spine, Carla slowly began to run her hands around his waist, her little fingers just slipping below the band of his shorts. She shifted slightly, leaning her body against his so that her hands could meet on his stomach. Her fingertips all found their way underneath the waistband and his abdominal muscles clenched as she caressed him just above the place he *so* wanted her to touch.

Carla began to kiss his salty back, her only focus this man's body and the feel of his masculinity. She did not want him to touch her. Not yet. She wanted to savour every part of him, explore and discover how far he would allow her to go. She had never been so aroused. She could feel the soft line of hair that led from his navel in a tantalising trail towards the centre of his heat. She continued to massage, moving in slow, tiny circles, each time reaching a little further down. She knew exactly what she was doing to him: she could feel his muscles tensing each time her fingertips brushed past his arousal; she could hear him softly panting. Slowly pulling her hands away she turned him round to face her. He was tense with longing and for a moment she met his gaze, without touching him. She then moved over to the bed and lay on top of the white cotton quilt, making a space for him to lie down beside her.

He did so, knowing that she was in charge and that he was to do exactly as she indicated. The excitement was intense and nothing like he had ever experienced before. Clasping his hands behind his head, he lay still and looked at her. She knelt up beside him and then, taking his head in her hands, she leaned down and kissed him deeply and sensually. He began to respond but she pulled her mouth away and looked into his eyes, starting to lick his lip with the tip of her tongue, following each lick with a kiss. He opened his mouth and she continued on the inside of his lips and his chin; moving further down she carried on loving him with her mouth around his neck and the base of his throat. The sensation was mind blowing. He still hadn't touched her and he had to fight the urge to reach out and caress her silky skin, knowing if he did that the moment would be ruined – the magic broken. He closed his eyes and revelled in every touch of her lips. Her mouth was now on his chest, her breath hot and urgent as she licked and kissed. She reached his nipples and he groaned involuntarily as her lips closed round one of them and she gently nipped him.

He felt dizzy, suspended in time, and he gasped as her lips travelled further and further down towards the top of his shorts. Was she going to go the whole way down there? He was briefly astounded that they had yet to remove a single stitch of clothing.

Carla decided she needed to do something about the pressing bulge in Adam's shorts and slowed the descending direction her mouth was taking to consider whether this would be too much for him. She looked up into his eyes: they were not saying *stop*, they were saying *please don't stop*.

'I want to kiss you here,' she said, running a finger along the length of him through his shorts. 'Is that okay?' In answer, he held her gaze and reached down to undo the top button of his shorts. Slowly and very tantalizing, Carla thought, he pulled the zipper down, lifted his hips, pushed his shorts and underpants down past his thighs, past his knees, and kicked them off, along with his socks, on to the floor at the foot of the bed. He was now completely naked. Carla drank in the sheer maleness of him, feasting her eyes on every inch of him. His tan stopped abruptly at his waistline and carried on down from his thighs. The paleness in between framed his proud, glistening erection. She bent and kissed the swollen end. Hands back behind his head, he closed his eyes and she felt his body tense. Still kneeling beside him, she began to rub and caress his strong, muscular thighs.

Adam was focussing all his concentration on not letting go and climaxing. Carla was running the show and she would let him know when he could explode. The fact that she was still fully clothed and pleasuring him was turning him on even more. The intensity of feeling was exquisite torture. He looked down and could see that, on his tip, a bead of his seed had formed in anticipation. It was almost too much when Carla followed his eyes and bent her head to run her tongue along his length and lap it up. She lifted her head and smiled as she then moved along the bed, came up alongside him and tilted his head towards her. Her kiss was passionate and deep. He raised his head and his arm came down to pull her closer to him, which caused her to gently pull away and push him firmly on to his back again.

Still kissing him she reached down, taking hold of him and beginning to massage his stiffness. 'Show me how you do it,' she said hotly into his ear. He took her hand and applied the pressure that suited him. It took only a few strokes for her to learn how he liked it, and then she took his hand away and knelt up, never taking her eyes from his face as she worked on him.

His excitement had reached fever pitch. He could no longer focus as the blood pumped round his body. 'Come for me, Adam,' he heard her say, and his orgasm burst through. He could hear himself crying out as he crashed through the climax with his arms above his head and his hands gripping the bedrail above him. When he came back to earth and opened his eyes she was still kneeling beside him, a warm, loving smile on her face.

'You're beautiful, Adam,' she said as she leaned over and kissed him softly on the lips. 'Now go and have a shower – you're in a right mess. I'll make drinks.'

Adam took a deep breath and let it out slowly as she disappeared out of the room. Did that just happen? He looked down and saw the evidence on his stomach. It certainly did!

Standing under the hot water of the shower, his mind was in a whirl and suddenly full of clichés: *seduced by an older woman ... every teenage boy's fantasy.* He did not think he had really thought of Carla as an older woman before; she was just Carla. But she actually had seduced him! He had not known that a woman could make a man feel that way. He had thought sex was all about the act of intercourse and nothing much else. Well, what a lesson to learn!

Carla had needed that time whilst Adam was in the shower to get her thoughts together. She realised that she had a huge amount to give to him and she had enjoyed the first experience. She tried to be philosophical, telling herself that if there were more, that would be great; if not, well, it would be a shame. She did not know when, where, or if they would get the chance to be alone together again, so she was not going to worry about it. Maybe she should try Trudy's advice and 'go with the flow'.

Adam was unable to sleep. As he lay in the familiar bed he had slept in since childhood, his encounter with Carla that day was still with him, as it had been all evening: he could not stop going over it again and again in his mind, still in awe of what had happened and how she had taken control. She had blown his mind, like a drug, and he wanted another fix. The thought of possible future pleasures kept sleep further at bay.

Carla had also woken something into existence in him that he needed time to get his head round – an awareness of love-making and a realisation of just how little he really knew about sex. Up until that day, sex had been something he did in the backs of cars or up against a random wall after a night out. Carla had shown him – given him – something else entirely: sex with her was like art – the art of loving – because that's what it had felt like – loving. He was amazed at how powerful it was to be simply looked at the way Carla had looked at him; her eyes had caressed him as well as her touch, and brought him to a state of excitement previously unparalleled. His body had exploded! But the thing that was both wonderful and terrifying at the same time was the intensity of emotions. Nothing about this experience had been just physical.

The problem was: what to do now?

Carla was asking herself the same question, that night, as she sat alone with a glass of wine after the boys had gone to bed following a trip to the cinema. When she had seen Adam standing there on the landing with such passion burning in his eyes, she had been lost – totally overcome by his power over her. Whatever doubts she might have about a sexual relationship with him, she now knew that the minute she saw him again she would fall under his spell.

With soft music playing in the background, she too ran through the afternoon delight over and over in her mind. The excitement of what she had done to Adam brought a flush to her cheeks and her heart quickened. Her main concern was that they would not know when to stop. But then, why should the end of their relationship be a problem, when it had hardly started? Then again, the point was that it did seem to have started. So how far should they let it go? Was it time to talk it through with Trudy? No. Trudy would want to know all the details and Carla was not prepared to share them with anyone, even her best friend.

After repeatedly going over the same predicament, she reached the one conclusion about which there was no question: she wanted Adam and the chemistry between them was very compelling.

Perhaps the wine was making her daring, she giggled, as she decided that there would definitely be a next time. She knew she was irresistibly attracted to him, so how could she help herself? She was available and so was he, so why should they not explore their relationship and enjoy the journey along the way? She actually felt privileged to be able to bring experience to this beautiful young man, and she snuggled into the sofa with her second glass of wine, as she thought of their next meeting.

*   *   *   *   *

Joyce looked at her son as he absentmindedly stirred his tea. They were sitting at the kitchen table together, as they often did on a Saturday morning, sharing a pot of tea, some Bourbon creams and the morning paper. Her 'mother alert' was always switched on and she was noticing that Adam's mind was elsewhere. She was not sure what was going on and she did not want to pry, but she could not help fishing around for whatever was keeping his thoughts so occupied.

'Did Mel tell you she's been offered a new job, love?'

'No? Has she? Where's that then?'

'Over at the garden centre on the A2 – as manager of the gifts department, I think. I'm surprised she hasn't mentioned it to you.'

'I haven't seen her since swimming on Wednesday. When did she hear about this?'

'Thursday evening,' Joyce muttered as she got up and started to clear away the dishes that were draining beside the sink. Well, there didn't seem to be a problem there, she concluded.

'How's work at the farm?'

'Same old same old. I'm not sure how long I'm going to stay there really, Mum. Still, it's a job.'

He went back to unnecessarily stirring his tea. The radio continued to chat away on the window sill; outside, children's voices could be heard from next door; a car alarm sounded in the distance. And an uneasy silence seemed to have suddenly enveloped them.

Joyce turned to face him and tried a last attempt. 'How are things going at Carla's?'

Adam looked up abruptly 'Fine!' he said, a little too quickly.

Joyce picked up on it straight away and understood, or thought she understood, what was consuming him. 'You like Carla, don't you, love?'

Adam could not quite meet his mother's eyes. 'She's a nice woman … yes … she's nice.'

'Mmmm. Just be careful, Adam. Don't go making a nuisance of yourself. You know what I mean.'

'I'm not fourteen, Mum! For god's sake!'

'All right Adam!' Joyce did not like his manner. 'I just care about you. You may be eighteen but you'll always be my boy.'

Adam immediately regretted snapping at her. 'I know, Mum,' he said apologetically and got up to go over to her. 'But you don't need to worry about me. I'm a big boy!' he mollified, putting his arm round her and giving her an affectionate peck on the cheek.

'Well, go and finish strimming that hedge then,' she said, nudging him and giving him a forgiving smile.

She finished putting the dishes away and looked out of the window as Adam got busy in the garden. He was so unutterably precious to her. 'Not worry?' she murmured aloud. 'You really don't know the half of it, my love!'

Mel immediately sensed that something was different when Adam got into the passenger seat of her car to go swimming the following Wednesday. He was quiet and a touch moody, but it wasn't just that: she knew him so well that she could feel that something about him had changed. 'What's up?' she asked him outright.

'What do you mean?'

'You're different, Ads.'

'Don't be daft. Come on, let's go. It's hot and I could do with a swim to cool down.'

Mel knew better than to push it and said no more about it as Adam asked her about her new job.

At the swimming pool, she changed quickly and was first out on to the poolside, where she waited for him to join her. He came out looking bronzed and breathtaking and she was proud to be with him as they sat on the edge of the pool adjusting goggles and briefly discussing tactics for their training session. Aware of the usual envious looks coming her way, she knew he could take his pick of women, and she found it quite endearing that he hadn't yet realised it himself.

He slid into the pool and pushed off, cursing himself, in the privacy of the water, for wearing his heart on his sleeve. Both his mother and now Mel had noticed that he was not himself. He needed to sort out his feelings. He couldn't sleep. He couldn't eat. Was this love? He didn't know, but what he did know was that he had never felt anything like it before. For a second he considered talking about it to Mel, but something held him back. What he was currently sharing with Carla was just too private to share with anyone; plus something told him that the news that he was currently being seduced by a woman old enough to be his mother would not go down too well with Mel. It occurred to him that there was no one to talk to about these feelings apart from the person who was causing them in the first place, and the irony made him smile.

Mel watched him go and mouthed the words *I love you* as he ploughed his way up the lane. Although she knew he did not love her in the same way she loved him, she consoled herself with the knowledge that they were close and she could call him her friend. Nonetheless, the awkward fumble behind the clubhouse the previous Christmas had hurt her deeply. She had never told Adam that, though. The time to talk about it had just never seemed right, and then days, weeks and months had passed until it felt wrong to mention it because it seemed like Adam had forgotten about it, as if it had never happened. But it had: she had kissed him, felt him, tasted him and aroused him.

Mel's erratic upbringing had made her old beyond her years and she had no expectations that their relationship would develop further; she could see that the feelings she wanted Adam to have for her just did not seem to be there. She had watched him turn from a clumsy, spotty youth to a muscular, sexual man in the period of a year, and during that time she had experienced stirrings of a different nature to just sisterly love. Now she knew she would never love anyone the way she loved Adam and it broke her heart, but she would never tell him. It would ruin what they had and she was not prepared to lose that for anything. She had no choice but to love him from afar.

*   *   *   *   *

Friday brought heavy plops of summer rain, which Adam quite enjoyed. Carla's car was parked on the drive when he arrived which also surprised and delighted him since it should mean she was at home. Remembering his manners, he rang the doorbell rather than using his key. His mother was on her way in the car, but Adam was hoping he might get half an hour or so alone with Carla before she arrived.

Carla greeted him with a slightly anxious smile, a rather false voice, and an indication with her eyes that she was not alone. 'Hi, Adam! You're nice and early. I'm glad you got here before I left for work – I don't have to write a list now.'

When he followed her through to the kitchen, a woman of about Carla's age was sitting at the breakfast bar on the stool he had become accustomed to occupying.

'Verity, this is Adam. Adam this is my oldest friend, Verity. We go back to primary school, don't we?' she said, giving her a hug.

Red, puffy eyes and a screwed up wad of tissues in her hand gave away the fact that Verity had been crying. 'Nice to meet you, Adam,' she said, blushing and obviously uncomfortable. 'You're not seeing me at my best, I'm afraid – girlie drama – sorry.'

Adam held up his hands, indicating that no explanation was necessary. 'I'll get straight on, ladies, and leave you to it. Carla, boys' bathroom shower?'

'Yes, please,' she replied gratefully. 'I'll be up in a minute before I leave for work. Is your mum on her way?'

'She's going to Sainsbury's for cleaning stuff, I think, but she'll be here after that.'

Carla nodded and gave him a brief smile. Glad to make a hasty exit, Adam took his leave and went upstairs to have a look at the shower. Minutes later, putting her finger to her lips, Carla joined him in the bathroom and pushed the door to. Knowing time was short, he pulled her straight into his arms and without hesitation brought his lips to hers. She stifled a small groan and momentarily relaxed into his arms. His tongue found hers and his arms tightened around her until he felt her stiffen and pull away. She looked flushed and breathless, and totally adorable. He smiled into her eyes and ran his finger gently down her cheek before bending to give her a quick kiss and moving back to the shower.

'So,' he said in an exaggerated tone, 'what appears to be the trouble here?'

Carla grinned. 'It's clogged up with scale, I think. I need a water softener fitted in here. Perhaps you can have a look into that for me?'

'Certainly, madam,' he replied.

They stood looking at each other. Adam wanted to kiss her again but he thought that would be a step too far, so he made to go out of the door.

Carla put her hand on his arm and in a whispered voice full of urgency she said, 'Meet me at lunch time – one o'clock by the clock tower.' And she was gone.

Adam was intrigued and excited. Going downstairs to fetch his tools, he noticed both Carla and Verity getting into their respective cars. They were still chatting and he left them to it, passing by with a wave as he went into the garage.

Carla drove to work feeling very unsteady: she was trembling, her heart was racing and she could still feel the way he pulled her body against his – the touch of his lips. It was the first time they had embraced like that, and it was wonderful to feel possessed, even if only for a few seconds. She was also excited. She had a board meeting to attend that morning and she would have to make sure it did not go on for too long, but after that she was pretty much free. She had hatched a plan that she wanted to act out. Her creative inventiveness was surprising her and she grinned mischievously as she thought about what she had in store for Adam later that day.

Verity was not sure what was going on between Carla and the chap who did her garden – the boys' rugby coach, apparently, and the son of Carla's cleaner, Joyce – but she had detected some kind of spark between them and doubted it was a good thing for Carla. The fellow must be at least ten or twelve years younger than her. She sniffed haughtily, as though there were someone there to share her disapproval. Carla had been sympathetic with her, that morning, but she had also seemed distracted and not really that interested in Verity's marital issues. But then who could blame her? At least Verity had a husband to moan about. Carla didn't have that luxury. She laughed out loud to the empty room at the irony of that last thought. Some luxury! Maybe it had actually been tactless of her to speak about Paul's impotency problems with Carla. Oh well! She hadn't seemed to be listening anyway.

She was not completely sure that Paul was impotent, actually. He hadn't wanted to perform on the previous two occasions that she had tried to initiate sex and after the first rejection, she had spent a good deal of time looking at her naked body in the full length mirror in the bathroom. She had deemed her shape to still be good: fuller hips and heavier breasts were an asset to a woman as she got older, weren't they? She had held her hair up and pulled in her stomach, seeing herself as she hoped Paul would see her. It was after the second rejection that she had decided there must be something wrong with him.

Her thoughts meandered back to Carla and the young man in her house. He was certainly handsome in a 'beach bum' kind of way: tanned face, sandy coloured hair and clothes which just hung effortlessly on his muscular frame. She briefly allowed herself a moment to imagine being in a naked embrace with him. His young body looked lean and taut. Paul's was pale and had sagged a little, but then he had never been muscular. Not like this Adam, who wouldn't look out of place with a surf board under his arm. He reminded her of Gareth – physically anyway. She had known Gareth since his early twenties and he had had the same unkempt hair and ease about him that was impossible not to find attractive.

As she started to unload the dishwasher, her thoughts found their way to Mr Goodban – sexy, unavailable, shy Mr Goodban. He had none of Adam's easy manliness; nevertheless, he had a smouldering sexual appetite that was ready for action at the drop of a hat. Well, he did in her fantasies anyway! She had seen him the previous Monday and although there had been no chatty tea break that day, she had taken delight in observing him from a distance. She also had her imagination to play with and the tantalising dilemma of what she would do if he ever made a pass at her. Verity's imagination was very active while she was busy with all that dusting and tidying.

Joyce made her way upstairs with a mug of tea for Adam. She had finished cleaning Carla's kitchen and was just about to change the beds and vacuum upstairs. 'Here you are, love.'

He was sitting on the bathroom floor, surrounded by bits from the shower, and looked up and smiled, showing a row of gleaming white teeth and those twinkling blue eyes. Her heart lurched. How could anyone, let alone a lonely woman like Carla, resist him? She had no reason to suspect that Carla did find her Adam appealing, but what normal, hot blooded woman wouldn't? She looked down at him and remembered him sitting on the floor playing with his toy cars and trains – her lovely little blue eyed, blonde boy, quiet and easy going, affectionate and willing to please. She would swing for anyone who hurt him. She really hoped he was ready for what women had to fling at him too; he was a real catch and the race would soon be on, if it wasn't already.

'Thanks, Mum. Nearly finished here.' Getting up he stretched his long body out of the cramped position in which he had been sitting. 'I just need to get this lot back in there,' he said, nodding towards the shower as he lifted the mug to his mouth.

'Does Carla pay you weekly?'

'Yep.' He pulled a plastic money bag – of the sort used by banks – out of his pocket and waved it at her. 'Twice as much as I get on the farm.' He gave a quick nod, re-affirming his point.

'I'm sure you're worth every penny, love, … every penny,' remarked Joyce with a sigh as she turned out of the door and made her way back downstairs to fetch the vacuum cleaner.

Adam almost asked her what she meant by that, except something told him that it was a conversation better not started. He puzzled over it for a few minutes as he reconstructed the shower, but then returned to the excitement of thinking about meeting Carla. He would have to get a wriggle on; there was no way he was going to risk being late.

126

The traffic was stacked up, as was usual on a Friday lunchtime and Adam squeezed himself through the hold up, grateful for his bicycle. He was locking it up next to the toilets behind Woolworths at ten minutes to one, in perfect time for his assignation.

Dodging the rain from doorway to doorway, he reached the clock tower, took a seat in the shelter of the ancient building and waited. His stomach was grumbling with hunger but he was too nervous to even think about eating. What was happening to him? He felt as though he were in a film – the drama was exhilarating and he was glad he had not confided in anyone; it would somehow spoil the excitement of secrecy and the anticipation of what was to come. This all felt like a dream – an erotic dream he did not want to wake up from.

Suddenly she was there beside him. 'Mr Barnes? How nice to meet you!'

He stood up quickly and rather awkwardly took her hand, shaking it and grinning at the feigned formality of her greeting. 'Nice to meet you, too, Mrs Trelawny.'

She nodded and began to walk out of the shelter of the tower. She was wearing a knee-length skirt under a summer raincoat drawn in at the waist; her hair was braided into a single plait, and he noticed she had on a pair of smart business court shoes. She looked so sexy he wasn't sure he could have an ordinary conversation with her. He suddenly felt very hot, thought his face was probably bright red, and ran a hand through his hair leaving it in an even more wayward shape than before.

'I thought we could hold our meeting at *The Accord*,' she told him in a brisk, business-like manner that turned him on even more.

The Accord was an upmarket hotel in the city centre. Adam had been in the bar area once or twice on nights out, but he had never been into the hotel proper, which made him a little concerned that his jeans, T-shirt and work boots would be inadequate for the occasion. 'Will I be okay in there dressed like this?' he asked.

'Of course! Oh, you'll need this.' She handed him a blue cardboard file with papers in it. 'No need to look at it until we get there.'

'Right,' he laughed, totally bamboozled by the whole charade, and followed her into the hotel and up to the reception desk.

The receptionist smiled. 'Hello, Mrs Trelawny. We have a table reserved for you, as requested.'

'Thanks Emma. Good to see you. How's little Kitty?'

'Much better now, thank you. Back to driving me mad, I'm happy to say.'

'I'm pleased,' Carla answered with genuine maternal empathy. 'Could you organise a pot of coffee for us please?'

Adam was impressed with a side of Carla he did not normally see: she was obviously known in this fancy place and had arranged all this. As he followed her to the rear of the lobby, where there were u-shaped booths with tables that would seat six to eight people, he felt proud and amazed that she was serious about spending time with him. She invited him to sit on one side as she slid her way along to the far end so that she was facing into the foyer and sitting at right angles next to him. He placed the folder on the seat beside him and Carla reached into her bag, took out a large spiral notebook and another file and opened them on the table while he simply watched.

When the large cafetière of coffee promptly arrived, he hardly noticed, his full attention being on this fascinating woman. He watched her mouth as she briefly conversed with the waiter. They laughed at a joke that Adam did not hear. There was a roaring in his ears as anticipation started and the swell of an erection pushed uncomfortably against the fabric of his clothing. He breathed slowly and deliberately to calm his racing heart, and moved in his seat to try to relieve some of the pressure down below. He cursed his lack of control, which seemed to result in an erection at the merest hint of an encounter.

The waiter disappeared. Soft music was coming out of a speaker just above their heads – George Michael wanted someone's 'faith'. Adam thought it very apt for this situation. Carla turned her mesmerising eyes on him and his heart seemed to momentarily stop. She said nothing, which she seemed to know drove him to distraction, and then slowly and deliberately ran her tongue across her bottom lip, never taking her eyes off him. Still she did not speak. The music, the heat in the room, Carla's moist lips – Adam was burning with pent up desire. His years gave him no clue as to how to deal with the situation, so he did nothing. He just watched and waited as Carla put her elbows on the table, folded her hands and, looking at him from beneath her lashes, began to slowly lick the edge of her knuckles with the tip of her tongue, moving her head very slightly from side to side. He remembered that tongue lapping at his tip just one week ago. He caught his breath, unsuccessfully attempting to regain control of his growing excitement.

At last, she spoke. 'Are you all right, Adam?'

He nodded. She smiled and shifted slightly, apparently trying to get more comfortable. Adam assumed she was also becoming heated and – dare he imagine – moist. He closed his eyes for just a second as he contemplated that thought. When he opened them, Carla was looking down at her book and writing some notes at the top of the page.

'So, what would you say is the one thing about your business that stands out for your customers?' Her voice had risen in volume and she had changed her demeanour entirely. What had happened? Then he noticed the approaching waiter.

'Shall I pour the coffee for you, Mrs Trelawany?'

'Lovely. Thank you so much.' She smiled gratefully at him.

Adam was not sure if he was equally as pleased or not, but at least it gave him a minute to compose himself again, and once more he shifted in his seat, trying to adjust the angle of his now bursting erection. Before Carla, he had always thought that the most important thing was to get to the act of copulation as quickly as possible. Now he was discovering how tantalising, how alluring, so sensual and sweetly tormenting all this could be.

Coffee steamed in the cups and Carla was taking a sip. He did the same, glad that he had something to do with his hands.

'Adam,' she said in a low, throaty voice, 'you are a very beautiful man. Do you know that?'

He shook his head and muttered, 'Not really.'

'Well, you certainly are. And you know what?' Again he shook his head.

'I want to pleasure you in so many ways. Would you like that?'

'There's nothing I'd like more.'

'There's a condition, and it may sound a bit presumptuous but it's important. The condition is that you mustn't fall in love with me. I don't want to hurt you. You can love me physically, as I want to love you; we can share physical love, play with it, experiment with it as we make love. But that's as far as it goes – no falling in love. If you can't agree to that then we need to end this now.'

Adam could see that Carla was deadly serious, but he was puzzled. It was all a bit too much for his eighteen year old emotional brain to take in. He didn't quite see the difference between physical love and being in love: it was all new to him. 'Okay,' he said carefully. 'I don't want this to end and I want you to show me everything about physical love. But I've never been in love so I don't know how it feels. I can't be more honest than that.'

Carla realised that she was expecting him to have more knowledge of love than was possible at his age. She leaned earnestly towards him. 'I am so worried about hurting you, my sweet Adam. Please understand that.'

Adam did not like the way the conversation was going: Carla was sounding like his mother again, which was really weird in this particular situation. 'I don't want to hurt you, either, Carla,' he said, erection having very definitely deflated. 'I get it – no falling in love.'

Carla sat back, stung by the sudden edge in his tone. What had she said to cause that? She stirred more cream into her coffee and took a sip. As she slowly replaced the cup in the saucer, it hit her. 'I'm sorry, Adam. I didn't mean to patronise you. I'm just worried about where all this could lead, and since I'm much older than you I feel responsible.'

'Responsible for me?' This just got worse!

'More for what's happening between us.'

'Aren't we both responsible for that?'

'Continuing to happen, then … Adam, I just don't want you to get hurt. Is that so wrong?'

'Carla, I'm a man!' This time it was Adam who leaned forward earnestly. 'I know I'm only eighteen, but I pay my way, I can get married, be a father, vote, go to war – do all the things men do. If I'm considered man enough for all that, including dying for my country, I think I'm man enough for this. If I get hurt, I'll deal with it, just like any other adult.'

'That was quite a speech!'

'Sorry,' Adam sat back, smiling ruefully.

'Don't apologise! I'm impressed, and you're *so* gorgeous when you're serious! I haven't really seen that before.'

'Can I ask you something?'

'Anything.'

'You're teaching me a lot – doing a lot,' said Adam, indicating their surroundings. 'You're amazing and beautiful and could have any man you wanted, so why me? What are you getting out of this?'

The fact that they could have a conversation like this – Adam being mature enough, composed enough and confident enough to tackle her as an adult – had gone some way to calming Carla's concern for him. His questions brought her full focus back to the power of his physical presence over her. She looked at him in astonishment for a second. Didn't he know how delicious he was? Was he so unaware of his own beauty and his effect on any female past puberty? Desire for him flooded her in a sudden torrent. Her eyes were alight with it as she inched sensuously closer to him. 'I have a woman's needs, Adam, and I can't argue with the chemistry between us: I need you.' Her voice sank to a slow, husky whisper. 'I need to feel you … touch you … taste you … explore you … I *want* you.'

Adam laid his head back a little and exhaled sharply as her words fuelled the excitement that had been re-ignited by the lust in her gorgeous green eyes and the clandestine movement of her body.

Without breaking her gaze, Carla indicated the file that she had given him earlier. 'Would you do something for me, please? Open the file and take out the top piece of paper. The writing is quite small so that no one can see, because the instruction is deeply intimate.'

With slightly shaking hands, he did as she asked and placed the paper on the table. The lighting was low and he strained to see what she had written, his eyes widening as he understood. The instruction was: *I want you to put your hand up my skirt and feel just how much I want you*. He looked up from the paper. Carla was visibly aroused and she moved in closer so that he could feel her leg resting against his.

Watching her face, he tentatively placed his hot hand just above her knee, and then hesitated. 'Higher, Adam, higher,' she murmured. Slipping his fingers under the hem of her skirt, he slowly and discreetly travelled the length of her thigh. Carla was now breathing heavily and looking straight ahead; he knew she would swiftly indicate if anyone was approaching them. He continued and reached her warmth. With a gasp, he realised she was not wearing any underwear. He could feel her – hot, soft and wet. She began to rub herself in tiny movements against his fingers. He wasn't sure what to do: should he reach further down to put his fingers inside her?

As if she had heard his thoughts, she breathlessly whispered: 'Just there, Adam, just there ... find my hardness ... there it is. Oh god, oh god, Adam. Yes ... yes ... don't stop.'

Moving gently and slowly massaging her soft folds, he had found Carla's pleasure spot and it was having a dramatic effect on both of them. He continued to massage, hardly moving his fingers as she seemed to be moving against them for maximum pleasure. He had never seen a woman aroused like this. Nothing he had ever experienced had ever been as erotic and exciting as this. Then Carla tensed and clamped her mouth shut as her orgasm shook through her body and she slumped forward a little, putting her hand on the table to steady herself. Adam felt the increase in her wetness.

She put her hand over his and gently moved it back on to his lap, looking around to see if anyone was watching before kissing her forefinger and putting it tenderly against his lips. 'Thank you,' she whispered. He was astonished at how erotic it was to watch a woman shudder through an orgasm. He had never seen it happen before.

Carla indicated the next piece of paper. He withdrew it and read: *You can smell and taste me on your fingers. Now I want you to go to the washroom and taste me as you relieve your tension.* He looked at her. She smiled and pointed towards the door that led to the gents. Luckily, it was close – she had thought of that too – and there was no one to see his bulge as he stepped through it to make himself more comfortable.

Composed, professional and every bit the business woman, Carla was sitting making notes in her diary when he returned to the table a short time later. Although the instruction papers were nowhere to be seen, the folder was still there. She grinned at him and pointed to it. 'One last one,' she said.

He took out the final piece of paper and read: *I am doing an overnight in Reading next Thursday night. Would you like to join me?*

'I would love to, Mrs Trelawny,' he responded eagerly, having no idea how he was going to get to Reading and not caring.

'I'm delighted,' she said with a wide smile as she closed her diary and put it in her bag, took the file from him and moved to stand up.

'Thank you,' Adam said, taking her cue and standing up with her. 'I've enjoyed our meeting very much – very informative. I look forward to learning more.'

They were both laughing as they left the hotel. Once outside, Carla shook his hand and they went opposite ways towards their respective afternoon's work.

He had watched them go into the hotel and then come out again almost an hour later. His coffee had gone cold as he sat and waited. They were obviously playing some kind of game, smiling politely on the way in, shaking hands when they came out, as though they hardly knew each other. Anyone with half a brain could tell it was all an act; there was more going on than met the eye. It made him feel sick.

Paying for his coffee with a couple of pound coins flung noisily on the table, he opened the café door and started to follow the youth up the street. He could just see his untidy fair hair bobbing up and down amongst the early summer crowds. He caught him up, staying a few steps behind, and watched him unlock his bike and cycle off towards to the roundabout. Damn! He would lose him.

* * * * *

Trudy was becoming a real little homemaker. She looked forward to Trevor coming round and he was due to arrive in just about an hour's time, after he had finished work at the police station. She poured herself a gin and tonic and sat down to watch the seven o'clock news while she waited.

At their first meeting, Trevor had seemed to be a bit of an emotional mess, not something Trudy really wanted to get embroiled in. Despite that, she had liked him and taken him back to her house, where she had simply sat with him and talked; in fact, they had talked most of the night. Eventually, they had made it to the bedroom, where Trevor had found that he had not had his balls cut off when his marriage ended and that there was life after separation. Mindful of her previous history with husbands, Trudy had made a promise to herself that this would be a relationship that she simply enjoyed – not one that she complicated and destroyed by making it legal.

The previous weekend, she had even met Trevor's two small children. Luckily, his wife had seen sense and allowed him to have them to stay every other weekend and for a night in the week. Trevor was a loving dad and those frightened little poppets of just two and four years old must have been missing him terribly, she thought. In addition, regular access had quickly transformed him into a funny, engaging companion and Trudy was completely thrilled to be classed as his 'girlfriend'.

She had almost dozed off when there was a tap on the door. Her cottage opened directly on to the street in a lovely, quiet part of the city, apart from the nights when theatre goers used her particular road as a cut-through to the city centre. She roused herself off the sofa and crossed the room to open the door. There he stood behind a huge bouquet of flowers. Corny but sweet, thought Trudy, kissing him and ushering him in as he came up from behind the flowers.

'Just a "thank you" for being so wonderful with the kids on Saturday.'

'Hey! No need!' she said, relieving him of the flowers. 'They're an absolute pleasure to be with. Anyway, I like watching you being a dad – turns me on!' she said, nudging him as she walked past him to get to the kitchen and find the number of vases that would be required to house all the flowers.

He laughed and followed her through. She had bought some ready meals from Marks and Spencer and added a bottle of bubbly as a special treat. Without asking, she handed him the wine to open – a little sign that they were settling into an easy relationship that didn't need explanation or instruction. By now, they were both experienced enough to allow things to grow naturally, without too much analysis.

'Oh, I saw Steve at work today.'

Trudy looked interested. 'Oh yes? How is he?'

'Same as ever really. What actually happened between him and Carla in the end?'

'Not a lot, from what I can make out. He just took her home and that was that.' Trudy had heard Carla's slightly confused story of events that night, but they hadn't really talked much about it since then. 'Did he mention it to you?'

'Well, he said something quite odd really. When I asked him what had happened he said that Carla had a Rottweiler on guard and he couldn't get past the front door; he also said he was going to call the dog wardens to sort it out. I asked what he meant by that but he wouldn't say any more, so I left it. Steve's not someone I would want to get on the wrong side of, if you know what I mean.'

Trudy looked thoughtfully at Trevor and made a mental note to speak to Carla about what he had said. She hoped Adam was not in any kind of danger.

It seemed to be taking an age for Thursday to come round. Adam had all of the impatience of youth but the longings of a fully-fledged man – a frustrating combination. Tuesday night was his night out with the boys, however, and during the rugby season it was training until about nine and then out for a few drinks. Tonight there was some fun training in the park by the city wall, which involved hill sprints and then swimming for an hour in the local private school's pool. By nine thirty, they were all relaxing and enjoying the summer evening, as well as the view: from the pub by the river there was a constant stream of foreign students going to and fro, many of them girls, who giggled to each other as the boys called out to them; some came over and joined them for a drink and whatever else was on offer.

Adam was preoccupied and just sat chatting to a few of his friends. In times past, he would have liked nothing more than the conquest of a pretty foreign student, but no longer. He suddenly felt much older than his years and soon after ten o'clock decided to make a move and walk the two miles home. Flinging his kitbag over his shoulder, he sauntered along the road enjoying the warm evening breeze and allowing his mind to occupy itself totally with memories of Carla's face, the feel of her skin and the sound of her hot, urgent instructions.

He was fairy oblivious to everything going on around him and didn't notice the car parked on the main road a hundred yards or so before the turning into his street. Nor did he really notice when it slowly drove alongside him and then parked someway ahead. If he had noticed, he would have thought it odd that no one got out after the lights and engine had been switched off. So when he was grabbed from behind and dragged into an adjacent alleyway, he was completely taken by surprise. His bag was flung over a nearby wall and he was slammed up against rough bricks. The first punch smacked him firmly on the cheek, crunching bone. The ringing in his ears was deafening as he fought to make sense of what was happening. A dark shadow was raining blows into his ribs and solar plexus. When it stopped he crumpled to the ground, fighting for breath. The last thing he felt before everything went black was something crashing into his skull.

The frantic knock at the door came just as she was about to go up to bed and Tom was watching the news. She had tidied the kitchen and quickly done the bit of ironing that was left in the basket. She would have liked to stay up until Adam came in, but she rarely did that anymore since he was now at an age when that could be any time; she always had an ear out for his key in the lock though. Hearing the noise at the door, she knew it couldn't be Adam forgetting his key – he wouldn't knock like that – and was hurrying along the hall just as Tom came out of the lounge. 'Who can that be?' she said as she passed him.

'Joyce, love, come quick!' It was old Mr Durrant from up the street. 'Come quick, it's your Adam! He's in the alley. Seems he's taken a right beating. Ambulance is on its way.'

Joyce went into automatic pilot. Without even looking at her husband she dashed out of the door to join her neighbour. 'Where, John?'

John Durrant led the way over to the alley further up on the opposite side of the street. A man she did not recognise was kneeling beside Adam, feeling for his pulse.

'Oh god! My Adam!' shrieked Joyce, kneeling down on the stony ground beside her son.

'Pulse is strong,' said the man who was with him. 'Ambulance should be here soon.'

Joyce stroked Adam's forehead; she didn't know what else to do. Looking up, she could see the flashing strobe lights of the ambulance approaching. Tom had followed her over and was crouching over his son, looking helpless.

Joyce looked at the man. 'What happened?'

'I don't know, I was walking past and I saw him in the alley. I thought it was a sack of rubbish but then I saw a foot and realised it was someone lying here.'

The ambulance crew arrived and quickly got to work, checking Adam's airway and feeling all down his body. The woman was saying, 'Hello Adam! Can you hear me, Adam?' as she worked. There was no response. Turning to Joyce, she said, 'Are you his mother?' Joyce nodded. She had gone into shock and the paramedic could see she would need to keep an eye on her too. 'Would you like to come in the ambulance with him?' Joyce nodded numbly and followed the crew as they put her unconscious son on to the stretcher and loaded him into the vehicle. By this time they had put him in a neck brace and he was fully clamped on to the stretcher. Once inside, the paramedic continued to check Adam as the ambulance sped through the streets, siren blaring; she also kept Joyce in mind, chatting to her as she worked, telling her what she was doing. A lot of it was precautionary but to Joyce, it all looked terrifying.

When they reached the hospital the activity around Adam went in to overdrive. Two doctors and nurses were in immediate attendance, one of whom was the registrar, calling out specific instructions to the others. Joyce was ushered away so that she would not hinder the proceedings. She went to wait in the relative's room and was soon joined by an equally pale and shocked Tom. They sat together, holding hands.

'I do love that boy, you know,' said Tom after a while.

Joyce could see tears in his eyes. 'I know you do, love. I know.' She patted his hand, her own eyes brimming.

'I saw his eyes flicker! Quick, Joyce!' Mel urged as she shook Joyce out of an exhausted nap. 'His eyes flickered!'

Joyce sprang up from her seat by the window to lean over her son. 'Adam love, it's Mum. Hello, my darling.'

Adam moved his lips, trying to speak, but nothing came out. He felt as though his mouth was made of corrugated cardboard, and trying to get his eyes to focus on his mother's face made him feel sick, so he closed them again. 'Mum ... drink,' he managed to squeak. Was that his voice? He felt water moistening his lips and he swallowed as it dripped slowly into his mouth. The pain was excruciating. He opened his eyes again and saw a face he didn't recognise.

'Hello, Adam, I'm Julie. I'm the nurse looking after you today. You've been beaten but you're okay. It's just going to take some time for you to recover. Your mum's here.'

'All right, love, I'm here with you.'

'He may need to sleep again, Mrs Barnes, so don't worry if he drops off. It's his body's way of helping the healing process.'

Adam once more drifted off into oblivion.

Now he could hear his dad's voice. He opened his eyes. The room was dark apart from a light over his bed. Moving his head slightly, he could see his parents facing him, side by side, on chairs beside the bed. 'Dad,' he croaked.

Both of his parents leaned forward. 'Hello, son.'

Was it his imagination or could he see tears in his dad's eyes. That was a first! His mum was holding his hand. 'How long have I been here, Mum?'

'Twenty four hours, sweetheart. You were found late last night and brought straight in here. Oh Ads, I thought I'd lost you.' She began to sob quietly.

Adam felt too woozy to say anything and once more sank into a dreamless sleep.

When he woke the next morning he was feeling far more human. A different nurse was checking the machinery at the head of his bed.

'Good morning, Adam. How are you feeling?'

'Better than yesterday, not as good as tomorrow,' he managed to quip.

'Good. You've had medication for pain, but let me know if it gets bad again. We've sent your mum and dad home for some sleep, by the way. They'll be back in later.'

'What day is it?'

'It's Thursday morning. Nine o'clock.'

Adam groaned. At six thirty that night he was supposed to be on a train to Reading to meet Carla. He had to get a message to her. But how? He tried to get his brain to work. The only option was to ask the nurse quickly before anyone else arrived. 'Would you do something for me?' he asked, summoning what little strength he had.

'What's that?'

'I need to get a message to a friend, but it's important that no one else knows about it. It's very private.'

'Sure. No problem.'

'Would you please call Majestic Marketing in Canterbury and tell them to get an urgent message to the owner, Carla Trelawny, saying I've been hurt and I'm here. That's all. She needs to know today, though, because I work for her on Fridays.'

The nurse looked slightly confused but had made a note of the names.

'Please!' he reiterated. 'No one must know, not even the other nurses.'

She could see he was getting distressed and how important this was to him. 'Now, you just relax,' she said reassuringly. 'I won't say a word and I'll go and do it right now, okay? I'll be back later to let you know it's done.'

He smiled weakly and watched her go, his eyes closing in spite of himself. He woke up some time later, moments before his mother came through the door. She was delighted to see him lying with one had behind his head, which showed improvement from the previous night.

'Here he is!' she said brightly, as if he were five again. 'Have you been awake long, love?'

'I don't think so, Mum. I seem to have lost all sense of time, though.'

'Do you remember anything about what happened, or who did this?' Joyce asked gently.

'I was walking home and some bloke came out of nowhere and beat the shit out of me. I don't know why. Did he take my wallet?'

'No, love, it was in your bag. Mr Durrant brought it over yesterday; it had been thrown into his garden. It was him who came and told us about the attack, too. Oh, sweetheart! I want to kill whoever did this to you! You could have died.' Joyce took his hand and held it to her cheek, overcome with emotion.

'Put me down, Mum,' joked Adam, not wanting to see her upset. 'I'm going to be fine.'

'Yes, you are,' she said, giving him back his hand. 'There's no swelling to your brain and that was what the doctor was most concerned about. You just need to rest and get better. Oh, and the police want to talk to you today. They talked to your dad yesterday – I was in here – but he couldn't tell them anything.'

'Not sure I can either, Mum. I couldn't tell you what he looked like; it was dark and it all happened so fast. He didn't say anything either.'

'Okay, love. Well, I'm going to just pop out and get a few things in town. I'll be back shortly but I just wanted to come in beforehand and see that you were all right. Can I bring you anything?'

'I can't think of anything, right now, thanks Mum.'

'Well, I'll bring you a few treats anyway,' she smiled, kissing him on the forehead and giving a little wave as she left.

The nurse who had tended to him earlier came in soon afterwards. 'I waited until your mum left,' she said quietly. 'It's all done: I left a message with someone called Jonathan. He said he would be sure to pass it on and hoped you would be okay.'

'Thanks,' Adam said with grateful relief. 'Can you give me something? I've got a splitting headache.'

'Of course. We can put it through your drip.'

It was only then that Adam realised he had a drip. His right hand and arm were bandaged too, and he hadn't noticed. He checked the rest of his body: his face felt swollen and all down one side was sore and stiff; he could move his legs but one of his thighs felt heavily bruised; the most severe pain, apart from the headache, was coming from his ribcage and he remembered the guy laying into him with his fists; he must have kicked him, as well. He also remembered the helpless feeling of being totally unable to fight back. 'Tell me straight. How bad has this been?'

The nurse looked at him thoughtfully. Underneath two black eyes and a bruised and grazed cheek, she could see he was handsome. The nurses had been talking about him at the shift hand-over that morning, saying somebody had been pretty intent on spoiling his good looks. She wondered whom he had upset to get beaten up so badly. Perhaps it was over a girl – maybe someone was jealous.

'You were lucky there wasn't more damage with the head injury,' she said. 'To be honest, suffering a severe trauma to the head could have killed you. The fact that you're young, strong and fit went very much in your favour. Who was it, do you know?'

Adam sighed. 'No idea. I don't think I have any enemies, and I try to steer clear of trouble.'

'Right!' she said briskly, getting back to the job in hand. 'Do you feel up to having a wash? It'll make you feel better and you'll no doubt have visitors again later, so it would be nice to be fresh and clean. You should also try to drink some water, and then later have some lunch.'

Adam nodded. He felt grubby and desperately miserable. His life had taken an exciting, challenging turn when he started seeing Carla and he was worried that she wouldn't want to see him again after all this. He couldn't imagine going back to his life the way it was before she changed everything.

Two nurses came in and expertly washed him with gentle care. They also moved him from one side of the bed to the other to change the sheets. When they had finished, and with the painkillers kicking in, he did feel brighter and was sitting up in bed drinking orange squash when his mother came back with the newspaper, magazines, fruit and biscuits.

She had hardly sat down when Mel arrived, looking tired and emotional. She sat on the edge of the bed and took his hand. Tears gathered and spilled down her cheeks as they looked at each other without speaking. Adam squeezed her hand and was shocked to find that he was also getting emotional and had a lump in his throat. It all felt awkward and uncomfortable.

Mel sniffed. 'I've been so worried about you, you bugger!' she laughed through her tears, instantly lightening the atmosphere..

'When did you find out?' he asked, his composure restored.

'Straight away, of course!'

'Mel's been here most of the time with me, Ads,' his mother interjected. 'You were asleep.'

'Really?' He took her hand again, feeling the need to bring her close. She felt like home.

'Who was it, Ads?'

'I've no idea and I don't get it. Maybe they thought I was someone else. They didn't steal anything and I don't think I've rubbed anyone up the wrong way – well, not off the pitch anyway.'

Even as he said this, the memory of a big, burly, tattooed man, walking away from him, the loser in their argument, came to mind. Surely it wasn't him! He was a copper! He wouldn't risk his job this way, would he? He knew that Carla had not seen Steve again. They had talked through what had happened that night, and although Carla wasn't too happy about him lashing out, she had said she was pleased and flattered that he had been looking out for her safety.

He dismissed the thought that it might have been Steve and listened while Mel updated him on all the people who had sent him well wishes or were planning to come and see him when he felt up to it. His mother joined in to say that she had been in touch with the farm and they would continue to pay his basic wage for another two weeks, when, hopefully, he would be back on his feet again. She ended by saying: 'I'll phone Carla tonight, Adam, and let her know what's happened.'

Adam just stopped himself from saying that he had already organised that. 'Thanks, Mum,' he said instead.

Joyce watched her son's face as she mentioned Carla's name, but she couldn't see anything that gave her any clues as to how he felt about her. Maybe she had imagined things that weren't there.

With the washing up done and the kitchen tidied after the evening meal, Joyce poured the tea and took a cup into Tom who was in his normal position in front of the television. He was watching football and she had no intention of watching it with him, so she decided to give Carla a ring and let her know about Adam. As she waited for Carla to answer, she realised that she was a little anxious about the conversation she was about to have but she couldn't really understand why.

Carla was playing monopoly with the boys when the phone rang, making her jump. Her mind had been on Adam and his injuries; she wasn't sure how badly he was hurt and she had been considering phoning Joyce but felt it would raise too many questions.

'Carla love, it's Joyce.'

'Joyce! How is he?'

Joyce was taken aback. 'You know?'

'About Adam? Yes, Jonathan, my PA told me. I was down in Reading at the time.'

'Oh, I see,' she said, although she was completely confused about the whole situation. On the spur of the moment, she decided she'd had enough of wondering: it was her son lying in that hospital bed and she had a right to know what was going on in his life, especially if it had anything to do with the attack. 'Carla, he was very badly beaten. He's going to be fine, thank God! It could have been a lot worse.'

'Oh my god!' Carla gasped quietly, looking over at the boys who now seemed to be sharing the Monopoly money out between them. 'Do they know who did it?'

'No love, they don't. Adam has no idea either. Er … Carla, I need to ask you something. Adam has been very distracted lately – a bit remote, if you see what I mean. He seems to be sweet on you and I know he's a man, but he's still my boy and I need to know: is there anything going on between the two of you?'

Carla felt her face burn, and, for a moment, she was speechless. She felt like a naughty, loose teenager who had been found out and the range of emotions running through her completely stymied her ability to respond. Again, she looked at her boys, whom she always encouraged to tell the truth. That decided her: taking a deep breath, she said, 'Joyce, I'm sorry I haven't spoken to you about this, although it's not really my place if Adam hasn't spoken to you about it. However, I will say this: Adam and I mean a lot to each other. I'm very aware of his age and, believe me, I'm not being flippant about it – but yes, we are having a relationship.'

There was a pause and Carla heard Joyce sigh.

'I thought so. How far has it gone? Is it physical?'

Carla immediately felt anger start to build in her chest. 'Joyce, with all the respect in the world to you and Tom, I'm not going to answer that. This is a conversation you need to be having with Adam, not me. It's not fair on any of us.'

Joyce sighed again. 'Maybe you're right, Carla. I'm just so scared for him right now. I think the world of you – you know I do – but Adam …. He needs someone special in his life – of course he does – but someone ... someone…'

'His own age, Joyce? Are those the words you're looking for?'

'Well, yes. I know you must be lonely, but –'

'Joyce, I'm going to stop you right there!' Carla was now at the bristling stage. 'In all fairness, you don't know anything about how I feel and I can assure you I was not on the look-out for a young man, however gorgeous. In fact, if you remember rightly, it was you who actually suggested he come to work for me. I know you're worried – I can only imagine the emotions you've been coping with – but please allow Adam to deal with this in his own way. I'm fully aware of boundaries, Joyce – the nineteen year age gap being the biggest – and I have not been pushing against them lightly.'

Joyce remained silent and Carla softened a little, regretting her outburst. 'Joyce, you have a wonderful son. He's special to both of us in different ways, and either one of us would do anything to protect him. But this is something that he, in fact we, both need just now: I think we're good for each other.'

Joyce began sobbing quietly, but managed to calm herself to speak. 'I thought I'd lost him, Carla. When I saw him lying there in that alley – so still – I thought he was dead.'

Carla's mind immediately jumped back eighteen months to the time she had seen Gareth like that. 'I understand, Joyce – you know I do.'

'I know you do, love, I know. And, Carla, I'm glad we've had this conversation, but can we keep it to ourselves? I really don't want Adam to know about it at the moment.'

'Neither do I, Joyce! Neither do I!'

Tom looked up as his wife came into the room. She had obviously been crying. He was not generally very good at dealing with erratic female emotions, but he knew that something must be really troubling Joyce as she was not prone to histrionics. Muting the roar of the football match with a flick of the remote, he turned his swivel chair round to face her, giving her his whole attention. 'What's the matter?'

'It's Adam.' As she spoke his face immediately clouded with worry. 'No, nothing like that,' she quickly explained. 'He's fine – a little too fine, if you ask me.'

Tom gave her a long suffering look. 'I can't cope with riddles at this time of night, Joyce. What is it about Adam?'

Joyce braced herself. 'He's having a fling with Carla Trelawny,' she announced, and then watched her husband's face turn from stony grey concern to pink-tinged delight.

'You're joking! Really? Our Adam and Mrs Trelawny?' He clapped his hands together in glee, threw his head back and laughed out loud. 'Bugger me, that's priceless!'

Joyce stared at him open mouthed. Rarely did she see Tom so animated, and in spite herself, she began to smile. 'Tom!' she said mid-laugh. 'You're unbelievable!'

'So is our son apparently!' His guffaws continued and Joyce just sat down and watched him. His merriment was catching and she suddenly felt much less bothered about the whole thing. Carla seemed to genuinely care about Adam and she no longer thought the attack might be connected – that was all part of worrying and imagining the worst. Well, she concluded to herself, I suppose it is a bit of a feather in our Adam's cap!

Wiping his eyes on the back of his hand when he was all laughed out, Tom looked at Joyce and leant over to pat her hand reassuringly. 'You silly woman, if the worse thing our Adam does is have a bit of hanky panky with an older woman, I think we'll be pretty lucky. Come on,' he said, standing up and taking her hand to pull her up, too, 'let's go to bed. The football's pretty shite, anyway.'

After switching off the lamps and straightening the cushions, she made her way up the stairs to join Tom, whom she could hear chuckling to himself again in the bathroom.

*   *   *   *   *

Adam had to spend a few more days in hospital, during which time he had a number of x-rays and

153

scans to ensure that everything was healing as it should. He had three cracked ribs, a 'depressed' cheekbone – which needed minor surgery – and multiple bruises all over his body. It appeared that whoever had attacked him had continued to lay into him even after he had lost consciousness.

On the Saturday, after coming round from the surgery on his cheekbone, he was sitting in bed with Mel, watching TV. She had plonked herself alongside him and they were sitting as they often did, just relaxing together. The door slowly opened and Adam could see Stefan's cheeky face peeping round the door.

'Hello, champ!' he said, beckoning him in. 'You coming in to say hello?'

Stefan opened the door wide and was followed in by Bryn and Carla, who looked flushed and unsure of herself – very different, Adam noted, to that day at the hotel.

'Hi, Adam, how are you now? Your mum's been keeping me up to date. Do you mind us all descending on you like this?' She glanced towards Mel and gave her a little wave. 'Hi, I'm Carla.'

Mel knew who she was.

Adam quickly introduced them and Mel stood up from the bed, not wanting to be there any longer. 'I'll leave you to fill Carla in on all the gory details, hon. I'll see you tomorrow.'

'Sorry, have we barged in?' said Carla apologetically.

'I need to go for a swim. It's usually a regular thing and I haven't been for days now,' Mel explained before leaning over and kissing the top of Adam's head. He looked up and smiled at her.

'See ya,' he said with relaxed familiarity as she left.

Carla sat on the chair next to the bed and just looked at Adam for a moment.

'I'm glad you came,' he said, watching her lips tremble a little as she smiled. How he wanted to kiss them!

The boys had brought Game Boys and comics with them and were soon on the floor in the corner, engrossed, having quickly lost interest in an inactive Adam.

'Why, Adam?' Carla finally said, taking his hand and stoking the bruises.

He took her hand in his. 'I don't know,' he shrugged, 'and I've stopped trying to work it out. Nothing was stolen and I can't think why anyone would want to just beat me up. Sorry I missed Reading.'

She waved her hand in dismissal. 'There will be other times.'

He flushed as he thought of her reaction to his touch in the hotel. 'I hope so.'

She nodded, her eyes shining with promise, telling him that she would wait for him to get better and they would continue their discoveries.

Carla had initially been perturbed to see a girl sitting on the bed with Adam. She was tall and athletic, with dark, shoulder length hair and even darker brown eyes, and she moved like a lithe panther, Carla thought as she wondered what her relationship was with Adam. She did not want to ask him. Was that because she was jealous? Then she remembered him mentioning that his best friend was called Mel and for some reason she had assumed Mel stood for Melvin, not Melanie. The fact that he did not seem remotely concerned about having a girl in his bed when she walked in reassured her that there was nothing between them apart from friendship. Her kiss to the top of his head had certainly been more that of a mother than a lover.

She was shocked to see Adam so battered. She had agonised over whether to come or not and had finally asked Joyce if it would be all right; Joyce had said she was sure it would be fine. As she sat holding his hand, it was clear in his eyes that he was delighted to see her. He was sitting up in bed, shirtless and bruised, and Carla had to control her urge to touch and stroke him. After they had chatted about what happened, she sat back and put her head on one side, just looking at him with a soft smile playing on her lips.

'What?' he said, laughing a little self-consciously.

She leaned forward, looking up at him through her eyelashes, and whispered: 'I want to kiss all your bruises – all of them. I want to heal you, Adam.'

His blood picked up speed as it coursed through his veins. He felt hot and heady. 'How would you do that?' He leaned towards her. 'What would it be like?'

She checked to make sure the boys couldn't hear. The noise of Stefan's Game Boy was probably drowning out the bedside conversation, but she felt uncomfortable with them in the room. Digging out her purse, she gave them a five pound note and said they could go to the hospital shop and buy some chocolate and crisps for themselves, and some

156

chocolate for Adam as he needed cheering up. They were delighted at the prospect of treats and something new to do, and both jumped up, babbling away to each other as they left the room.

Carla sat back in her chair so as to give the impression that they were just chatting about nothing in particular. 'Are you sure you're ready to hear this? I intend to make you very excited and I wouldn't want anything to hurt.'

'I'm full of painkillers. Tell me!' Adam urged.

She regarded him playfully and began to describe what she would do to him. 'First I'd take you home to my place. Then I would run you a bath. I would help you take off all your clothes and gently guide you into the lovely, warm, soothing water.'

Adam was hanging on her every word, his excitement already starting to show under the hospital blanket. 'Go on,' he encouraged, praying that no one would come in.

'Then I would wash you, very gently so as not to hurt you. I would run my hands all over your chest, just like I want to do right now.' She looked hungrily at his torso and the hair that covered the top of his chest so invitingly. 'Then I would slowly rub and massage both of your legs, running my hands up to the tops of your thighs. I would massage you all around your beautiful hardness, but without actually touching it. You would be so erect and ready by then, that I would help you out of the bath and dry you very carefully. As I dried you, I would kneel in front of you and … Adam, I think you should do something about what is going on under the blanket.'

Adam was hot with arousal. 'Please touch me, now, Carla.'

'No, Adam,' she chided, 'absolutely not. But *you* can touch you.' She leaned forward and lifted the sheet for a moment, drawing in her breath with a little gasp when she saw how hard he had become. Then she sat back in her chair again. 'Touch yourself, Adam.'

She watched him slide his hand slowly under the covers, take his throbbing ache and bring himself to climax as she murmured erotic, throaty sounds, feeling her own heat and wetness increasing as his exquisite face contorted with the waves of orgasm.

Passing him tissues to make sure he cleaned up, she sat back with a warm gaze. She could see that the whole thing had completely exhausted him, so she helped him to lie down and tenderly kissed his cheek before going out to find the boys. They came back with chocolate and hugs for Adam, and then Carla took them off for tea with her mother in the city centre. Adam drifted into a contented doze.

He spent one more day in hospital and was making such a rapid recovery that the doctors were happy for him to go home. He was relieved to be getting out of the four walls he had been looking at for the past five days and was looking forward to some of his mum's home cooked food. He had lost some weight and he knew she was eager to feed him up.

Joyce had made a special trip to the supermarket in preparation for her son's home coming. She had also spent extra time cleaning his bedroom and had even put flowers on the window ledge. It would probably be totally lost on Adam, she knew, but it made her feel good.

She hadn't slept much while he had been in hospital. The sight of him lying unconscious and bleeding on the ground in that alley had shaken her to the core. But now, after thinking he was dead – how still and broken he had looked – she was soon to have him back home. He would still need to sleep quite a bit the doctor had told her, whilst his body healed, but he would very soon be back to normal – if there is a normal after the fright we've all had, she muttered to herself.

The shock had also set her mind to thinking about other matters, and she had come to the conclusion that she would soon have to talk some things through with him. There were things he needed to know, but she had to find the right time to tell him.

Carla thought a lot about her visit to Adam's hospital room. When she had walked in she had wanted to gather him into her arms and hold him close. Mel's presence had put a stop to that. There had been something about the way they were sitting together: totally at ease; no need for speech. It had reminded of the way she and Gareth were together – easy, uncomplicated.

She actually couldn't quite work out if she was jealous or not. It was the look that Mel had given her that gave her concern. Mel may be just a friend in Adam's eyes, but Carla doubted very much that the feeling was mutual. Still, she reminded herself, she had made it quite clear to Adam that their relationship was about present, mutual need – not about building a long term relationship. Was that what she had been proving to herself by instigating the erotic session for Adam under the bedclothes? She was hugely shocked by her own wantonness. It was a side of herself she had not been aware of before, and she couldn't understand why she was intent on taking her relationship with Adam down this particular route. Maybe it was the addictive chemistry between them – they could not get enough of each other.

Which could not possibly last: there would be an end; of that she was certain, even though, in her weaker moments, she did fantasise about what a future with Adam would be like. It started off well, but always ended with her desperately trying to keep up with him. She imagined him looking at younger women when she was approaching middle age, and it hurt. It wasn't something she was prepared to endure. Nevertheless, something had happened when she had walked into that hospital room – something had shifted and it frightened her. Was it because of Mel, the 'best friend'? She was his age and she was stunning. Adam hadn't noticed. Soon he would, and Carla felt threatened by that. Why? she wondered, confused by her own feelings.

She finally came to the conclusion that it was because she just wanted more of him. He felt, smelt and tasted like nothing she had ever experienced, and he was a dangerous pastime that could lead to trouble – all in all, an intoxicating combination. Looking back at her life, she could understand why.

She had met Gareth when she was nineteen. He had been her first serious relationship and they were inseparable from the start. Like many other couples, they started married life with a white wedding; four years later they welcomed their first baby, and their life together continued to unfold. Gareth had been a thoughtful, helpful, romantic husband and a loving and involved father. What he had lacked as an income provider he had more than made up for with his dedication to their family and his skills around the house. Plus, she had never had any complaints about his expertise in the bedroom. On the contrary, there had even been a significant and delicious change in the year before he died: he had begun encouraging her to take the lead, be more adventurous, pleasure herself whether he was there or not, and create erotic fantasies for them to act out. This had all added new dimensions of fun and intimacy to their sex life. Carla had wondered if it was what all couples experienced as their children got older, but she had never discussed her marriage with her friends, and wasn't about to start; she had just lived and enjoyed it – until he had been killed, wiped out by someone else's folly, and her beautiful marriage had ended.

Within seconds, she had ceased being a wife and become a young widow, with two children to bring up on her own. Her place in life had been turned on its head, a state of affairs that had eventually brought her two choices: to sit at home and cry into her wine glass, or make a new life and do something that got the blood rushing in her veins again. She had chosen the latter, and Adam Barnes was reaping the benefit of those lessons she had enjoyed so briefly with Gareth. She wished, now, that he had begun teaching her ten years earlier, because her libido was travelling at a hundred miles per hour, as if to make up for lost time. She could hardly keep up with it; and with Adam, she was acting out what her newly discovered imagination was presenting to her.

All of these thoughts were spinning in Carla's head on the day Adam was discharged from hospital. She knew he was home because he had called her before leaving the hospital, and she couldn't help feeling a little jealous that Mel would be at home with him – part of the family – whereas, she would not be able to see him for a few days.

Sighing, she got into bed in her plush, fully fitted bedroom, and sank down under the soft covers. As she reached out to turn off the light, the phone rang. She picked up the extension on the bedside table. 'Hello?' Calls late at night made her nervous.

'Hi.'

Her breath caught in her throat. 'Adam! Are you okay?'

'Yeah, I'm here in my lonely little bed thinking of you in your lonely big bed. Fancy playing a game?'

Carla giggled and snuggled further down the bed, wriggling her toes in anticipation. 'What did you have in mind?'

*   *   *   *   *

Adam's recovery moved on swiftly. He was young and strong and used to bruises, so, once he felt better he was soon up and about and getting bored being stuck at home. The police had come round to see him a couple of times; they seemed no closer to finding out who had attacked him and why – mainly because

162

they had no leads – but they assured his parents that the incident would not be ignored. Adam could not come up with a possible motive: was it retribution, or to teach him a lesson? He didn't know. The incident with Steve crossed his mind again but he didn't mention it to the police. It was far too tenuous and he had to have more information before he named a copper. It was something he would talk over with Carla the next time her saw her.

He would be back working there in a few days' time and he was hoping she would be there. After their very erotic phone sex the night he had come home from the hospital, he was looking forward to seeing her with sweet anticipation, eager for physical contact. Carla infiltrated his mind twenty four hours a day; he was obsessed with her; everything about her fascinated him. There were times when he wondered where it was all going, but not for long; he was enjoying the present too much to be too concerned about the future.

He was pleased that he had taken the initiative by phoning her, that night. He was trying to follow her example and become more creative, often lying in bed doing his best to dream up new ideas that might please her. It was all new to him and he was still shy about voicing those ideas but he was learning fast. *When the student is ready the teacher will appear*. Where had he heard that? Was it in a film?

Carla was ashamed to admit to herself that the sexual encounters with Adam were more exciting than anything she had ever experienced before. Her relationship with him was entirely different to her solid partnership with Gareth. She would always love Gareth – that wasn't the issue – she was just becoming more and more aware that she had the capacity to love another man, albeit differently to the way she loved Gareth.

She was sitting at the kitchen table with a coffee, listening to the boys making a loud racket upstairs and enjoying hearing their happiness. Stefan had a friend over and it always excited them when there was another person to play with. The phone rang, making her heart skip a beat because she immediately thought it might be Adam.

'Hi doll!'

It was Trudy.

'Hello my darling, how are things? I haven't spoken to you for ages. What have you been up to?'

'Wouldn't you like to know!' replied Trudy.

Not really, thought Carla, knowing what Trudy's life was like at the best of times. 'I don't really want to know, Trude, but I have the feeling you're about to tell me. How's it going with the sad, solemn Trevor?'

'You'll be pleased to know that with a bit of Trudy magic, sad, solemn Trevor is now happy-go-lucky, sexy Trev. It's amazing what a bit of loving can do, don't you think?'

Trudy's comment was thick with meaning and Carla could tell she was baiting her, trying to get her to spill the beans about Adam. 'Well, funny you should say that and I have to agree, because there is a bit of that going on in my life at the moment, as well.'

'Ha! I knew it. So come on then, what's he like in the sack?'

'I don't actually know yet.'

'You're joking! You haven't slept with him? What have you been doing, kissing behind the bike sheds?'

'Rest assured, Trudy, you would be very impressed with what's currently going on with me and Mr Barnes.'

'What do you mean?'

'Well…' Carla hesitated. How much did she want to tell her friend? Once again, she was feeling very possessive of her private moments with Adam. They were very sexual, but there was a certain level of affection that created a powerful, intensely personal magic that was theirs alone; she was not prepared to talk about that to anyone. 'Let's just say we're learning a lot from each other.'

'That sounds extremely intriguing. Tell me more. '

'Adam is an eighteen year old with the body of an Adonis, the face of an angle and maturity beyond his years. He has a willingness to try anything and learn, so suffice to say we're having some fun playing a few games.'

Trudy was amazed but also very impressed. 'Good on you girl' she laughed, not pushing for more details. This was a side of Carla she had not witnessed before so she thought it best to let her set the pace and content of discussion. 'Listen though, in all seriousness, my house is your house if you need somewhere to meet. I don't like to think of you having to make out in the bushes in City Wall Gardens.'

'Now there's an idea!' laughed Carla. 'Thanks Trudy, but I'm not going to hurry this. I want Adam to learn that there is much more to sex than shagging.

Opportunity is always scarce, of course, but it only makes things even more exciting and we snatch what can only be described as golden moments of bliss.

'Gareth taught me a lot about that: he suddenly seemed to think that we needed to spice up our love life and it was great. I don't know what gave him the ideas; I just wish he'd had them years before.'

Trudy was a little taken aback by the comment about Gareth. That sort of thing would have rung alarm bells in her head, but there was no point in investigating further – too late, for one thing, and why put questions in Carla's mind? 'Well, my lovely friend,' she said instead. 'I'm glad you're having some fun, you deserve it.'

After that, Carla managed to divert the conversation away from her love life back to Trudy's. Trevor had apparently turned out to be a bit of a catch and there was something in Trudy's attitude towards him that was different to the other men in her life. She also seemed very taken with his children and Carla was pleased for her.

As the call ended, however, she was slightly perturbed by something Trudy had told her: she had recounted a conversation that Trevor had had with Steve a few days before Adam was attacked. He said that Steve had referred to a Rottweiler that was going to be dealt with. Through her drunken haze of that night she could remember him referring to Adam as her Rottweiler. Although she realised there was no proof, she was shaken to the core by the possibility that she might have been the reason for the brutal attack on him.

She went into the kitchen to get her mobile phone and open the last text she had received. She had not recognised the number when the text came, but as soon as she saw the message she had known who had sent it. *Hi. I have been persuaded to get one of these after getting beaten up. Not sure it would have helped. Keeps Mum happy though. This is my number. A.'* She had just sent a quick reply then, as she was busy sorting out after-school snacks for the boys. Now, she sent a text asking Adam to call her immediately if he was free.

Seconds later her phone rang. 'Is everything okay?' Adam asked anxiously. 'Your text sounded urgent.'

She recounted what Trudy had told her. 'It would be terrible if you were beaten because of me,' she ended.

'I thought of Steve,' said Adam, 'but only because he's the only person I've alienated. But it doesn't make much sense if you think about it: he's a copper and I imagine they'd throw the book at him for GBH so I can't imagine he'd be fool enough to risk his pension just to have a pop at me.'

'Then what do you think he meant by saying you were going to be "dealt with"?'

'I hit him, remember; he didn't even hit me back. He probably meant a bit of harassment – the odd stop and search to teach me a lesson – that's all. The attack was so random it seems more likely it was some poor deranged guy who hadn't taken his tablets.'

'So you haven't mentioned it to the police?'

'No.'

'Have they come up with anything – the police?'

'Nope, and I'm not holding my breath. Let's change the subject: when am I going to see you?'

Carla laughed, wanting to believe what he said about Steve and happy to change the subject. 'I don't know. It's pretty full on here at the moment: I've got three proposals to write and Stefan's got a friend over for tea.'

'Okay,' Adam sighed. 'Will I see you on Friday?'

'I'll try and think of something,' she promised. 'I want to see you too.'

Carla poured herself a large glass of red wine. It was seven o'clock, Stefan's friend had been picked up by his mother and the boys were watching a bit of television before going to bed. Carla sat down in her home office, fully intent on beginning work on the proposals. Twenty minutes later she knew they would have to wait until morning: all she could think about was Adam. She kept picturing his face as she brought him to orgasm the first time they had been intimate. He really was exceptionally delectable.

A plan started hatching in her mind. Feeling like a teenager, she picked up her mobile phone and with pulse racing, she texted: *Would you like to come out to play?* She pressed *send* before she had time to change her mind and put the phone in the kitchen where the signal was most strong, at the same time trying to pre-empt disappointment by telling herself Adam might have gone out for the evening, anyway.

Twenty five minutes elapsed. Carla was gazing out of the kitchen window feeling like a rejected sixteen year old, when she heard the familiar beep of a message coming through. Remaining calm in body but not in mind, she picked it up and opened Adam's text. *I knew this thing would come in handy. I'm hoping you might be in the mood to give me some more instruction.* Laughing with delighted relief, she picked up the house phone and dialled.

'Mum, would you do me a favour and pop round to watch the boys in about an hour. I need to go out for a bit. I'm not going to be long.'

Her mother readily agreed; she loved to help and liked to feel she was needed. Carla wondered at times what she would do without her; she certainly was her rock. Her mum also respected her privacy, something she very much appreciated, and she knew she wouldn't ask where she was going. Nevertheless, she would have to give some thought to sharing what was going on with her. Going back to her mobile phone she wrote: *See you in the car park by the City Wall Gardens. 9pm. You'll recognise me. I'll be wearing a raincoat but very little else.*

Send.

Beep.

She smiled and read*: That takes the 'flasher mac' to a whole new level. See you at 9.* She looked at the clock on the kitchen wall: she had an hour before she would have to leave – just enough time to sort out the boys and get ready.

Just before it was time to go, Carla could hear her mother in the lounge, talking to the boys, who were ready for bed but had been allowed to stay up for a story with Nana as a special treat. Carla was standing in the bedroom looking at herself in the mirror: basque with suspenders, black stockings and a pair of court shoes she wore to work – had to be sensible with the footwear. She put some subtle perfume on, brushed her shoulder length hair through once more and checked her makeup – not too much – just some mascara, which defined her green eyes well, giving them that sexy, smoky look. Gareth had said that men rarely liked too much makeup on women and she hoped Adam was of the same opinion.

'Mum, thanks so much for this. I recorded *Morse* for you. If you want to watch it, it's on the tape in the machine and set to go.'

'Okay, love, thanks for that.'

'I won't be too long.'

'All right, see you when you get back.'

Adam felt slightly sick with excitement. He had managed to have a quick bath and his hair was still damp. He ran his hands through it and his fringe fell obstinately back over his eyes; he really needed a haircut. Since he hadn't seen Carla for a while, his anticipation was starting to build and he had to keep himself in check, at least to get out of the house – his mother was watching him like a hawk. He had told her he was going to meet a few of the boys in the town and had ordered a taxi, promising her he would also get one back, or a lift.

The taxi dropped him off by the bus station and he walked through to the car park, not really knowing where she was going to be, but confident he would spot her car since the summer evening was still quite light.

He saw her pull in and drive to the far end of the car park, near the entrance to the park. As he walked over to meet her, he caught his breath when she got out of the car. Her hair was loose and she was wearing the raincoat as promised. They walked up to each other and for a few seconds just stood, Adam looking down into her face and smiling, she looking up at him, being coy and incredibly sexy. Without speaking, she took his hand and they walked through the gateway into the green of the park. She seemed to know exactly where she was going so Adam just followed. There were a few people about, walking their dogs or making their way into the town, and half way along the path was a little teashop, now closed for the night. It backed on to a wooded area and Carla led him round to the back wall. His excitement was mounting and he could feel himself getting hard already; his mouth was watering with imaginings of what was to follow.

They had not yet spoken, which seemed to be Carla's preference and certainly heightened the excitement. Being careful of his ribs, she guided him to lean back against the wall; he stood with one foot against it and his hands in his pockets as she moved in between his legs. She took his face in her hands, ran her fingers through his hair, soft from just being washed, and then ran her hands over his broad shoulders and down, slipping them up his T-shirt sleeves, feeling his skin; she closed her eyes and sighed, brought her body closer to his.

Deciding to take the initiative, he took his hands out of his pockets and pulled her to him so that she could feel his urgency pressing against her body. His ribs reminded him of their presence but he didn't care as he lifted her face to his and began kissing her, deeply and slowly. He had learnt that she liked things slow, passionate and tender, and he got the result he had hoped for when he felt her go

171

limp in his arms and moan softly. Then she pulled back and stood just a foot in front of him, simply looking him up and down, caressing and undressing him with her eyes. He felt on fire and knew she could see his arousal. He didn't know what to do with himself.

'We're going for a drink – just a quick one,' she said.

His eyes opened in surprise. 'Really? What if we're seen?'

'Do you have something to hide?'

'No,' he smirked, 'apart from this.' He pointed to his groin.

'Ah, yes – that! Well, I can't promise it's going to get much better when you see this.'

She slowly undid her belt and then one by one popped open the buttons. Adam watched and waited as she looked around to see if anyone was nearby, and then she parted her coat.

Adam gasped. 'Oh my god, Carla, you're gorgeous!'

She moved a few inches closer and put both hands on his chest. 'Touch me, Adam,' she whispered softly. 'Touch me very gently and very slowly.'

He slipped both of his hands inside her coat and reached down to the tops of her thighs and buttocks, running his hands up and down, feeling the suspender clips and the exposed skin where the tops of her stockings ended. He thought he was going to ejaculate there and then. With a bit of concentration he probably could have, but he was learning to savour the build-up, knowing that the climax would be all the sweeter for the delay: he had discovered foreplay. He moved his hands up to her waist and continued to explore, while she simply stood with her eyes closed and her face tipped up towards his. When his hands glided up along her basque and cradled her breasts she gasped but did not move or interrupt the flow of his touch. He so wanted to take her, lay her down and make love to her dressed like this. But then she opened her eyes knowingly and stepped away, tying her belt firmly.

'Come on. We're going to have a drink and be amongst lots of people – only you and I knowing what I'm wearing under here.' She lowered her voice to a breathy whisper. 'Then we'll drive somewhere quiet … and you can touch … more.'

The pub was busy and there was nowhere to sit so Carla stood to one side of the room while Adam waited at the bar to be served. Feeling young, carefree and sexy, Carla kept her eyes on him the whole time and he couldn't stop looking over at her, the two of them exchanging mischievous grins. Eventually, he got served and came back to her with two sparkling waters. As they stood close, sipping their drinks, Adam restlessly shifted his feet and Carla could see he just wanted to drink up and go, but she was intent on teaching him the joy of slowing down and savouring the moment.

'What would you like to do to me, Adam?' Her voice was low and husky.

He didn't reply immediately and she could see in his eyes that a whole host of thoughts were flying through his head. She waited, wanting to see if he could voice his desires.

'I don't know where to start.'

'Would you like me to help? I'll tell you what I would like to do to you, shall I?'

He nodded.

She ran her eyes up and down his body, listening to his breathing become more rapid and shallow. She discreetly lifted the bottom of his close-fitting T-shirt and, with one finger, checked to find out whether his jeans had a zip or button fly – it was button. She drew in a breath and looked up into his eyes, he returned her look with the desire his body was already expressing.

'We're going to go to the outskirts of the city, Adam,' she said purposefully, 'to a quiet, very private, wooded area where we can be alone. I'm going to take your T-shirt off, kneel down in front of you and …' She paused and dropped her eyes for a second to indicate his fly. '… I'm going to unbutton this, slowly, one button at a time, and release your stiffness. And I'm going to kiss you there.' She casually ran the tips of her fingers over his swelling, sending sensations juddering through his groin. He gasped and glanced around the room to gain control, taking a gulp of the sparkling water. 'Now, what would you like to do to me?'

Still he looked confused and a bit shy. She kept silent and encouraged him with her gaze.

'Carla, there are so many things I want to do to you. I lie in bed at night and all I can see is you: I imagine us lying together. I imagine…' He faltered and she nodded, urging him on. 'I imagine being deep inside you, looking at your face as I put my hand in the small of your back and lift you up to me as I move in and out of you…. I can't think any more … all that's in my head is what's under that coat.'

She could see that he was reaching a state of arousal in which the blood was pumping so fast that he couldn't think straight. She remembered Gareth saying that there were times when he was so turned on that he lost all sense of reason – his body took over and all thoughts were lost. It was obviously time to take this delicious man somewhere where they could enjoy some flesh on flesh. She took his glass and placed it with her own on a nearby table.

Inside the car, Carla unbuttoned her coat and drove off, her stocking-clad legs visible in the orange light of the streetlamps. Adam wanted to touch, so badly. He reached out his hand, but Carla gently replaced it in his lap. 'Not while I'm driving,' she chided.

She parked at the far end of the parking area beside the woods, away from the two cars already there, and they both got out. Holding hands, they walked down one of the pathways deeper into the woods and away from any possibility of prying eyes. Carla then led him off the path, leant against a tree and turned to face him. He immediately reached for her belt and opened her coat while she stood passively allowing him access. He slid her coat off her shoulders and the moonlight filtering through the trees gave him a dappled view of her femininity. She trembled and softly groaned as he softly ran the tips of his fingers down her shoulders and up and down her arms.

'Touch me, Adam,' she murmured, still without moving.

Moving her hair away from her shoulders, he bent and tenderly kissed around her neck. She tipped her head back, surrendering to sensation as he kissed and licked her in the same way she had done to him on their first encounter. 'Oh, yes, Adam,' she responded to the hot, incoherent words he breathed in her ear. Kissing her lips he entered her mouth with his tongue and swirled around the tip of hers. She tasted of desire, slightly metallic and it drove him on. He crouched in front of her, taking hold of her hips and running his mouth over the laciness of her underwear, breathing through the material so that she could feel his hot breath on her skin. As he knelt on the ground, twigs cracking under his weight, he could hear her panting and entering a level of desire from which there was no return. He began kissing her thighs above the tops of her stockings, giving her little nips between kisses. She moaned and started to push her groin towards him, but he was learning to tantalise. The old Adam would have pushed his fingers inside her panties and delved. But now he was learning that the waiting was as sweet as the action itself, so, instead, he stood up while she remained motionless … waiting. He understood that she wanted him to take control, so he took his T-shirt off and dropped it on the ground. She slowly breathed out, touching his chest with her finger tips, brushing his nipples; her touch made him draw in his breath and momentarily close his eyes.

'You said you were going to undo my jeans and kiss me there.'

She smiled, crouched down and began to seductively pop open his fly buttons. She put her nose on him through the cotton of his pants and smelt in his heat, glancing up at him as she did so. Her eyes having accustomed to the dark, she saw him drop his head back and heard him sigh. She pulled his jeans over his muscular buttocks and down to his knees; then she did the same with his pants. His manhood sprung free in front of her face and she took him in her warm hands, stroking and kissing him, causing him to openly groan and repeat her name. His stomach muscles were taught, his hands entwined in her hair as she ran her tongue along his shaft from base to tip. She could tell she was bringing him close to orgasm, and feeling his hands tighten in her hair, she pulled away.

But then he surprised her by again assuming control: he took her by the shoulders, brought her back up to a standing position, turned her to face the tree and put her hands up against it. She was unsure what he was going to do but she let him continue, and as she was leaning forward slightly it felt natural to part her legs. His hands ran down her body, and she could feel him kissing the backs of her thighs and her buttocks through her panties. It was delicious and she allowed herself to disappear into the sensations that his breath, tongue and lips were creating. With his full body pressing against hers, he then slid his hands round her waist and she felt his fingers find the inner edge of her panties, slide it to one side, find their way to her arousal and slowly begin to massage her right where the sensation was the sweetest. At the same time, she could feel that he had bent his knees and was sliding his hardness up and down against her buttocks. In no time she could feel the familiar tightening in her groin as her orgasm began to reach the edge. Adam was panting loudly in her ear as his movements continued, almost pushing her off balance. Her mind was now spinning and her head felt light and airy. His fingers relentlessly worked their magic and just as she started to climax he slipped one inside her. She exploded with tight squeals of uninhibited pleasure.

Her orgasm was the ultimate turn on and Adam closed his eyes to calm himself as she bucked and cried out. He felt her juices flow through his fingers and he marvelled at how different this was with Carla than any of the other girls he had shared intimacies with. He had stopped pushing against her buttocks because the plumpness against him was bringing him too close to his own climax and he had other ideas about how he wanted to finish his pleasure. As she calmed, he withdrew his fingers and she turned to look at him. He spread her wetness over the tip of his erection and massaged it slowly as he bent his face to hers and said through a kiss. 'Let me lose myself into your mouth.'

Carla kissed him hungrily for a few more seconds and then once more crouched down in front of him, this time pulling her coat over and kneeling for better support. Adam looked down and watched as she took his length into her mouth, and then closed his eyes as her lips lightened around his shaft; he moved gently back and forth in time with her head movement. His orgasm seemed to split him in two; he grunted, clasped his hands either side of her head and shot his seed deep into her mouth while she held him there as he pulsated. His mind seemed to shatter into a thousand pieces and then re-gather itself as consciousness returned.

Licking him dry, Carla wiped her mouth on the back of her hand as though she had just drunk after days of thirst. She then lovingly dressed him.

They silently walked back to the car and before they got in Adam took Carla in his arms; leaning against the car, held her close for a long time, just stroking her hair and never wanting to let her go. So few words had been spoken, yet so much had been said. His emotions were rising from somewhere deep inside and he felt as though he wanted to cry; he realised he was falling and falling – his heart was no longer his own. This was a first for him, and suddenly, with sweet fear blooming in his chest, he realised what the feelings meant.

*   *   *   *   *

It rained so hard the next day that there were summer floods in a host of areas across the country. The sky was slate grey and Carla found her attention continually being drawn away from her work to watch people wrapped in raincoats scurrying about, and groups of tourists, some dressed in matching waterproof ponchos, chattering away in the street below. It was a miserable day, but Carla liked the smell of summer rain on the tired, heat bashed pavements, and it freshened the air.

Her mind constantly kept drifting back to Adam and their wonderful interlude the previous evening. He was such a delight, so eager to learn, and there was something special about him that transcended his age, looks and raw sexiness. She could not put her finger on it, but it was something to do with his core being, and she was aware that whenever she spent time with him she was left feeling more attached to him and more reliant on his presence to make her day complete. He was no longer just 'a friend with benefits'.

Adam at home, being an eighteen year old, sometimes crossed her mind: his bedroom with things left over from childhood still around – a childhood that had ended just a few years before. But she did not dwell on such thoughts: she had never known him as a child and had first met him as Stefan's rugby coach. To her he was a man, albeit a very young one.

Shaking her head to rid herself of such random, sporadic thoughts, she returned to the proposal writing she had tried to complete the previous evening. She managed to get her focus back and had just about completed the first one when the phone rang. It was Barry, who was on reception that day.

'Carla darling, there's a Mrs Simpson in reception for you.'

Carla wracked her brain but could not think who Mrs Simpson might be. 'Where's she from, Barry. I'm not expecting anyone.'

'She said it was a personal matter.' Barry lowered his voice. 'She seems a bit nervous too. Anyway, I've sat her in the meeting room.'

'Thanks, Barry. I'll be right out.'

Carla was puzzled: a personal matter? Could it be about Adam? Maybe it was something to do with one of the boys. Well, there was only one way to find out.

The woman was sitting on the edge of a chair facing the door when Carla walked in. She appeared to Carla to be in her late forties, attractive in a voluptuous way, with short, straight, dark hair which was well cut around her face. Her clothes looked expensive and the handbag on the table bore the Gucci logo.

'Hello Carla. Is it okay to call you that? I'm Sandra Simpson. I'm an old friend of your husband's.'

They chose a table at the back of the restaurant, away from other customers. With profound indifference, a waitress sauntered over with menus and handed one to each of the women without a word of greeting. Carla automatically sighed in annoyance at the bad service, even though her mind was going a hundred miles a minute with half-formed questions.

Before the waitress had time to turn and walk away, Carla said, 'I don't need a menu. I'll just have glass of Pinot – a large one – thank you.'

'I'll have the same, please,' Sandra added.

The waitress made a note on her pad and sloped off to give bad service to a group who had just come in.

Carla turned to Sandra. 'Why do I have the feeling that you're about to tell me things I don't want to hear?'

The other woman picked up the paper napkin that was on the table in front of her and started to nervously play with it. 'I'm so sorry to bring this to you, Carla. Yes, I'm about to tell you things that will no doubt upset you, and I wouldn't be doing it if I had any other choice. Please believe me – I'm not doing this for myself, but for someone else.'

Carla felt prickles of anxiety popping up all over her body. 'I think you should just come out with what you came to say,' she said shakily, in the most composed voice she could muster.

'Of course,' answered Sandra, shaking her head as though frustrated with herself. 'The fact is that three years ago Gareth and I had a nine month affair.'

The words were out. They could never be taken back. A split second was all it took for them to register in Carla's mind and cause her world to tilt. Everything she knew, or thought she had known, was no longer what it seemed. She felt herself falling without moving, blood pounding in her ears; she felt the walls closing in on her; the noise of the restaurant intensified to an unbearable level. Bile rose in her throat and she stumbled her way from the table through the restaurant to the ladies and into the nearest cubicle, where she was violently sick. Once her body had stopped heaving, she stood with her head against the cool of the partition wall and breathed slowly.

Her hands were shaking and her head pounding as she flushed the toilet and went out to the sink. She looked at herself in the mirror. The face looking back did not look like her. And why would it? She was now someone else. All that she had held sacred about her relationship with Gareth had been dashed on the rocks by a stranger who had just walked into her life. How could she possibly move on from this?

Common sense kicked in: she couldn't stay in the ladies toilet of *Cruzo's* all day; she had to pull herself together. Step one: go back out into the restaurant and sit down with the woman who had known her husband as intimately as she did; the woman he had fucked; the woman who had probably wanted to take him away from her; the woman who had just turned up and destroyed everything she held dear. Go back out there, she must. So with all the grace and poise left in her, she walked out and crossed the room to sit down and begin one of the most painful conversations of her life.

Sandra was sipping wine, which had arrived during Carla's absence, the crumpled napkin clutched in her free hand. For the most fleeting of moments, Carla felt sorry for her.

'Are you all right?' Sandra asked.

Carla sat down and brushed aside Sandra's concern. She hadn't cared three years before; why should she care now? In a voice still shaking with emotion, Carla said, 'I want to know everything. Everything!'

Sandra kept it short: Gareth had been doing some maintenance work at the tennis club where she was a member. One day her car wouldn't start and he gave her a lift home. She asked him in to have a drink as it was a hot day and they got chatting. She made a pass at him that he didn't rebuff. The affair lasted nine months, at which time she could feel that things weren't right and that he was starting to feel regret. She finished it then: she couldn't bear the thought that he was about to reject her, so she made the first move. That was how their relationship was -

she ran it: he seemed to want to be led and she enjoyed being in charge.

Carla was finding the whole thing surreal. It was as though Sandra was talking about someone completely different – not her Gareth. Questions were flying into her mind. 'Are you married?'

'Not now, and I'd been divorced for two years when I got involved with Gareth. I suppose I was feeling lonely, and that's why I did what I did. I'm not proud of myself, Carla. I knew Gareth was married – he made no secret of it – and I knew he would never leave you. In fact, I could tell he was very much in love with you.'

Then *why*? thought Carla. 'Was it just sex?'

'To be honest, yes. I didn't want to think so at the time, but it really was. He was pretty inexperienced and seemed to enjoy some of the things I arranged for him.'

Carla held up her hand. She had said she wanted to know everything, but this was already getting into the realms of too much information – she didn't want details. There was also the minor revelation that the story of the older woman with the inexperienced younger man was almost repeating itself with her and Adam, the difference being, of course, that both she and Adam were at liberty to have a relationship.

Sandra was wisely remaining silent and Carla decided to divert the conversation. 'You said it was for someone else that you came to tell me this.'

Sandra took a deep breath as if in preparation, and Carla's intuition kicked in: she knew – she just knew – where this was going. Reaching into her handbag, Sandra pulled out an expensive looking purse and extracted a photograph, which she handed to Carla. 'This is Sophie,' she said. 'Gareth is her father.'

Carla stared down at little blonde-haired Sophie, the innocent result of adult lust. Stefan's eyes looked back at her – Gareth's eyes. This wasn't just Gareth's daughter: this was also Stefan and Bryn's little sister. A vision of her two boys walking through the park each holding one of Sophie's hands flashed before her eyes. She looked up and saw tears in Sandra's eyes and, to her horror, she felt her own throat constrict.

'Carla, I'm so sorry to bring this to you, just as I'm truly sorry that I instigated an affair with your husband. But I can never regret Sophie. I never thought I would be blessed with a child and Sophie is my life. But the thing is: my parents are dead, I'm an only child and if anything happens to me, Sophie will have no one. I'm forty nine – old enough to be her grandmother really – and Sophie is the reason why, rightly or wrongly, I'm here. One day I'll want to tell her that she has brothers, and I know I have no right to ask, but, for Sophie's sake, would you please consider making her a part of your lives, even if only in a tenuous way? I would never blame you for hating me. I just ask that you give Sophie a chance to be part of her brothers' lives, if you can.'

Through this whole long speech, Carla did not attempt to interrupt or respond, but sat repeatedly looking from the picture to Sandra and back again, unable to form a single thought.

'This has been a terrible shock for you,' said Sandra, 'and I think it's best that I go now.' She pulled a card out of her handbag. 'These are my details. I'd be so grateful if you would call me when you've had time to think about this, but I'll understand if you don't.'

Carla said nothing as Sandra got up, gathered her handbag and walked over to the desk to pay for the wine. Carla's wine still stood untouched. In the next instant, Sandra was through the door, out into the rainy street and gone; and Carla was left with a bombshell, a glass of wine and a picture of a small girl with her husband's eyes.

She spent another half hour sitting at the table where her life had been turned upside down. So many emotions – betrayal, hurt, sadness, anger – were coursing through her. She was glad of the chilled wine as it calmed her shattered nerves, but it was also making her feel even more unsteady, especially on an empty stomach. She could use some support and was blessed with great friends and a family, all of whom would be there for her, she knew. But she was not sure she wanted to share this earth-shattering news with anyone just yet. It made such a mockery of her relationship with Gareth. She wondered if he had known about Sophie – she had forgotten to ask. She thought not. She felt immense rage towards him for his infidelity, and it was painfully frustrating not to be able to shout and swear at him, punch and kick him, lock him out of the house or dump his clothes in black plastic sacks. But maybe that was all for the best; she didn't much see herself as a drama queen.

Sitting in the corner of the dingy little restaurant, she could not help going back three years, searching her life for the clues she must have missed. How was their relationship then? How could she not have noticed anything different? Oh, but wait a minute! Something was nagging at her now fuzzy brain. Hadn't that been when Gareth's love making skills had suddenly become more adventurous and creative? Yes! And now she knew why! That woman had taught Gareth how to make exciting love; he, in turn, had taught her, and now she was passing on those lessons to delicious young Adam. Carla had to stop herself laughing out loud with the irony of it all.

She really needed to get out of there. She was feeling quite dizzy and faint, and had to gather up her resolve to get herself up and out, and find her way back to the office. Jonathan was in reception talking to Barry when she got there.

'Carla! You okay?'

'Actually, no Jonathan … not feeling too good. Would you… er … drive me home in my car? Er … we'll pay for a taxi to get you back…. Oh, and the Chich … Chich-e-s-ter House proposal is on my desk and just needs setting out properly…. Other two will have to wait.'

Jonathan helped her to her car and into the passenger seat, where she sat back with her eyes closed during the journey home. Back at her house, he got her upstairs into her bedroom, drew the curtains and helped her off with her shoes. Leaving her flat out on the bed, he went down and got two pain killers from the kitchen cupboard where he knew she kept the medicines, filled a glass with cool, filtered water and took them back up to her.

'Come on, let's get you sorted,' he said. 'You need to be more comfortable.' She groaned as he helped her up and unzipped her dress, which she stepped out of as it fell to the floor. He found a pair of sweatpants and a T-shirt and proceeded to dress her; after that, he sat on the bed while she obediently took the tablets and then he let her lie back down, covering her with the blanket from the bottom of the bed, and giving her a kiss on the forehead. 'Go to sleep. I'll call your mum and ask her to pick up the boys,' he said on his way out.

'Thanks Jay. You really are a love.'

'All in a day's work, my sweet. Take the day off tomorrow.'

She woke in the late afternoon feeling a lot better. Banjo, who was lying on the floor beside the bed, looked at her with expectant eyes. 'Walkies?' His ears pricked up and he followed her downstairs where she pulled on a raincoat and wellies, pocketed her mobile phone and put his lead on. They made for the park in a warm, blustery wind and Carla could feel it blowing away the cobwebs as she set her mind to go over the day's events; she had a lot of thinking to do. First she had to absorb the fact that her husband, soul mate, love of her life – her *Gareth* – had succumbed to the advances of a sexy, older woman. That was hard enough, but now she had to work out whether she was willing to bring her dead husband's illegitimate child into her life. How would she explain *that* to the boys?

She watched Banjo innocently bouncing from one very important smell to another and she envied him his simple life; his biggest decision was where to lie down and what to sniff next. Now that she felt more calm, she knew it was time to talk through her dilemma with someone – it always helped. She dug her mobile out of her pocket and speed dialled

Trudy's number. It went through to voicemail so she left a message asking if she could come round later that night, after the boys had gone to bed.

'You don't seem very surprised Trude!'

Trudy nearly spat her wine out. 'Darling, that's not fair! You're talking to someone who's lived a very colourful life – as you know – so when it comes to men, nothing surprises me, even with your very gorgeous Gareth. Look, he didn't have an affair and then leave you to start a completely new life, did he? What he actually did was learn from it and better his life with you, or so he thought. Anyway, men keep their brains in their dicks, we know that.'

They were curled up on the sofa in Carla's lounge, the children were asleep and Einaudi was softly playing in the background. When her mother had brought the boys back around six o'clock, Carla had considered telling her about her devastating discovery, but decided to leave it until she had processed the information fully herself. She thought it would really upset her mother because she had adored Gareth, as had everyone it seemed, and the way Carla was feeling she wasn't sure it would do either of them any good to talk about it yet.

She was quite surprised at Trudy's laid back attitude about the whole situation. But then, she was also aware that Trudy had a way of cutting through the crap and seeing things as they really were. They both sat quietly listening to the bewitching piano until Trudy had her next thought.

'Carla,' she said. 'I cannot begin to imagine what it must be like to lose the love of your life the way you did; and finding out about a wayward part of his life, on top of that, makes it doubly horrendous. It's going to hurt whichever way we look at it, but let's try to be as objective as possible because that sometimes helps. Right now, I expect you're thinking Gareth was not the man you thought he was. Right?'

Carla nodded.

'But is that really true? Yes, he gave in to the sexual advances of another woman; yes, he was weak, but that doesn't make him a different person to the one you knew and loved. Think about it: if this woman had not come along to see you today, would Gareth have been anyone other than the man you knew him to be? No. So what's changed? Nothing, except that you know about an event in his life and your *perception* of him has changed – nothing else – and our perception is just the way we think about something – an opinion – that's all. And I ask you, who is in charge of your thoughts?'

Trudy waited.

'I suppose I am,' Carla finally answered with a slight frown.

'Absolutely! So, my darling, at the end of the day, the lovely Gareth did make mistakes and act inappropriately, but the sad fact is, the lovely Gareth is no longer with us. You have the choice about whether or not to let this event sully the memory of the man you love and the father of your children.'

'That's all very well, and it makes sense,' said Carla, still frowning, 'but it's easier said than done. Right now, my heart doesn't give a toss for all that: I have all these *feelings*. I'm *devastated*, Trudy!'

'Darling girl, of course you are! And I'm not suggesting for a second that you ignore those feelings. That wouldn't help, at all, because they'd be in there festering away. But neither would it help for me to just sit here and make sympathetic noises. Just bear with me, darling. I'm only planting seed thoughts for you to consider – a way of looking at this new reality you're faced with that will help you get through the hurt with the least amount of emotional fallout.'

'Okay, I'm listening. That 'no nonsense' approach of yours is really why I wanted to talk to you, anyway, because I have no objectivity about any of this and I need a way to deal with it sooner rather than later. I know crying my way to the bottom of a wine bottle and wailing from the roof top may help in the short term, but I need to think about the long term implications for everybody concerned – especially my boys … and hopefully for Sophie too.'

'Exactly! I'm only clarifying what you already know, which is that this whole thing happened three years ago and no one can change the past, so the fact is that it would still have happened whether you knew about it or not.

'The reality, now, that you have to deal with one way or another is that Gareth is gone and can't be held accountable; Sandra Simpson has come into your life and you now know there is a very real and innocent child – the boys' half-sister – to consider. You *are* going to be able to handle the practicalities of this situation in the best possible way for everyone concerned, you know. You're strong, my darling.'

'I don't feel it,' sighed Carla, sitting back and resting her head wearily. She did, however, feel that perhaps everything could turn out all right eventually. She could see that Trudy had indeed helped by acknowledging her as the injured party but not getting into dissecting and analysing the emotional storm battering her psyche, or taking the moral high ground against Gareth or Sandra. Carla didn't want that – the very thought of it felt draining – and she did not want Gareth denigrated either. Enraged and confused as she was, nothing could shake her belief in the core goodness and decency of the loving man with whom she had shared her life. Thanks to Trudy's disinterest in emotional wallowing, Carla could feel something like a glimmer of space opening up inside her, in which measured thought could eventually hold sway. But not yet – she still felt indescribably hurt.

Late in the night, after Trudy had gone, Carla sat in bed looking at family pictures: Gareth playing with Banjo – shirt off and tanned in the garden; Gareth walking towards the camera with a little Bryn on his shoulder – stunning, dark, sexy eyes burning into the camera lens; Gareth lying on the bed in just his jeans – her favourite shot – leaning on his arm and looking straight out at her from the past. She looked back into those eyes, remembering just how wonderful he had been in his carefree, wholesome way.

She could not, however, prevent herself wondering about when the pictures had been taken. Was it during those nine months? She began to sob and pushed the photos on to the floor, much to Banjo's startled surprise. She sobbed for the deceit; for not realising that something was missing in their marriage; for the little girl with Gareth's eyes who had never known him. She sobbed well into the small hours and eventually fell into a troubled sleep fuelled by too much wine and a day full of heart-rending revelations.

The next day dawned bright and clear. Carla woke up to the sound of the boys, already downstairs, and her mother's voice gently chivvying them into eating their breakfast and getting ready for school. She sighed, turned over and slipped back into a restful slumber. The next she knew her mother was knocking at her door and bringing her in a cup of tea.

'How are you feeling today, love? I thought I'd pop down to sort out the boys. I just had a feeling that you may not be quite yourself: Jonathan said you wouldn't be going to the office today.' She sat down on the edge of the bed. 'So, are you going to tell me what's been going on?'

Carla sat up and told her what had happened the previous day. Her mother was saddened but not unduly shocked, which wasn't at all what Carla had been expecting.

'I always knew Gareth was very hot blooded, Carla. I think he probably had some Latin blood in him somewhere along the line, what with that olive skin. He had a big capacity for love and he just didn't choose very wisely when he was dishing it out on that occasion, but he came to his senses. His love for you never wavered – he just got greedy. It happens in marriages more often than not, and more often than not the spouse is none the wiser and life goes on. You'd be none the wiser if it weren't for the child. It's long after the fact, but now you do know and you have to cope with it somehow.'

Carla sighed. 'Oh, Mum, I feel like I'm in a whirlpool of horrible emotions. It would be easier if I could just hate them, but I can't, I just can't.'

'Then be thankful; hate will eat you up. Just give it time, love, and the pain will fade, just as the pain of losing him has been fading over the months since his death. Don't let this disrupt your recovery.'

'I'll do my best, Mum.'

'You've been so chirpy too, lately, and looking quite radiant, I wouldn't be surprised if there's a man on the scene. Am I right?'

Carla was looking at her mother with her mouth agape in disbelief.

'No need to look at me like that! I gave birth to you. There's not a lot I don't notice about you.' She patted Carla's hand. 'Don't worry: you don't have to tell me anything until you're ready. I just like to see you happy.' She kissed her daughter and went downstairs to clear away the breakfast things. She knew very well who was making her Carla glow, and she wasn't about to judge; she just wanted her to have some joy in her life and not get hurt.

Carla shut herself off from everyone and watched her favourite films all day. She didn't answer the house phone or switch on her mobile phone, and her mother was having the boys for the night so that Carla could have some time to contemplate how to deal with everything.

When evening came, she drove Banjo to the cliffs at Dover and they walked for miles before it got dark. It was blustery and drizzling with rain, but she didn't care. She cried into the wind and cursed her beloved, late husband for being unfaithful and for being dead. She wanted to be able to slap him and shout in his face, and then she wanted to hold him tight and never let him out of her sight. The wind blew and she walked faster and faster, looking out over the vastness of the channel. She even looked up to see if she could see Gareth's face in the sky – a vision – but she couldn't. What surprised her were the two other faces that came to her instead: a tanned, smiling young man with cornflower blue eyes, and a little girl who looked back at her with haunted, pleading eyes.

Carla let all the tears come. This time they flowed for the love she had been given over the years and still had around her in abundance; they flowed for the love she was lavishing on Adam, and the love that this little girl may need one day. She eventually stopped howling into the wind and sat on a rock, exhausted by her outburst, and thought about love: it had torn her apart, but it was also the one thing that held her together and made life rich and full. With the wind and sea bearing witness, she made a heartfelt promise to focus on love and endeavour to choose it in every circumstance, because the alternative was bitter and dark and lonely. She was in pain now, but even that let her know that she was fully alive, and she, of all people, knew how important it was to live every minute to the full, every day as if it were the last – because one day it would be.

*   *   *   *   *

It was ten thirty at night and Adam was worried. He had called Carla's office earlier and been told that she wouldn't be in that day. He had called the house and her mobile and got no answer. In fact, he had been calling her for two days now, the last time just moments ago, and still she was answering neither her mobile nor her landline. What could have happened? Where was she? He was due to work at her house the next day, but he couldn't face a sleepless night of not knowing. Picking up courage, he jumped on his bike and made a dash across the city, arriving at her house to find her car on the drive. He could see that the lounge lights were off and assumed she had gone to bed, but then he leaned against the car to catch his breath and discovered the bonnet was warm, so she must have been out and just come home. He had to find out what was going on.

With a racing heart, he rang the bell and stood waiting for a moment. He then stepped back as he heard an upstairs window being opened. 'Carla?' he called. 'It's me.' He could see her face in the light of the streetlamp and she wasn't smiling.

'I'll come down,' she said, and disappeared.

The Carla who opened the door was a very different person from the confident, sassy one he had played erotic games with in the woods two evenings before. Now she looked tiny, washed out and dishevelled. He was about to speak but she just turned back into the hallway, leaving him to follow her. Shutting the porch and front doors behind him, he went through to join her in the kitchen, worried that he had done something wrong. But then in the glow of the under-cupboard lighting, he could see that her eyes looked dark and swollen from crying. Without hesitation he crossed the floor and folded her into his arms.

It was exactly what Carla needed – no questions and strong arms. Adam wrapped her close into his sweatshirt. He smelt of washing powder and outside, and she lost herself in the soothing comfort of him stroking her hair and planting small kisses on her head. The warmth of his touch, his tact and gentleness, would have made her cry if she had not been completely drained of tears already. She was thankful that he had instinctively known what to do, but as they gently swayed together in the lengthening embrace, she got the feeling that he did not know what to do next.

She had come back from her walk in a much calmer state, but she did feel drained and just wanted to sleep. She wanted to sleep, however, with this man by her side. Looking up into his handsome face, she pulled his head down and kissed him sweetly and invitingly, but without fire and passion. She needed the night to be all about love, not sex, and she took his hand, opened his palm and kissed it in a way she hoped would show him that she needed comfort tonight. He looked into her eyes and gently stroked her cheek with his knuckles.

'Shall we go to bed?' he asked

She nodded. He had no idea what was wrong but assumed she would tell him in her own time, which did not appear to be now. Yet, he had never felt closer to her and wanted only to do what was right for her.

In the bedroom, he kicked off his shoes and stripped down to his jeans. He then helped her out of her T-shirt, under which she was not wearing a bra as she had been getting into bed when he arrived. She pushed down her comfy pyjama bottoms and kicked them aside; for the first time he was seeing her fully naked. She did not move, allowing him to run his eyes over her. She was beautiful – not perfect, but beautiful – and he drank in every inch of her, noticing her nipples harden under his gaze. All he wanted was to be inside her.

He took off the rest of his clothes, and now it was her turn to look. As she reached up and stroked the contours of his chest, he took her hand and led her to the bed, pulled back the duvet and got in, making room for her to get in beside him; she followed him in and moved straight into his arms. Light and tender kisses accompanied their caresses as they moved together, his body moulding around hers. Then, laying her back against the white sheet, Adam parted her legs and moved on top of her.

Carla felt as though she were someone else. It had been a surreal few days and now here he was, this strong young man, about to enter her for the first time, and the moment was exactly as she needed it to be: they were not fucking; they were making soft, gentle, tender love. She could feel him butting up against her thighs and she opened her legs, reaching down to bring his tip to her entrance. Adam looked deeply into her eyes as he entered her, gently pushing right in. Her eyes closed momentarily as she welcomed the invasion. She had forgotten how good it was to feel the heaviness of a man on top of her. The rhythm started, slow, long and in unison, both of them panting. She wanted it to go on forever. Reaching down she grasped his buttocks, pulled him deeper into her and wrapped her legs around his back. She worked with him, watching his face. His eyes started to mist slightly and she could see him lose focus. The tension in his body increased, he cried out as he came and she pulled him in deeper.

As he came back to her, he smiled the heart breaking smile that was his alone and she caressed his face and lightly kissed him as he took his weight off her and lay down beside her. Within a few minutes he was snoring gently and Carla slipped out of bed to wash off the stickiness oozing down her thighs. He had turned and his broad back was facing her when she came back so she spooned herself around him and draped her arm across his hip, kissing his back and bringing her pillow down so that she could stay next to his warmth and love. And then she slept.

The familiar chink of bottles and the sound of the milkman's running feet slowly filtered into her consciousness and brought her mind, if not her eyes, into the new day. Something was different. With her eyes still closed, she could sense his masculine presence in her bed, and she liked it. Her mind, still foggy with sleep, drifted back to early mornings just after Gareth had died. She would lie in this bed and sense him, strain to hear him, hoping it had only been a terrible dream that her man had been taken from her. Sometimes, she had thought she could feel him move in the bed next to her and had opened her eyes, picturing the familiar contours of his face, or the side of his head, or his lithe, strong shoulders. But there was only the space where he should have been. And her heart would break anew.

Today, though, was different: Adam was with her. She opened her eyes and looked at the clock: six fifteen. The milkman's float whirred off up the road and the sound of the birds in the hedge took its place. She felt a stirring in her abdomen as she remembered watching Adam lose himself inside her. The night's sleep had refreshed her and she was becoming aroused. She wanted this virile body again. This time, however, she wanted things to be a little different.

With as little movement as possible so as not to disturb him, Carla rolled over to look at him and her heartbeat moved up a gear. He was lying on his back, the arm nearest to her stretched up behind his head and his face turned away; the covers were pushed down to his waist, leaving his chest bare. For a time she was content to just look at him while he slept, studying his features: his profile was strong, straight and very masculine, suiting his physique. His hair was unkempt and badly in need of a cut, but it was like him: free to go its own way. His eyebrows were darker than his sandy coloured hair, but it was the flecks of blonde in them, she realised, that made his blue eyes so startling. Her eyes ran down his shoulders; she loved the way his arm muscles bulged with his hand behind his head and wanted to kiss that part of him – but not yet.

He stirred, as though sensing the caress of her eyes, and turned his head, opening eyes full of sleep and bewilderment. Her stomach flipped when his look softened at the sight of her and he smiled, turning on his side and reaching out to stroke her arm lovingly.

'Well, hello,' he said huskily. 'Feeling better today?'

She nodded and snuggled close into his chest. His arms encircled her and his chest hair tickled her nose as he pulled her closer. She could feel his body in full response and in one move he lay flat on his back and pulled her on top of him, the suddenness startling her a little, and she giggled. But then she saw the lust in his eyes and became more serious, opening her thighs so as to feel his erection hard against her.

'I want you,' he said, 'and I want you to show me how you come. You didn't reach it last night did you?'

'No, sweetheart, I don't need to come every time. I wanted to watch and feel you come. Sometimes it's just as fulfilling to focus solely on you and your build up and release; then I can clamp round you at the right moment and bring you in deeper as you reach your climax. I could feel you pulsating inside me last night; it was luscious.'

Adam had never slept the whole night with a woman. He had experienced plenty of sex, but it had always been a rush to get in, explode and get out again – never a slow, languorous sharing. Carla was introducing him to more than he imagined possible. Waking up with her beside him, for instance, knowing he could just roll over and make love to her was erotic in the extreme. And she was so cute, sexy and young-looking, all tousled and with no makeup – so different from the part of her that was the equally sexy owner of a business.

He felt somewhat guilty that she had not climaxed the previous night, but his orgasm had been so powerful that it had pretty much wiped him out and the need to sleep had overwhelmed him. He had woken in the night to go to the bathroom and he had considered pleasuring her, but she was sleeping so soundly and was obviously having some kind of emotional upset in her life, so he had slipped back in beside her and drifted back to sleep. But here she was, lying on top of him in the early morning light. Now, he wanted to watch her reach her pleasure and he wanted to do it right. She had wriggled her body around on his, pushing the air from his lungs with her weight, and even that was erotic and sensual. He was powerfully turned on.

'Okay, so this is how we're going to do this,' she said with a naughty look in her eyes. She put his arms above his head and clamped her hands down over his wrists, kissing and tasting him as she moved to straddle him. He groaned as she manoeuvred the angle of her body so that he would slip easily inside her and his eyes opened wide as he felt himself enter her. How she loved his inexperience for giving her such opportunities to witness that look of surprised pleasure! 'Now, I want you to tip your hips up towards me.' She took in a sharp breath as he did so. 'Yes,' she said breathlessly. 'Now, don't move too much; I need to get the angle right and then I'll do the moving, okay?'

'You're the boss,' he grinned and lay back as she held him down and started a slow, rhythmic, back and forth movement. He had never seen anything more sensual than this woman taking her pleasure from his body, and hoped he could control himself long enough for her. He focused on her face and her gratification rather than his mounting desire to ejaculate inside her. Her eyes closed and he felt her grip on his wrists tighten. Her movements became more precise and measured. He could tell it was more about positioning than tempo so he kept his hips still and pressed into her. She continued grinding into him and he could feel her getting hotter with the exertion. The way she was holding his wrists, the heat from her thighs, how she was clamped around him making little movements up and down and the intensity of her expression – it was all driving him wild. All of a sudden she slowed even more, her eyes opened and burned deeply into his, and she literally stopped breathing as an orgasm rattled through her body. He could feel her contracting around him inside and that was just too much for him: as she slumped forward releasing his wrists, he grasped her hips, moved them up and down a few times and then emptied himself into her.

They both lay panting, glued together with heat and dampness. Carla raised her head and tickled his face with her hair. He laughed.

They showered together and then dressed, after which Carla took Banjo and went to join her sons for breakfast at her mother's house, whilst Adam made toast and coffee and sat on the deck contemplating the day ahead. Today they would need to spend some time talking, he thought. He was a bit frightened of emotional stuff but he felt he had to overcome that if he was to continue with Carla. She had a past and a family; she was a respected professional and she was nineteen years older than him: there was a lot at stake for her. They needed to talk about how – or maybe even *if* – they wanted to go on from here; he needed to know how she really felt about him, now that he realised he could get hurt. He was at a cross roads in life, he knew that. His work wasn't remotely enough for him; there had to be more, but he didn't know which way to go. With one thing and another, he felt he was treading water.

Carla made her way back home after taking the boys to school and having coffee and a very interesting chat with her mother, who had said that anytime Carla needed a bit of time to herself, she would step in to help. She had also said that Carla should never be concerned about what other people might think when it came to life decisions; as long as she wasn't hurting anyone, she should just do what was right for her and made her happy. Carla wondered what had prompted her to say all that, although she hadn't pressed her mother further because she had too much on her mind as it was. But she was getting the strong impression that her mother might have guessed that Adam was more to her than a gardener.

As she walked back home via the park with Banjo, she thought about how her relationship with Adam was developing in ways she had not bargained for – feelings were gathering that frightened her. She had opened a Pandora's Box, it seemed, and she might have to accept that this was not something of which she was in complete control. Ironic, since it was the element of control in making love to Adam that was an important part of their relationship to this point, and so very different from her sexual relationship with Gareth. Gareth had encouraged her to take control, but it was only at his suggestion; he could take it back anytime, so that wasn't real control.

She had been very clear that love in the sense of the whole life partnership thing, was just not on the agenda for her and Adam, and it still wasn't. But she was no longer so certain that her feelings towards him were just physical. She had only ever been in love with Gareth and she was beginning to recognise that it was certainly love she felt for Adam, but it was different. Just as she loved her boys, their father, her family and friends in different ways, she was now finding she could be *in* love in different ways. She felt quite enlightened by this and calling Banjo, she picked up speed to get home and see the man who was currently turning her heart and her resolve upside down.

Joyce wasn't at all surprised to see Adam's bike already at Carla's when she pulled up in the car. Since Carla had told her about the two of them, her concern for Adam had not abated but she was doing her best to stand back and be glad of their present happiness. She wished Adam had felt he could confide in her, but he could be very closed at times and only fed her snippets of information about himself. She sighed, knowing he was cutting the apron strings, as any young man should, and she had to let him get on with it. He had to learn about life just like everybody else, and she had to let him go even though it was far from easy.

Carla was just coming along the road with Banjo and she waved and smiled. She looked so young, Joyce thought – wearing wellies, jeans and a floppy sweatshirt, she could easily pass for a girl in her twenties.

'Hello, love,' she said.

'Hi, Joyce, I'm home today. I haven't been too well, so I took a few days off.'

'Sorry to hear that. Are you all right now?'

'Much better, thanks. Fancy a cuppa?'

'You just relax and I'll put the kettle on.'

As Joyce made her way into the house, Carla went round the back to see Adam, who was already halfway through cutting the hedge. His T-shirt had already been discarded and was lying on the deck where he had thrown it; his torso glistened with sweat.

'You're mum's here,' she said, appreciatively casting her eyes over his toned body. 'Does she know you stayed here last night?'

'Not from me she doesn't. Why, has she said something?'

'No, not yet, but if she does I don't want to lie to her. I'm not ashamed of us.'

Adam beamed and touched her cheek. 'Me neither. Let's see what happens.'

Joyce had already made the tea when Carla came back into the kitchen and at Carla's suggestion, they sat at the breakfast bar together.

'So have you had a bug then, love?'

'Well, no, I've had a bit of a shock – no, a huge shock, actually.'

'Oh dear, it sounds like it knocked you for six if you've had to take time off work.'

Carla brushed some invisible specks from the granite top. She trusted Joyce and she wanted to talk to someone older and wiser – someone not as close to her as her mother – and get their view of Gareth's infidelity. 'I'm dealing with it, Joyce, but I'll never be the same again.'

'Good heavens! What on earth has happened?'

'To cut a very long story short, a woman came to my office the other day to tell me she'd had an affair with my husband three years ago.'

Joyce's hand flew to her mouth. In one way she was flabbergasted: she'd had Gareth up on a pedestal, seeing him as everything a man should be, including faithful. But no one was perfect, herself included, and she was in no position to pass judgement on him. Plus she knew other women must have found him as irresistible as she had, so although she was shocked, she was not totally surprised. 'Carla, love, I'm so sorry. That must have been a terrible shock for you. Who was this woman?'

'Her name is Sandra Simpson, and I have to admit I can see why Gareth was attracted to her: she was quite a bit older than him, sensual and probably very experienced in the art of love – she told me she knew he loved me but liked what she gave him. Joyce, even though I'm so hurt, if I'm honest the more I think about it the more I understand it. When Gareth and I met at nineteen, neither of us knew anything about sex; we just got on with it and enjoyable as it was, we didn't realise there could be so much more to it – I'm not embarrassing you, am I?'

'Of course not, love. You say anything you want.'

'Well, I think she taught him what we'd been missing because he then taught me, and our sex life moved to a whole new level in the last year of his life. And unfortunately, that's not all.'

Joyce coughed as she swallowed some tea. 'There's more?' she spluttered.

Carla got off the stool and retrieved her handbag from the hook on the back of the door. After rummaging around in it for a moment, she found the photograph and handed it to Joyce.

Joyce could immediately see whose child it was: it was there in the eyes looking back at her from the picture. 'So they had a child?' she breathed, almost to herself.

'If it hadn't been for her I would probably never have known about the affair. Joyce, I just don't know what to feel. It's bewildering – one minute thinking *how could he?* and the next being half way to understanding it.' Carla leaned back against the sink and covered her eyes, unwilling to display the sudden eruption of yet more tears. Her shoulders shook and Joyce immediately went to her and held her.

'You just let it all out, love,' she soothed. She was facing the window, and over Carla's shoulder her eyes found their way to her son in the garden. Watching Adam's strong arms swinging the hedge trimmer took her back to another set of strong, young arms belonging to the intoxicating German who had taken her to levels of physical love she had never believed could exist outside the covers of magazines. She knew the feelings Gareth had apparently succumbed to, and with the same result – hers being out there in the garden. Kristophe had been their lodger for five weeks one summer, while he worked on the ever-expanding engineering links between England and Europe, and she had been the older woman then. What a strange turn of events, she suddenly realised, like father like son – well as far as the older woman with two children is concerned – no husband involved though, thank goodness. Kristophe had also been older than Adam now was too. His blonde Teutonic bearing and attentiveness had left her breathless and unable to resist temptation. Is that how Carla feels about my Adam? What a peculiar way history has of repeating itself, she concluded.

Carla pulled away and reached over for some kitchen roll to mop up her red, puffy face.

'Does Adam know?' Joyce asked, recognising that pain was juxtaposed with passion in Carla's life and she knew all about that herself. She sat back down and sipped her tea, listening for Carla's tone when she answered; she wanted to be able to talk to Carla about Adam without either of them getting het up.

'No, not yet.'

'He was here last night, though, wasn't he? He didn't come home.'

'He was, Joyce, and he was wonderfully supportive without asking a single question. I was very upset and he was just there for me. You have an amazing son.'

'Yes, he's a very caring person, and mature for his age – too mature, I sometimes think – but still daft enough to think I don't know anything about what's going on with him.'

'I take it he hasn't said anything to you about us yet?'

'No, and I doubt he will. I'm his mum; he doesn't think I have a love life let alone know about what he's sharing with you. I know it's pretty special. Just seeing you in the garden together just now – the body language says it all. And I hate to admit it, but I think you *are* good for each other, just as you said – for the time being anyway. I have to be honest though, I wouldn't want to see the two of you as permanent.'

'And you won't, Joyce. Both Adam and I are very clear on that.'

'Well, that's good to hear. I've had my misgivings, as you know, but if it had to happen – a relationship with an older woman, I mean – I'm glad it's with you, Carla.'

'Thank you – I think,' Carla laughed, glad that they were able to talk so openly with each other. She'd known Joyce for a long time but now they seemed to be getting close, as friends, and it had happened because of Adam. It could have gone either way, to be sure, Carla realised, if it weren't for Joyce's generous understanding, for which she found herself grateful: she would not have wanted to alienate this woman, whom she liked so much and who had been largely responsible for maintaining the smooth running of her household since Gareth's death. Love was the operative factor, she realised: they both loved Adam, albeit in different ways, and it had drawn them naturally closer.

Joyce broke into her small reverie. 'Well, I've enjoyed talking to you but I must get on. The house won't clean itself.'

'It can wait another half hour,' said Carla warmly, with a dismissive wave of her hand. 'I'll put on a pot of coffee, shall I?'

'I wouldn't say no to a caffeine lift!' Joyce was feeling somehow lighter, having been able to say what she felt and being reassured by Carla that she and Adam weren't thinking long term. She also felt a bit stronger in herself as that worry eased, and decided to stop putting off the time to tell Adam what she must, seeing Carla's news as maybe the signal she needed to get things out in the open. With that thought, she broached the subject of Gareth's child. 'So, this little girl then?'

'Yes, Sophie,' said Carla, busying herself with cafetière and ground coffee. 'She's two years old and she's the reason that Sandra came to find me. Sandra has no husband and no extended family, so, obviously, at the moment, Sophie has no family except Sandra. She's concerned that if anything happens to her, Sophie will have no one.'

'So this Sandra is thinking that Sophie has two older half-brothers?'

'Exactly!' said Carla. 'And I'd probably do the same thing in her shoes. Wouldn't you?'

Joyce nodded emphatically. 'Absolutely, love. I'd do anything to protect my own.'

Carla moved round the kitchen, getting two of her good china cups and saucers from the cupboard and cream from the fridge. 'And I appreciate that it must have taken some courage on Sandra's part to approach me,' she said. 'But I'm still so angry with Gareth, and I'm not sure I want the boys to know that they have an illegitimate half-sister.'

'Ooh, illegitimacy is a thing of the past, Carla; there's no such thing as an illegitimate child any more, I'm glad to say. In my view, labelling a child because of who got together and created him or her was always a travesty. The innocent little person who's been brought into the world and has to grow up in it doesn't deserve that.'

Carla looked up from pouring the coffee. 'Have I hit a nerve, Joyce?' She was genuinely concerned: Joyce sounded so vehement.

'Just something I feel strongly about, that's all. I'm older than you and I remember people being called that – well, they were called bastards, which meant the same thing in those days,' said Joyce evasively, wondering what Carla would say if she knew that, technically, Adam would once have been called illegitimate. Well, Carla would know soon enough and then she'd know what nerve she'd hit. 'Sophie can't help who her parents are,' she added.

'You're absolutely right, and I have to remember that when I get caught in emotional quicksand. It would be terribly wrong to deprive her of the only family she has, apart from her mother, because of my bitterness. Anyway, I promised myself I wouldn't be bitter. It won't be easy explaining it all to the boys, but I'm sure I'll find the right words somehow.'

You and me both, God willing, thought Joyce. 'Of course you will, and I'm sure they'll enjoy having a little sister to fuss over,' she reassured Carla.

Carla sighed and came to give Joyce a hug. 'Thank you for being so wise,' she said. 'I'll call Sandra later and ask her round for a talk. It will be a start.'

* * * * *

It was crunch time: Tom was out at a snooker competition that evening, and Joyce had no excuse

212

for putting off any longer what she had been dreading for years. She felt familiar shame and guilt wash over her, but she knew it was the right time for her Adam to know the truth. Not only was he now a man, but he was involved with someone who could undoubtedly help him through it. She heard the bang of the door around six o'clock and her stomach churned with nerves.

He came into the kitchen and sat down at the old kitchen table that had been there his whole life. He looked at his mother, obviously nervous himself, and the atmosphere between them suddenly felt strained. She felt his eyes on her as she took a bottle of wine out of the fridge and poured two glasses, putting one in front of him. He looked at her askance – they had never been drinking buddies – but then she went round behind him, stooped and hugged his neck, kissing his cheek at the same time and relaxing inside as she felt him relax.

'Cheers, Mum,' he said as she sat down at the table with him.

She smiled. 'Cheers, love.'

'You spoke to Carla then.'

'I did.' She waited while he slowly and solemnly nodded his head.

'You okay with it?' He looked up at her with concerned eyes.

'Why wouldn't I be?'

He shrugged. 'Because she's a lot older than me?'

'True, but I can't keep you a boy any longer. You have to make your own decisions and your own way in life and be man enough to deal with the consequences if things don't go according to how you'd like them to. It doesn't mean I don't worry about you, mind!'

Adam raised his eyebrows in surprise. 'Great!' he said with a slow, relieved smile, a sense of freedom washing through him. 'I wasn't expecting that.'

Joyce knew the moment had come. 'Look, love, there are no blueprints in life, no master plan that everyone has to follow. Things happen: people die who shouldn't die; people fall in love when they shouldn't. Which brings me to something I think now is the right time to tell you. You're at the age when you're stepping out into pastures new, and to help you to do that you need to know exactly where you come from.'

She paused. Adam was frowning slightly, his eyes fixed on her face, obviously waiting for what was coming. She took a gulp of wine to calm her nerves. There was no easy way of saying this.

'Ads, your dad is your dad in every way except biologically. Nineteen years ago I had a very short affair with a man who came to stay with us. He's your biological father. He doesn't know about you and Tom is your dad in every way that counts – he always has been and always will be. He knows you're not his biological son but he loves you as if you are. We always knew this day would come because you need to know, but we wanted you to be old enough to understand.'

She stopped the rush of words, looking into Adam's face for his reaction. He sat as still as a stone, looking back at her as if he no longer knew her; he looked at his hands and then stared out of the window, saying nothing.

The harsh sound of his chair scraping the floor broke the silence as he stood up and walked out of the room. Seconds later, Joyce heard the front door slam – not in anger, just the way he always slammed it. She thought she knew where he was going and she was glad in a way: she had always known that this information would not be something with which she could help him come to terms; he had to do that for himself, and he knew best who could help him. She sat and cried, drank all the wine including what Adam had left, and Tom came home to find her cried out and slumped over the kitchen table. 'I told him,' she muttered.

'We'll talk about it in the morning,' he said gently, helping her up and taking her upstairs to bed.

*   *   *   *   *

Mel was checking herself in the mirror, about to go out: hair and makeup were okay and she liked her firm, athletic shape, although she didn't think she was very sexy. Until recently, she had thought that was why men didn't seem attracted to her, until she got tired of feeling like a wallflower and had spoken to her friend Josie about it. Josie had no such problem: it seemed men were lining up to take her out. Her response to Mel's dilemma had been short and sharp.

'What do you expect?'
'What the hell does that mean?'
'Adam Barnes!'
'What about him?'

'Mel! Adam Barnes is the reason no one asks you out: they all think you're with him because you spend so much time together. He's a dishy rugby player – no one's gonna want to argue with *him*, or think they stand a chance while he's around.'

So now she understood: everyone thought she was taken! *'If only!'* she said aloud to her reflection just as a knock at her studio flat door made her jump. 'Who is it?' she called.

'Mel, it's me.'

Adam's voice sounded flat and miserable and she hurried to open the door. 'Bloody hell, sweet! What's wrong?' she exclaimed, standing back to let him in and eyeing his white face and sagging shoulders.

He stumbled in and sat down, putting his hands over his face. Mel sat down beside him, put her arms around him and stayed quiet as his shoulders began to shake and she could feel him crying. What could have happened to make her Adam cry? Tears welled up in her own eyes as she stroked his hair and he lent against her.

Finally he stopped. 'Tissue?' he sniffed.

She went and fetched a whole toilet roll for him. After a noisy blow of the nose, he screwed up the tissue and flung it into the nearby waste paper bin.

'What the fuck is going on, Ads? Is this something to do with Carla Trelawny?'

He looked at her in amazement. 'How did you know about Carla?'

'Adam, I'm not your best friend for nothing. Anyway, everyone knows: you'd have to be blind not to see what's going on there.'

'Oh my god! Is it that obvious?'

'Yep! Have you been dumped?'

'No, I just had a bloody big shock and I wanted to see you.'

He turned doleful eyes on her, melting her heart. She felt herself falling into the blue depths of them but managed to grab hold of herself. Something had happened and she wanted to help; at the same time, she was secretly pleased that it was her he had come to when upset.

'My mother has just blown my fucking mind. Apparently nineteen years ago she had a fling with some guy and I'm the result. Dad's always known – well, the person I thought was my dad but isn't. I can't take it in. My whole life feels like a lie. Who the fuck am I?'

A lot of things suddenly made sense: why there was a wide gap in age between Adam and his older brother and sister – they had been well into their teenage years before he turned up – and why he looked so different – they were small framed and dark with brown eyes, while Adam was much taller and broader with light hair and those oh-so-blue eyes.

She didn't know what to say for the best so decided just to say what she thought, which was what she always did, as Adam knew; he wouldn't be suddenly expecting her to be someone else. 'I know it'll take a while to settle in, Ads, but in the cold light of day, nothing has changed: you still have a mum and dad who love you and a great family. Your family has given me more love than any blood relative I've got. So, okay, you've had a big shock – I appreciate that – but don't go overboard with the dramatics. Don't take what you've got for granted;

217

umpteen thousands would give their eye teeth to be in your shoes. Just think how much your dad must love you to overlook the biological details. I wish my biological dad loved me half as much as that.'

Adam sighed heavily, 'Yeah, I suppose you're right – you usually are.'

'I know it's not how you feel, right now, but I'm on the outside looking in and it still looks bloody good to me! Your mum is fantastic. She didn't have to tell you this and it can't have been easy for her. Why did she suddenly tell you, anyway?'

'She thinks I need to know where I come from.'

Mel waited for him to continue. 'And?' she encouraged as he gazed into the distance.

'Actually, I don't know much more than that, except that he was someone who stayed with them for a while and he doesn't know about me. I couldn't take it in so I just walked out – didn't think to ask questions.'

'Do you want to stay here tonight? You could call your mum and let her know where you are and that you're okay – she'll be worried.'

On impulse, he put his arm round her and pulled her to him. 'Thanks,' he said, kissing her lightly on the end of her nose, 'but you look like you were off out somewhere before I turned up, so I'll make a move.'

'I was only going to *Maze*. Why don't we both go?'

'Why not?' he said, pretending enthusiasm.

Mel knew he didn't much like going clubbing and would always choose a swim and a few drinks or a film given half a chance, but she had learned not to change her plans for Adam. If he wanted to be with her, he would come to the club, and anyway, it would take his mind off things. 'Come on then.'

By eleven o'clock Adam had already drunk more than he would usually drink in a whole week. He could see a lot of people he had known for years at the club and spent quite a while chatting to a few of his rugby friends at the bar before joining Mel's group of girls at a corner table surrounded by sofas. She was dancing a lot, so he sat and waited for her to come back.

It was dark and noisy but when someone came and sat down beside him he recognised Becky's friend – Ruby … Rosie? She was saying something to him but he couldn't hear her clearly and between the alcohol and the background noise, he couldn't be bothered to make an effort. He grinned and nodded a few times, hoping she'd get bored and move off. She stood up and he thought, with relief, that she was going to do just that, but then she turned and gave him a resounding slap on the face before stomping off. It hurt but not nearly as much as it would have done if he hadn't been drinking. *What was that for!* he wondered, knocking back another of the pints that was lining up for him on the table and looking around for Mel. She seemed to have been swallowed up by the crowd, which he hoped meant that she hadn't seen him being slapped round the chops. If she had, there would be questions he did not want to answer.

The beer was followed with a shot of whisky, which he didn't like but he wanted to keep his emotions dulled – he just felt he didn't know himself anymore. The music got louder – somehow distorted – and someone came to sit next to him on the sofa. Was it Mel? No. Where was she? Someone was in his face, speaking in a pathetic attempt at a sexy voice. 'Hello, handsome!' the voice said. 'Want a drink?' He nodded and 'sexy voice' went off to the bar. To Adam, it seemed like only seconds later that the drink was put in his hand and he knocked it back. It tasted sweet but he didn't care – he wanted oblivion. Someone was unbuttoning his shirt, touching his bare chest; he felt someone's mouth on his nipples but couldn't see who it was. He felt sick and dizzy and everything seemed insanely topsy-turvy. What was happening to him? His jeans were undone, warm hands were touching him; he didn't want this but couldn't seem to stop it. He tried to push the hands away, but it wasn't working.

He heard Mel's voice; she was shouting and swearing. Why was she angry? What had he done? His face was being slapped again, not so hard this time and on both sides.

'Adam! Adam! Wake up!'

He forced his eyes open and suddenly, as he raised his head and tried to focus, vomit rose in his throat and he threw up all over himself and on to the floor.

'Oh fuck, Adam!'

He tried to say something but his mouth couldn't seem to get the words out. Mel was there with him. He could feel her, and she was shouting for people to come and help. Yes, he needed help. Several pairs of strong arms got him up and he did his best to walk as he was guided across the dance floor and out into the fresh air of the night, where he promptly threw up on the pavement.

As he sat on the kerb with his legs in the road, resembling some kind of tramp, Mel turned to Josh, who had helped her get Adam out of the club. She had bumped into Josh on the dance floor and they'd gone back to the table together, to find Adam semi-conscious, partially undressed and being sexually assaulted by some man. Mel was so outraged she had grabbed the guy by his shirt and flung him across the floor. Josh had then made sure he was unceremoniously dragged to the door, where the security guards ejected him.

Meanwhile, Mel had been sorting out Adam: she had done up his shirt and jeans and slapped his face to bring him round. As he had struggled to get himself upright, she'd smelt the empty glass he had dropped on the sofa beside him. It must have been some kind of cocktail – not what Adam would have liked, at all, she thought. In the next breath, he had thrown up all over her. 'Better out than in!' she had sighed.

Mel was now cursing herself for leaving him alone. Some friend she was, knowing what had just happened in his life – this was all her fault and she deserved to be covered in his vomit. 'Josh, we'll have to walk him back to my place,' she said. 'He's a vomiting fountain at the moment and no taxi will take him.'

'You're not wrong,' nodded Josh. 'Come on, then.'

Taking an arm each, they hoisted Adam to his feet and began the long trek back to Mel's flat.

Adam came to some hours later as he vomited yet again. Someone held the bowl for him, gave him sips of water and then settled him down again to sleep. He knew it was Mel, but he just couldn't raise his head or speak. The next time he opened his eyes it was light. He groaned; his head felt as though it was being repeatedly smashed against a wall. Mel stirred beside him and her soft hands stroked his forehead.

'I'm going to be sick,' he muttered, promptly retching. Nothing came up: he was running on empty. He looked at Mel with aching eyes; she was lying next to him in her pyjamas. Had there been any sex? He couldn't remember anything, and he felt so ill he just wanted to die.

'Lie back down. I'll get you some fresh water.'

While she went over to the kitchenette, Adam checked to see what he was wearing – nothing except his pants. He ran his hands through is hair, which felt disgustingly sticky and stiff. He just couldn't remember. 'Where are my clothes?' he said hoarsely.

'Washed and hanging in the bathroom to dry. You were sick all over them.'

He groaned, clasping his head and sinking gingerly back down on to the pillows.

'You stink,' she said, putting the glass of water on the bedside table.

'Thanks! What's the time?'

'About eight, I think.' She checked her watch. 'Yep, five past. Have you got to be anywhere?'

When he said he didn't she went back to the kitchenette to put the kettle on. The clicking noise of the switch shot straight through his head. 'Oh fuck!' he gasped. Minutes later she was back with a glass of fizzing Alka Seltza for him. He wasn't sure he could keep it down but knew it was the best thing for him at that moment.

Mel stood over him to make sure he drank it. The least she could do was look after him now, after letting him – and Joyce for that matter – down so badly the night before. She had called Joyce soon after they'd gone out, to tell her that Adam was with her and that she would keep an eye on him. Joyce had sounded distraught, which Mel couldn't do much about, but she could have looked after Adam, especially when she could see he was getting more and more drunk. She hadn't bargained for a spiked drink, of course, but that was no excuse.

Now, he was in her bed and her heart went out to him, he looked so awful – pale and sweating – so she would stay with him today and get fluids into him. She hoped he hadn't got any blood poisoning but she thought he had been so sick that there couldn't possibly be anything left.

His phone began to ring and he put a pillow over his head with a groan. Mel grabbed his jacket and got the phone out of the pocket. Carla's name was coming up on it.

'Hello?'

'Oh, hello. Who is that?'

'Mel.'

'Oh, hi Mel. It's Carla.'

'Yes, I know.'

'Is Adam there?'

Adam had gathered who it was and was gesticulating for Mel to give him the phone.

'Hang on. I'll pass you over to him.' She gave him the phone walked off into the bathroom.   It suddenly occurred to him on some level that there could be a problem between Carla and Mel. He couldn't worry about that now, though: he was having issues staying upright.

'Carla.'

'Where are you, Adam?'

That tone like his mother's again! 'I'm at Mel's. I managed to get my drink spiked last night and I've been as sick as a dog. My head is banging!'

'Oh dear, that sounds nasty,' said Carla without much sympathy. 'Your mum called me last night, Adam, and told me about your dad. She thought you would be with me. She's sick with worry about you, sweetheart.'

'I know. I just left without talking to her, which was a bit harsh. But it's a big deal – I had to get my head round it.'

'Well, come over for tea later and after the boys have gone to bed we can talk about it, if you want. There's something else I want to talk to you about, as well.'

'Okay.'

'Get plenty of fluids down you, and vitamin B.'

'Okay. See you later.' As he disconnected and flopped back on to the bed, his head was reeling but he wasn't feeling so sick: the fizzy salts were working.

Mel came out of the bathroom, dressed and glowering.

'You okay?' he asked, not much liking the expression on her face.

She nodded, putting on a jacket and gathering up her handbag and a shopping bag. He watched her. Long limbed and strong, Mel always reminded him of an Amazon woman – the kind who would have been the head of the clan in prehistoric times. It wasn't a thought he had shared with her as she would probably have punched him.

'I'm going to the shops. I'll get bread. You need toast. Go back to sleep,' she said, staccato fashion, and was gone.

He sank back down into the soft bed, tried to ease his banging head by relaxing his forehead and neck, and thought about the women in his life: his lover, his best friend and his mother. He loved them all, but, right now, he could not deal with any of them.

Three hours later, during most of which he slept, he was starting to feel more human. He had sipped water and eaten toast and hadn't been sick again; his naturally strong constitution had taken over and his system was returning to normal, although he never wanted to touch alcohol again.

Mel had looked after him in a straight forward, not overly sympathetic way, which suited Adam. They were sitting at the breakfast bar sharing more toast in companionable silence, and Adam was risking a cup of tea. He thought it best to avoid the subject of Carla because he could sense Mel's disapproval. She was tough – she'd had to be with her upbringing – and she could be quite formidable at times. He thought she was probably angry that he hadn't confided in her, but he hadn't told anyone; people just seemed to have worked it out.

He was looking forward to seeing Carla that evening. They wouldn't be able to really talk until after the boys had gone to bed, but he didn't mind; he liked being around the boys and it was enough just to be around Carla, too, sometimes. He could watch her doing some ordinary, everyday thing and imagine her face in the throes of passion – eyes closed, mouth open and head thrown back.

He was also glad of the prospective evening because the hangover had depressed him and he had felt wretched about his mother's revelation. It had floored him completely. She had sliced off half his identity and left a vacuum he did not know how to fill – he didn't even know what his biological father looked like. Who was this guy? Where was he? Did he even want to know? One minute he did and the next he didn't; he felt raw with the re-occurring sense of shock that kept hitting him. And he was *angry*; he wanted to hate his mother for letting everyone down with her behaviour. And what about his dad? How did he react when he found out?

Mel read his thoughts. 'Are you going home to see your mum?'

He shook his head.

'Come on, Adam. Don't punish her any more than she's probably punishing herself.' Mel's dark eyes searched his face.

'Thing is, I keep thinking about my dad, Tom .... I have to say that now don't I?' he laughed with heavy irony. 'How did he cope? What did he do when he found out? How did he feel when this screaming wretch came into the world as a constant reminder of his wife's infidelity? How did he feel, year after year, as I was growing up and probably looking more and more like the other guy – because I sure as hell don't look like anyone else in my family, do I? I don't know whether to be grateful to him or punch him for being spineless?'

He stopped and swallowed, trying to keep back welling tears. Mel took his hand and held it without saying anything.

'Why did she even tell me?' he continued. 'Or rather, why the hell didn't she tell me before now? Do the other two know? They used to call me "golden boy". Maybe they knew all along and I fucking didn't! It's like I've been living as somebody who didn't actually exist; my whole life has been a lie! How can anything ever be the same again? It can't! Because I'm not who I thought I was. You know, right now, I just want to leave and not come back – go off somewhere where nobody knows me and start being this new person. I could go travelling abroad. That's what people do, isn't it? They go and "find themselves", don't they? That's what I need to do, because I've just fucking lost myself!'

Adam stood up and went to stare out of the window.

Mel had never heard him rant before. It was all stuff he needed to get off his chest so she had just listened without commenting. Now, she sat and contemplated this angry man with his back to her, breathing heavily with the force of his emotions. How she would have loved to go and take his face in her hands, kiss his sadness away, and then take him back to her bed and sooth him with her body. But there was another woman doing that for her Adam, so she had to be content with friendship as she always had; and though it was not enough, it did have merits: she had his trust in a way no one else had; it was her he had come to when he was hurt and confused, not Carla, and she would be there when the older woman tired of her young lover. She would pick up the pieces, until the next woman came along.

The walk over to Carla's was refreshing and made Adam feel a lot better, although he was barely aware of the fact since he was deep in thought. The last few weeks had been a roller-coaster: first Carla, then a beating, a change of identity, all that weirdness the night before. He felt dirty and ashamed for getting so drunk and allowing that creep to try his luck – Mel had told him she'd found him being felt up by a guy and he was quite thankful that he'd been virtually unconscious when it happened, shuddering to think how far it might have gone, were it not for Mel coming to the rescue. He smiled as he imagined her flinging the dirty bastard across the floor.

Mel was a puzzle. He was beginning to wonder about her feelings for him. They had always loved each other because they were as good as brother and sister, but there was something else going on. Despite the time behind the clubhouse at Christmas, he had never looked at her in a sexual way. Just for a moment, as he walked along the dual carriageway, he imagined having a different kind of relationship with Mel. He inhaled and blew out a rush of air. No! He really couldn't go there. Things were already complicated enough.

He deliberately turned his thoughts to Carla. She had sounded very much the older woman on the phone and he had felt like a little boy. Although he had mixed feelings about that, he reminded himself that he was happy for her to be in control and call the shots, for the time being anyway. She'd said she had some things she wanted to talk to him about. He hoped it was nothing too heavy. His head was aching with all the emotion flying around.

Stefan and Bryn were sitting at the breakfast bar when Adam arrived, and Bryn jumped down to run over and give him a huge hug. Adam looked at Carla, sharing his surprise and ruffling the little boy's hair as he smiled widely at her over Bryn's head. Carla looked emotional as she returned the smile and turned away. Adam could see that something about this little tableau had hit a chord with her. He went over to Stefan and shook his hand, rugby style. Sefan grinned at him through a mouthful of beef burger which he quickly swallowed.

'Garden after tea?' he asked hopefully. 'I need to do some more throwing practice.'

There was nothing Adam felt like doing less at that moment, but he nodded and said: 'Why not?'

Carla cleared away and washed up, watching her boys through the window over the sink and listening to the screeches of delight as Adam engaged them in lots of rough and tumble. She was so pleased to see Adam. There was no doubt about it: she had been jealous that Adam had gone to Mel when he was upset and had wondered, again, about their relationship. Were they more than just friends? The fact that he had stayed the night with Mel made Carla feel as though pincers had got hold of her insides and twisted and twisted, as thoughts of that raven-haired beauty running her hands all over Adam's body consumed her. She had not been pleased with herself for allowing those thoughts: Adam was a free agent and she had known the risks from the beginning.

She had also been worried about Adam after Joyce called in such distress, berating herself for having told Adam the circumstances of his birth. Carla had listened in stunned silence as Joyce filled her in on the details. The Joyce she knew was someone very different from a wife giving in to romantic temptations of the flesh, but that, she realised, was because she had only known her in middle age, somewhat worn down by life, and she was a little ashamed of herself for never recognising that Joyce might have had longings and fantasies the same as her own. Who knew what had gone on behind the face of age? There must always be a story, thought Carla. And this one strangely reflected so many similarities to her own: she was standing where Tom had stood, Gareth in Joyce's place, Adam where Sophie was.

She had tried to console Joyce, telling her she had done the right and brave thing, and there was never going to be the perfect time when Adam would absorb the news without a significant reaction. Carla had a lot of respect for what Joyce had done; she wondered what she would do in similar circumstances. After all, Joyce could have kept her secret, probably even from Tom. Thinking of her, Carla picked up the house phone and dialled.

'Joyce, it's Carla.'

'Hello Carla, love. Is everything okay?'

'Yes, I just wanted to let you know that Adam is here now, playing with the boys in the garden. He went on a bit of a bender last night, apparently. His friend Mel took care of him and nursed him through a hangover this morning.'

'She's a good girl. They just about grew up together, you know, and they're very close. So Adam is all right?'

'Seems fine to me, Joyce. I'll send him home later. I think he's going to need an early night in his own bed.'

'Well, thank you for letting me know, Carla. I won't wait up, though; I'll see him in the morning.'

Adam waited downstairs while Carla put the boys to bed. He looked through the CD collection, wondering which would have been her choice and which Gareth's. He found *Faith* by George Michael and put it on, remembering the hour he had shared with Carla in the hotel restaurant. His eyes grew heavy and he dozed. When he woke it was to see her kneeling in front of him, her hands on his knees. She leaned over and kissed him, long and deeply. He felt the stirrings but before things started to heat up she pulled back and sat down at the opposite end of the sofa, kicking off her shoes and pulling her legs up.

'It's been a bit of a hard time for both of us, hasn't it?' she said, snuggling into the soft cushions.

He immediately felt selfish: he had been so caught up in his own drama, he had completely forgotten about her being desperately upset a few days before, 'God, yes! How are things with you? Are you okay now?'

'I'll probably never be okay about what I learned on Wednesday, Adam. My life changed, just like yours did yesterday. I spent some time thinking about it, talked it through with some people who are important to me and I think I've worked out how to deal with it.'

'Do you want to tell me about it?'

Carla picked at the tassels on one of the cushions, intent on choosing the right approach, given that Adam might see his mother in Gareth's role. 'I am going to tell you, but not because I need to lean on you. – And don't look hurt, Adam. That's not what our relationship is about, remember? It can get too complicated otherwise. You did your bit for me the other night by making beautiful love to me and making me feel wanted and loved. That was exactly what I needed that night because I found out that Gareth had been unfaithful to me a year or so before he died.' Her voice cracked slightly and she paused, looking down at the cushion while she got her emotions under control.

Adam sat still and said nothing.

'Ironically,' she continued, 'Gareth fell for the charms of an older woman and for nine months they carried on a passionate, sexual affair. It ended because, with the best will in the world, sex cannot replace love and Gareth was in love with me. The woman told me she knew that, so she virtually told him to go back to me. Of course, what he had learnt from her, he brought back with him. He taught me things I could never have dreamed of, I was so innocent. I could tell he had changed: he was so much more expressive, attentive and inventive, but I didn't realise why until now. I had just a few short months of this new, passionate man. When he was killed, grief struck me like a ton of bricks – I thought I could never love that way again, and I doubt I ever will. He really *was* the perfect life partner for me.

'When he died, my new found passion died with him, or so I thought. Then this beautiful young man came into my home and into my life. I'm not sure what you felt Adam but, for me, it was like an electric current whenever you were around. You showed me that not only was I still desirable but that I could feel passion again, and that I could pass on what I'd learned to you. I've also discovered that I can love again, too, in a different way. The love I feel for Gareth will always be his, and the love I feel for you will always be yours. We love many different people in many different ways – and love has no rules.'

Adam puffed out air and his eyes were wide. 'That's some story Carla. I don't know what to say.'

'You don't have to say anything, because it's my story. And there's more.'

'There is? Blimey!'

Carla laughed at his surprised face. 'No one ever said life is straight forward. Gareth had given this woman a child – a little girl called Sophie who's two years old: an innocent result of the complicated lives us adults create for ourselves. And I have to admit, though it pains me to do so, that she was born out of a loving relationship, even though it was a short one. Stefan and Bryn are her half-brothers and she has a right to know them, as they do her, so I'm going to bring Sophie into our lives, and also make sure she knows Gareth's parents – her grandparents. Explaining all this to the boys won't be easy, but there are enough of us to help them accept it and work it out in their own way, if necessary. I'm hoping I'll find the right words so that they'll be delighted to find they have a little sister.'

Carla was now close to tears and she noticed that Adam was too. As she reached across to take his hand, he dashed away a tear that spilled down his cheek.

'Adam, there's far more to learn about love than just sex. Over the past few days, I've been working through this problem and, like I said, I had some very good friends to help me. One of them was your mother. She told me her story about how you came into the world and she and your dad have helped me more than you'll ever know.'

They were now both allowing the tears to come.

'Adam, both you and Sophie came into this world through love and are loved every day of your lives. What really matters, now, is what you both do as people and what love you bring to others.'

Adam took Carla's hand and pulled her to him, burying his face in her shoulder as sobs heaved through his body. She held him until he pulled away and yanked a handful of tissues from the box on the coffee table.

'I want to stay, but I think I have to go home and see my parents,' he said.

* * * * *

The table was booked for eight thirty that Sunday evening and Trudy had arrived a few minutes early. What with the men in their lives it had been difficult for her and Carla to find time to see each other, so she was looking forward to a good girlie chat. Her life had changed quite dramatically since she had met Trevor: she now found herself sitting on benches in play areas and wallowing about in the shallow end of the local leisure pool. Before Trevor came on the scene, if she had been told she would be engaging in such pastimes early on a Sunday morning, she would have laughed like a drain. Even more surprising was the fact that she was enjoying them, along with the rest of the time she spent with Trevor's children, who were sweet little chatterboxes; she loved their innocence and seeing the world thought their eyes.

But tonight it was all about the grown-ups. Trudy was aware that things had progressed between Carla and Adam. This concerned her, but with her track record in relationships she was not about to judge other people's choices. Besides, she did need to get to know the fellow a bit better before forming an opinion about any of it – the age gap included.

Beaming and looking ten years younger, Carla approached the table wearing a white open-necked shirt tucked into well-fitted jeans; her dark, straight hair shone as it bounced on her shoulders with the rhythm of her step.

So that's what a relationship with a very young man does for you! thought Trudy. 'Darling, you look bloody gorgeous – quite shaggable, in fact. Pity I don't swim in that pool – I'd sweep you up and eat you whole.'

Carla laughed and leant over to kiss her friend. 'Sorry, love, you're not my type. You're far too old!'

'Bitch!'

A young, dark haired waiter with even darker eyes and a shy smile came over to their table as Carla made herself comfortable.

'Can I get you ladies a drink?'

'I can think of a few things you could get me, my sweet!' Trudy felt a little daring, as though she had been let off the leash to go out and play.

'Two large glasses of chilled Pinot, please,' said Carla, rescuing the embarrassed boy, now a startling shade of fuchsia, who smiled and turned, visibly relieved to get away.

'You scared him, Trude! Maybe he's new at this job and not used to predatory females yet!' Carla said.

Trudy huffed and looked down the menu. 'I'm thinking steak with salad. How about you?'

'I'm starving! Something with carbs for me – pasta would be good.'

'You've lost weight, haven't you?'

'A few pounds, I think. I haven't eaten properly for a few days.'

Trudy tapped the side of her nose knowingly. 'Lots of excitement and sex will do it every time. So, how are things? I want all the details.'

The waiter arrived with the wine and after nervously putting the glasses on the table, took their order and beat a hasty retreat.

Carla told Trudy of her decision regarding Sophie.

'You're certainly doing the decent, ethical thing, Carla. It'll be hard on you emotionally, but well done you.' She rubbed the top of her friends arm in a congratulatory way. 'Have you contacted her mother yet?'

Carla shook her head. 'No, I just need to think things through for a couple more days. But I will call her during the week and ask her to come over.'

'Well, let me know if you need me there for moral support.'

'Thanks. I think I'll be fine though. She'll be more nervous than me I imagine – being inside Gareth's house and on my territory, so to speak.'

'You seem remarkably in control considering you've just had a massive shock. I'm proud of you.'

'Thanks Trude, but you wouldn't have been so proud if you'd seen me on Thursday night up on the cliffs, wailing like a banshee.'

'No change there then – you've always been a wailer!'

'Not like this and not out in the open. Then Adam came round and made it all better.'

'Ah, the lovely Adam! I'm thinking I should get to know him a bit better. What's the score between you?'

'Well, it's gone beyond physical insofar as I do love him, in a way. But I think it's based on needing each other emotionally right now. Yes, there's definitely a physical need, too, but it's more than just lust. Having said that, anything more is unlikely.'

'There's nothing to say you can't spend your life with a younger man, Carla,' Trudy said.

'No, I know. It's not that. I could never be in love with Adam the way I was with Gareth – that deep, earth-shattering love, where you're in so deep you can't get out, even if you try. With the recent turn of events, I'm not sure I want to love another man that way, anyway.'

Trudy laughed, quite delighted with the way Carla's mind was working. 'You're starting to think the way I do.'

Carla adopted an expression of mock horror. 'Oh-my-god!'

'No, seriously. Don't you think that life is too short to just do things the conventional way: grow up, meet a boy, fall in love, get married, have kids, live happily ever after? Pah! How many people out there go to bed each night feeling unfulfilled and dissatisfied with their lives? How many fantasize about how they'd like things to be, daydream about making love to someone else or waking up in another country – basically wanting to feel alive?'

'I know,' agreed Carla. 'We spend too much time trying to be what other people think we should be, and sometimes it's not until something happens to radically change our lives that we realise how pointless sadness and dissatisfaction are. I was happy with Gareth and would never have wanted that to change, but his death taught me that we don't know what will happen from one minute to the next, and we have to make the absolute most of every day.

'I'm in the process of giving my life a thorough audit. I'm happy with my career, having built up a successful business which has fulfilled my ambitions and is, for now, enjoyable. When or if I stop enjoying it, I'll do something else. In my personal life, being with Adam is a wonderful way to buck the trend and do what feels good. It may only boil down to him having a crush on me and me lusting after him, but it works well for us and it's what I want, at the moment. I want to unleash everything on him that he can handle, so that he

238

experiences more in his young life than people three times his age ever have. And it's not all one way: I'm learning a lot about myself in the process and having my own fantastic experience with him at the same time.'

'Sounds like my kind of philosophy, darling. Ah! Food!'

As the two of them enjoyed their meal, Trudy remarked on Carla's shift in perspective. 'You really are being philosophical about everything and choosing how to think about things instead of just bewailing your fate, aren't you?'

'You planted the seeds, Trudy, so you can take a large part of the credit. I could have gone on much longer feeling like a victim if you hadn't given me the idea that it's all about perception. I've discovered that my perception directly affects my emotions, and I'm opting for perceptions that help me feel better. It's not the easiest thing to do, I must admit, but the effort pays off.'

'Taking responsibility for your own happiness, is what you're doing, my darling – happiness comes from the inside out, not the outside in. Not a lot of people know that!'

'In your own inimitable way, you're an absolute tonic, Trude!' laughed Carla. 'You've often said things that baffled me in the past, but I'm beginning to understand you have your own peculiar brand of wisdom.'

'I wish! I wouldn't see myself as wise after all my mistakes! But this is the only life I have and I've never wanted to waste time sitting in a corner feeling sorry for myself and waiting for other people or circumstances to change. My life is far from a good example for anyone, but my mistakes haven't been mistakes for me: they've taught me a lot, of course – as mistakes do – but more to the point, I wouldn't be who I am without them, and I *like* who I am!'

'Me too! Just by being who you are, you give me courage, do you know that?'

'You'll have me weeping in my wine, Carla Trelawney, and I won't be thanking you for that!'

'Your glass is empty! Anyway, I'm going to stop procrastinating and contact Sandra Simpson tomorrow morning.'

'Go for it, girl! And keep me posted!'

* * * * *

Carla picked up the phone as soon as she got to the office, not giving herself any time to dither. 'Sandra? Hi, it's Carla Trelawny.' Carla heard a sharp intake of breath on the other end of the line.

'Oh, Carla! I'm so glad you've called, although to be honest I didn't expect to hear from you. How are you?'

Carla gave s short laugh devoid of humour. 'It's been a roller coaster of a few days, as I'm sure you can imagine. It's not every day that you discover that your dear, dead husband was unfaithful to you for nine months and fathered a child.'

'That's very true,' Sandra said carefully. 'But I don't think you've called to berate me, have you Carla?'

Carla was pulled up short for a second, realising that this woman was not about to indulge her guilt-inducing digs. Sandra had already made it clear how sorry she was at their first meeting and she was refusing to be cowed or manipulated into more abject apologies. Carla had a sudden, grudging respect for her: Sandra had made all this very clear with just a few words. 'Sandra, I'm sorry. That was crass and unnecessary.'

'That's all right, and totally understandable: in Gareth's absence, I'm the automatic target for your anger.'

Carla felt her cheeks burn and her indignation rise at the patronising tone of the older woman. She knew, however, that she had started the unpleasantness and so chose to rise above her emotions; they were dealing with highly emotive matters so care had to be taken, biting words held back, or this could degenerate further. 'I know where my anger belongs,' she said gently, 'and now that's out of the way, I'd like to invite you round to the house to meet the boys and share a bottle of wine with me – maybe have a chat to answer questions we probably both have.'

Sandra paused for a moment, and Carla waited, wondering if she would refuse.

'I'd very much like to, Carla. When were you thinking of? I'll have to arrange for someone to look after Sophie.'

Carla took a deep breath. 'Why not bring her with you? She may as well meet the boys when you do. I was thinking of tomorrow night, but we can make it tea time instead.'

'That would be great. You know how hard it is to get sitters at short notice.'

Carla didn't because her mum had always been there. Knowing Sandra had no such luxury, Carla was once again reminded that her blessings far outweighed her burdens.

She came home early from work the following afternoon and began to prepare a shepherd's pie. As she washed and chopped and mixed, she thought about Sandra and the relationship she'd had with Gareth. It was strange but she was finding that she wanted to know and understand more about what they had shared. It was painful, thinking this way, but something in her needed to know. Was it unnatural? She didn't know, or much care. Gareth had shared with *her* what he'd learned from Sandra; he had wanted her to have the pleasure he had discovered, as well as himself. What more would he have shown her, had he lived?

She popped the shepherd's pie in the oven and got vegetables from the fridge to prepare for steaming later. *I'm cooking for my husband's mistress!* she thought. *What would he think if he could see this?* She had to chuckle to herself at the strange games life played, and recognised that the more she allowed her thoughts and feelings about the affair, the more manageable they seemed.

At six o'clock Stefan and Bryn came running in response to the knock at the door, and joined Carla in greeting the guests. Sophie was adorable: along with his eyes, she seemed to have inherited her father's sunny disposition and immediately settled down on the floor beside the boys. They were watching cartoons; she had brought a doll and two puzzles which she set out on the floor and began to assemble, as though staking her claim in this new and unknown territory. The cartoons soon lost their appeal: Bryn was drawn into helping Sophie with the puzzle pieces, the two of them chattering amiably to each other; Stefan got bored and went upstairs to play on his Game Boy.

The strange little group, linked like discordant musical notes in a new arrangement, were awkward, at first, as they sat down to share a meal, but Bryn and Sophie's chatter quickly eased away any tension. The children were then allowed to watch a film while the mums cleared away in the kitchen. Looking in on them a short time later, Carla saw that Sophie was curled up with her doll and fast asleep amongst the cushions on the sofa. It was time to talk with Sandra, and though she felt sick with the fear of what she might discover, Carla remained resolutely determined to satisfy her need to know.

'Sophie is a delight, Sandra,' she said, once they were each sitting with a glass of red wine. 'She's a credit to you.'

'Thank you,' Sandra smiled, thoughtfully twirling the stem of her glass between her fingers. 'So where do you think we go from here, Carla? You must have something in mind.'

Carla tilted her head to one side and regarded the other woman. She was still very beautiful and although she looked her age, she had a soft femininity about her that Carla could see a man of any age would find attractive; in her way, she was ageless. 'I'll come straight to the point, shall I?'

'I'd appreciate that,' Sandra nodded.

'I've thought about and agonised over our conversation last week.'

243

'As I did about coming to you in the first place,' interjected Sandra.

'Of course,' Carla conceded. 'It can't have been easy. I think it would be good for us to be in touch and for Sophie to be part of Stefan and Bryn's lives. I'm sure it's what Gareth would have wanted. Am I right in thinking Gareth didn't know about Sophie?'

Sandra nodded. 'Yes, I had every intention of telling him but I couldn't seem to pluck up the courage, and something was also telling me that it wasn't the right time for him to know. I think I was right on that score, wasn't I?'

'Yes, one big secret is bad enough. I'm relieved he wasn't hiding a child from me, too. You know Sandra, I don't really know how to say this, but you taught Gareth a lot.'

Sandra looked a little puzzled. 'About what?'

'Physical love, lust, desire, how two people can pleasure each other. I know because he became a different person, sexually, and I suppose I have to thank you for that. The last year we had together was quite wonderful.'

Sandra looked down into her glass, thoughtful for a moment before she spoke, as if deciding whether or not to say something. 'Carla,' she finally began, 'when I was a bit younger than you are now, someone taught me those things. He was only in my life for a very short time one steamy summer nearly two decades ago. I had just gone through my first divorce, which was a painful one, and I was feeling ugly, discarded and unwanted – ridiculous when I think back, but the feelings were very real to me at that time. A big blonde German, with a heavy accent and a body to die for, seduced me and made me his for two whole weeks. I knew from the beginning that it would not be for longer because he had told me. He was a mystery, never wanting to talk about himself, so I knew very little about him; nevertheless, he taught me that life is for living and showed me how two people can bring each other to pinnacles of physical bliss. I tried to bring that bliss into my second marriage, but after we married my husband became pretty much totally resistant to the idea of me taking any kind of sexual lead. Unfortunately, the relationship was ultimately unsuccessful for lots of reasons, and the physical side was probably a symptom more than a cause, but it was a big disappointment to me. Gareth, on the other hand – dare I say – was very open to everything.'

Carla winced. Her stomach twisted but she'd expected this to be the effect on her, so she simply nodded to let Sandra know she was not about to react badly to anything she said. 'It's odd, but I seem to need to know everything to be able to move on. It hurts like hell, but the thing is: it's imagining that's worse that actually knowing.'

Sandra took a sip of her wine and Carla waited; the conversation was not easy for either of them.

'Carla, I didn't keep count, but during that nine month period I probably only saw Gareth ten or fifteen times. And you have to understand, his heart was never mine. I knew and accepted that – I had no choice. You had a very firm grip on his heart and so did your two little boys. It was as if I was his teacher and he my pupil in the ways of the flesh; he was certainly a joy to teach and I'm glad it made a difference to your lives in a positive way. Kris would be happy to know that, wherever he is now.'

'Kris?'

'My German lover. You know, Gareth reminded me of him a lot – he had the same stamp, if you know what I mean.'

Carla nodded. Something was pecking at the back of her mind but she couldn't think what. Maybe she would think of it later. 'What sort of things did you teach Gareth?'

'What do you want to know?' Sandra asked warily.

'I suppose I'm trying to find out if there were things I missed – things you showed him that he would have shown me, in time?'

Sandra laughed, throwing her head back. Her eyes sparkled as she fondly rubbed Carla's forearm to show she was not being patronising. 'You really are courageous. I like you. I can see why Gareth loved you so much.'

Carla felt a bit uncomfortable. She wasn't enjoying any of this and the other woman's attitude was disconcerting, as, deep down, Carla had expected to feel more in control and the other woman to be more timorous. As it was, Sandra was a strong, confident woman.

'There were obvious things that I introduced,' Sandra began in answer to Carla's question, 'such as how to pleasure a woman, how exciting just watching is, dressing up, sex in unusual places and at unusual times, watching erotic films. But really, Carla, the overriding theme, which is what Kris made clear to me, was that, within reason, anything goes and relationships are kept alive by variety, or innovation. I always told Gareth that there were no rules and, as long as both parties were in agreement, there were no boundaries. I also encouraged him to talk about his most erotic fantasies – those that he thought were most outrageous and only happened to other people or in books or films – and to re-enact something he'd thought of earlier in the day.'

Sandra paused to make sure Carla was not finding the conversation too much. As Carla seemed fully attentive and calm, she continued. 'In my opinion, too many relationships die because of boredom: one partner doesn't want to try anything new, for whatever reason, and, eventually, the more progressive partner is very likely to stray. It's a shame, as I'm sure you'll agree.'

'Yes I do, and you've given me a lot to think about.'

They were interrupted by a little voice at the kitchen door. 'Mummy, bed now.'

Sandra smiled and got off the kitchen stool to pick up her daughter. Little arms went around her neck and Sophie snuggled into her.

'Thanks, Sandra.' Carla was feeling mellowed by the wine, especially now that the stress of the evening was over.

As she waved them goodbye and then went to get the boys to bed, she acknowledged to herself just how brave Sandra was and wondered if she could be that brave. Then again, maybe she had been just as brave by bringing Gareth's mistress and their daughter into her home – into her life. She gave herself credit, too, for being able to listen with equanimity to a fuller disclosure of Gareth's adultery.

Throughout the evening, the conversation played over and over in her mind. She came to the conclusion that emotions could overwhelmingly complicate life, or simplify it, depending on how any situation was viewed. When she got into bed, just before she switched off the light, she picked up the phone and dialled his number.

Adam had just gone to bed himself after an evening at the rugby club, although he could not yet play. The injuries he had sustained were more or less healed, although his ribs were a little tender at times, but he had to stay clear of strenuous activity for another four weeks, which was just about when the season was due to begin again. He missed his team mates and as summer training had started he often popped down there to see them, sometimes going in to have some physiotherapy on his neck and shoulders.

Carla's phone call was well-timed as, like her, he had just switched off his light. She had talked to him, in that soft, sexy way that made every fibre in his body tingle. She asked him to describe his fantasies and, taken by surprise, he couldn't think of anything to say, at first, but then the scenarios he had often played in his mind came flooding back to him as Carla's voice whispered in his ear. She was suggesting that they try and act some of them out and encouraged him to tell her in as much detail as possible. As he talked he became more and more aroused, and more inventive as a result. She was quiet for a moment after he stopped talking and he wondered if he had gone too far.

'Adam,' she finally said in that sexy voice, right into his ear. 'Are you aroused?'

'Very.'

'Touch yourself.'

He didn't need any persuasion.

'I'm going now and I want you to bring yourself to orgasm, imagining those fantasies. Close your eyes as you come, and picture the scene and how erotic it's going to be. Goodnight, sweet Adam.' And she was gone.

That night Adam dreamed vividly and woke, once more fully erect, with the dawn chorus. His imagination was starting to kick in when he was asleep now and after he had relieved his tension he decided it was time to show his teacher how well he was learning.

*   *   *   *   *

The notice on the changing room door said: *Due to burst pipes the men's and ladies' changing rooms have been flooded. Please use the family changing cubicles. We apologise for any inconvenience.*

'Damn!' Mel exclaimed. 'I was really looking forward to doing some timed swims tonight.'

Adam came up behind her, having paid for the *Pay and Display* ticket. 'We can still go in,' he said, handing her back her car keys.

'But there aren't many family cubicles.'

'Come on, you can share one with me!'

He laughed to see Mel actually blush. It didn't happen often and he liked it; it made her seem more vulnerable, less self-contained. 'I won't look,' he promised with a grin.

She quickly recovered herself. 'No, but I might take a peep at you!' she retorted.

'Be my guest, Melanie. You've seen it all before,' he said, paying for their tickets and leading the way through to the cubicles.

He quickly undressed and put his clothes in his bag. Much to Mel's disappointment, he already had his trunks on underneath his jeans. She was also annoyed with herself that she'd had no such forethought and had to get into her swimming costume. She turned her back and undressed, aware of Adam enjoying the view, teasing her by standing and watching. Refusing to allow him to embarrass her any further, she tutted, wrapped a towel around herself and proceeded to wiggle out of her clothes, but just as she was pulling her costume up her towel came loose and even her fast reflexes could not keep it from falling to the wet floor. She screeched and Adam laughed.

'It's okay, I'm not looking!' he chortled, peering through his splayed fingers. 'Hey, what's that? I didn't know you had a tattoo?'

In the small of her back was a tiny, round tattoo – a circle of about an inch and a half across, containing the letters *A* and *M*.

By this time Mel was at her wits end and not thinking; she turned round giving Adam a full frontal as she tried to hide the tattoo from his prying eyes.

'Oops!' exclaimed Adam, full of fun and laughter.

Mel was not amused and concentrated on wrestling herself into her costume and pulling the straps over her shoulders, before angrily ramming her belongings into her kitbag and wedging it into their shared locker. Adam was contrite. She was obviously quite upset and embarrassed, so he took her hand and pulled her close for a semi-naked cuddle. He associated her with warmth, home and safety; her smooth, firm skin smelled of fruity soap and he felt something stir inside him, confusing him. As his main concern was not to get an erection whilst wearing his swimming trunks, however, he ignored the feeling, smacked her on her behind and walked off toward the pool, leaving Mel in a puddle of mixed emotions.

It was Mel's turn to buy the cokes in the bar afterwards. She came over to the table carrying the drinks and gripping two packets of crisps between her teeth. Adam grabbed a packet as soon as she put everything down, tore it open and delved in; he was starving.

'So when did you get the tattoo?'

'A couple of years ago, and I've regretted it ever since.' She was blushing again.

'Why? It's nice. Why A and M? They're our initials.'

'No shit, Sherlock!' Mel sipped her coke through a straw and then stirred the ice around in the glass with it.

'So why do you have our initials tattooed on your back?' Adam asked innocently, crunching through a mouthful of salt and vinegar crisps.

Mel just looked at him as if contemplating whether or not to answer him. Adam kept quiet, looking back at her, becoming aware that there was something of significance he was missing.

'Because, Adam, you're my best friend; you always have been and you always will be. I wouldn't have had it done if you had been my boyfriend, because then I would have had to have flowers or something put over it when we split up. We'll always be friends though, so it was a safe bet.'

Adam wasn't sure that really explained it, but he thought it was rather nice and leaned over to give her a kiss on the cheek. 'I love you Mel.' She smiled and for the first time he really noticed her flashing dark eyes and wide, sensual mouth.

'And I love you, Adam Barnes.'

They sat grinning at each other until Mel laughed. 'I think that's enough of the sloppy stuff, don't you?'

'You can't beat a bit of slop on a Wednesday evening, though! Cheers!'

They chinked their glasses together and moved on to safer subjects.

*　*　*　*　*

Adam arrived home from work the following day to find a police car parked outside the house. He took his bicycle round the back, put it away in the shed and called out to his mother as he walked in through the back door.

'In the front room, love,' came her answer.

Adam nodded hello to the two police officers, whom he recognised from their earlier visits, briefly wondering why they hadn't all sat in the large kitchen at the back of the house instead of the little room at the front of the house, which was just big enough to house a sofa, a chair and the TV, and was now looking comically cramped. PC Williams was sitting on the sofa next to Joyce; DC Richards, the one in charge, was sitting in the chair, and Tom was leaning against the window sill.

'Do you have some news?' Adam asked.

'No, we're here to ask you again, Adam: over the past few weeks have you thought of anyone who may have held a grudge against you?' asked DC Richards. 'If you argued with anyone or upset anyone, at all, it's very important that you tell us, even if it seemed unimportant to you at the time.'

Adam went and stood next to his dad and looked nervously at his mother before speaking. 'There was a guy – a policeman actually. I punched him.'

'Adam!' his mother sat bolt upright in surprise. 'Why didn't you say so before?'

'Because he's a copper, Mum. He wouldn't beat me up, would he? But he's the only bloke I've upset recently.'

'Do you know the officer's name?'

'Steve Bishop.'

'You say you punched him,' said DC Richards. 'Why was that?'

'He tried to take advantage of a friend of mine when she was drunk.'

'Who was this friend?'

'Carla Trelawney. I was babysitting her boys and this Steve guy brought her home. He tried to get rid of me, but I wouldn't go because I was worried about leaving Carla with him. Then he accused me of wanting to take advantage of her, so I punched him.'

'Did he hit you back?' asked Tom.

'No, Dad, he just told Carla to keep her Rottweiler on a leash and left. I haven't seen him since.'

'The fact that he's a policeman doesn't mean he's not responsible for the beating. *Being* a policeman, he'd know all kinds of thugs and could have had you beaten by someone else,' said Tom.

Adam glanced at his mother, who was staring at the detective. He wasn't sure he wanted her to hear all this – there had been enough emotional turmoil over the past few weeks – but there was nothing he could do about it.

'Is that what could have happened?' she angrily asked DC Richards. 'Is it possible this thug of a policeman had my son beaten to a pulp?'

'All I can tell you, Mrs Barnes, is that we'll follow up every lead. Now, is there anything else you can tell us about this incident, Adam?'

'I believe he said something about the Rottweiler being "dealt with" to Trevor May. He's a copper too.'

'Yes, we know DC May.'

'Well, he told a friend of Carla's about this remark – that's how I came to hear about it.'

'What else did he say?'

'That's all I know.'

'You've been very helpful, Adam,' said the police officer. 'I just wish you'd told us this before.'

'I really didn't think it was him. And I'd hit him so I didn't really want to stir things up and have him on my back for false accusations or something.'

'Adam's not in any danger is he, Officer?' Joyce was obviously anxious.

'I don't believe so, Mrs Barnes.'

The two officers stood up to leave. 'Give us a call if you think of anything else, Adam,' said DC Richards.

'Okay,' Adam agreed, pretty shocked by the idea that it might have been Steve – albeit once removed – behind the beating, after all. He was also experiencing a sense of relief that the question of why it had happened might be closer to an answer. He hadn't been comfortable walking around the town at night since the beating and not understanding the reason for it: he had been either cycling or getting a lift.

* * * * *

Carla knew there was never going to be an ideal, or even a right time to tell her boys about Sophie. She had spent hours agonising over how to start the conversation and accomplished nothing beyond tying herself in knots; in the end she decided to just do it and deal with any resulting fallout.

After they'd had their tea, one evening, Stefan and Bryn sat side by side on the sofa, relaxed but regarding her with solemn expressions, having been told that Mummy wanted to have a serious talk with them, but not to worry that they were in trouble for anything – it wasn't anything like that.

Carla sat on the footstool, facing them, and was surprised to find she felt no nervousness; she just felt an acute sadness that she may be about to bring disappointment to the two people she loved more dearly than anyone else in the world. 'Okay boys, we have some things to talk about which may be quite difficult to take in. Everything is all right, so don't look so worried Bryn, I want to talk to you about Sophie – the little girl who came to our house the other day, remember?'

Both boys nodded and Stefan looked as though he was about to speak, but Carla held up her hand so he sat back, resigned, folding his arms and eyeing his mother with some suspicion.

'Do you remember Sophie's mum?'

'Yes. I can't remember her name, though,' said Bryn.

'Her name is Sandra, and a few years ago, before Sophie was born, Daddy and Sandra met and became really good friends.'

'You mean they had a love affair, don't you Mum?' Stefan interjected in a voice much older than his years. 'Brendan Lafferty's dad had one of those with his next door neighbour and Brendan's mum punched him because of it. Brendan saw it happen!'

'Yes, all right, thank you, Stefan!' Carla interrupted his graphic account and checked Bryn's face for shock. There was nothing. He seemed more interested in a car that was doing a three point turn in the road outside.

'Daddy and Sandra had a friendship that lasted a few months.'

'Mum, did you punch Dad when you found out?'

'*No Stefan!* I didn't. And would you please stop referring to punches; it's really not relevant.' Carla took a deep breath, intent on keeping the conversation going in the way she had decided it would. 'We all really loved Dad, and we still do, and it's very hard when you find out that someone you thought was perfect was, in fact, not perfect, after all. Everybody in the world makes mistakes – everybody – including mums and dads, and Daddy just made some mistakes.'

Now it was Bryn's turn to contribute. 'Yes, I made a mistake when I let Stuart get past me and score a try at that match where there was that big fight with all the mums and dads, didn't I Mum?'

'That's right, Bryn, and we still love you and your team are still your friends, even though you made a mistake.'

Bryn seemed satisfied with this explanation. 'So what were you going to tell us about Sophie?'

Carla once again took a deep breath. 'Well, after Daddy and Sandra had been friends, Sandra then had Sophie.'

The boys were now looking blank.

Carla continued regardless, ready to answer questions after she had got it all out. 'So that means that Sophie is Daddy's little girl, which means she's your sister.'

'Our sister!' The duet rang around the room.

'Well – half-sister. Your daddy is also her daddy, but she has a different mummy, so that makes her a half-sister.'

The clock ticked loudly on the mantle-piece while the boys absorbed this revelation. Carla sat patiently waiting. It was Bryn who seemed to get it sorted out in his head first.

'I like Sophie,' he announced. 'I'm glad she's my sister. Is she going to live with us? Are you going to be her mummy now? Can I take her to school for "show and tell" on Monday? '

Carla had to laugh. 'No, Bryn. Sandra is her mummy and she won't be coming to live with us, but she will come to visit.'

'Hooray!' shouted Bryn. 'Can I go out and play now?'

'Yes, darling.'

Bryn jumped up from the sofa, closely followed by Banjo, and ran out into the garden. Stefan remained where he was, looking accusingly at Carla through dark eyes. She had known he would be the one to struggle with this news.

'You okay, sweetheart?'

He nodded, lowering his eyes and picking at a piece of dried paint on his shorts. 'Dad shouldn't have done that. He was our dad, not anyone else's. '

'You're right, honey, and it's been hard for me to understand too: I was angry when I found out but I'm not going to love Dad any the less. He wasn't perfect, Stefan – none of us are – but he was the best dad and the best husband, and that's what I'm going to remember. Dad was such a wonderful person in so many ways and we have lovely memories of him to keep.'

Stefan got up and came to put his arms around his mum's neck, snuggling into her for just few seconds, before running off to join his brother in the garden, leaving Carla massively relieved that it was now out in the open instead of being hidden away like a dirty secret. She knew it would take time for Stefan in particular to come fully to terms with it, so she would certainly keep a close eye on him, but the worst was hopefully over

*   *   *   *   *

Carla decided it was time she threw a party – a garden party, now that it had all been tended so beautifully – to officially celebrate the fact that she had come out of mourning and was getting on with life as a changed person. The weather forecast was good for the coming Saturday, so Carla opted for that day, called everyone who had helped her reach this turning point and was delighted when they all accepted her invitation.

That Friday, when Adam arrived for his day's work, Carla had not yet left for the office and gave him a list of things to do in preparation. She looked stunning in a short, red shift dress and shoes to match; her dark hair shone, as did her eyes. Adam stood leaning against the kitchen counter with his arms folded, watching her as she went through the list with him; he was listening, sort of, but mostly he was loving her with his eyes.

She recognised the way he was looking at her, stopped talking, let the list fall from her hands on to the breakfast bar, and allowed her eyes to travel over the glorious creature in her kitchen. It was a hot day and he was wearing a vest top, shorts and flip flops, looking, as usual, tanned, toned and sexy as hell. The Adam she had known a few months ago would have dropped his gaze as she met it, but not this one: he simply added a ghost of smile to his open appreciation of her. She started to feel heated and her breathing changed as excitement grew. She wanted him; he obviously wanted her. She really didn't have time to play … but …. She went and stood inches away from him and looked up into his face. Was he going to take the initiative?

Adam put his hands on either side of her lower back and pulled her against his body, slightly opening his legs so that she could come in closer. She ran her hands over his shoulders, making small circular movements on his skin, and he quietly moaned as he bent to take her mouth with his. His kisses were urgent and demanding. This was not a time for gentle love making. This was a time for passionate, possessive sex. Adam's hands travelled over her hips and eased her dress up in order to touch skin. The sensation of his hands on her bare legs made Carla draw breath and she felt that wonderful, familiar contracting of her groin that his touch awakened.

'Carla, I want you,' he whispered hotly into her mouth.

She answered by moving herself against him, rhythmically and with definite purpose.

Joyce was expected to arrive at any time, so, moving Carla away from him, Adam took her hand and led her into the utility room, in which there was just one high window of frosted glass. Carla slipped off her panties and popped them into the nearby washing machine while Adam dropped his shorts and trunks and was obviously totally ready for her. There was an exciting urgency, even a sense of the forbidden, as he lifted her dress above her hips and with his finger traced a line through her pubic hair to find her wetness. She was very ready for him. He lifted her up on to the edge of the washing machine.

With her arms entwined around his neck, she wrapped her legs around his waist and slowly edged off the cold metal on to his warmth and stiffness. Adam held her under her buttocks and thrust into her. She moved her body in time with his and kissed him, whispering words of encouragement as every muscle in his body worked towards a powerful climax. She held his head as he came and he buried his face in her shoulder, stifling the noise as he grunted and groaned.

As he calmed, Carla held his face and kissed him, grinning into his eyes. He really was so unbelievably gorgeous and she felt privileged to be part of his life. 'I've got to go,' she said. 'And I think I just heard your mum's car!'

Adam's face was a picture as he suddenly reverted back to an eighteen year old who had almost been caught by his mother in a compromising position. Carla giggled impishly as they hurriedly dressed.

She was busy with her handbag, getting ready for the day, by the time Joyce had let herself in and come into the kitchen. Adam was out in the garden. *Close one!* he chuckled to himself as he rummaged in the shed for extra chairs for the party.

Joyce had to smile: she had been around long enough to know when two people had been up to mischief. Carla was unnecessarily looking for nothing in her handbag and she had spotted Adam disappearing into the shed.

'I'm off then, Joyce,' Carla called as she grabbed her jacket from the coat hook.

'All right, love. Have a good day – that's if it can get any better!'

Carla looked at her blankly from the hallway.

Joyce chortled gaily and waved her away. 'See you tomorrow, love, and thanks for the invite. We're looking forward to it. Mel says she can come after work, if that's all right.

'Of course, that's fine,' Carla hurriedly replied, her cheeks pinking as it dawned on her that she hadn't managed to pull the wool over Joyce's eyes. 'See you then,' she added, as she pulled her handbag over her shoulder and went on her way.

Joyce continued to smile as she went about her work that day, paying special attention to the downstairs toilet as that would get a lot of use the next day. Carla was expecting an interesting mix of around twenty guests, including kids; it would be interesting to see everyone together. She was surprised that Carla had specifically called her to ask her to invite Mel, seeing as Mel was probably competition that Carla would not relish. But then, maybe she had got things wrong: Carla had surprised her in lots of ways – she was a real one off.

She had also been surprised by the turn for the better that the Barnes household had taken since she had told Adam about his biological father. Her marriage had taken on new dimensions – something she had to admit she would never have expected after all of these years. She could actually trace it back to when Adam was attacked, and she and Tom had been sitting side by side looking at their son as he lay unconscious in the hospital bed. She has always known Tom loved Adam but it came as a complete revelation to see just how deeply, and it had caused her to regard her husband in a different light.

Then, after the initial trauma of divulging the truth to Adam about his birth, it was as though the Berlin Wall had been pulled down all over again. Adam had come back from Carla's that Saturday night and sat down to talk to both her and Tom together; they had stayed up until two in the morning talking everything through. Tom had been able to voice the absolute truth of his feelings because that was what Adam had asked of him and nothing less would do. Tom had said that he loved Joyce too much to ever hate her for what she had done; in fact, he loved her more for her courage and honesty in telling him and giving him the choice of whether or not to end their marriage. 'Secrets and lies fester,' he'd said, 'whereas, openness and truth lead to healing.' And as for Adam, how could he not love a baby who was in his care and protection? He had related how he had held Adam moments after his birth and immediately bonded with him, just as he had bonded with his brother and sister. The hardest part for him, he'd said, was keeping it a secret from Adam, and Simon and Jacqueline too. He didn't like secrets, no matter how necessary they were, and he felt much lighter now that that burden had been lifted. It had all been emotional and tearful; Adam had hugged Tom, telling him what a great dad he was and how much he loved him, and confirming that whoever had physically made him, Tom was the only dad he would ever want.

From then on, the communication channels between Joyce and Tom had opened wide. They'd spent the next day walking in the hills together and had stayed overnight at a little hotel near Tunbridge Wells. Tom had called in sick on the Monday and they had made leisurely yet passionate love several times in the big, anonymous hotel bed. A new era in their long marriage had begun. Joyce was discovering her love for her man all over again, while he laughed more, talked more and loved more, both of them saying it was as if magic had happened.

When she had realised just how difficult it had been for Tom to carry that secret around all those years, she had loved him so much and respected him for never taking his feelings out on her, let alone Adam. He was such a *good* man, her Tom.

That evening, before the party the next day, Carla took the boys round to Verity's for tea. Paul was always late home from his London job so Carla was able to spend some time alone with her friend. After they had fed the children on lasagne and peas, they sat out in the conservatory, drinking tea while the children played in the tree house at the far end of the large garden.

'So, tell me what's been going on, Carla. I haven't seen you in so long.'

Carla smiled over her cup. 'I've been having quite a strange time, what with one thing and another, but the main thing is that I feel I can start planning for the future again.'

'In what way?' Verity asked, kicking off her shoes and curling up in the soft cushions of the wicker chair.

'I'm not sure yet, but I think things will start to make more sense soon. I'm not going to rush anything and I have the boys to think about, but there may be some big changes in my life. I'm just mulling things over.'

'Carla! Have you met someone?' Verity leaned forward eagerly. 'Hey, don't tell me you're going to marry the gorgeous gardener!'

Carla laughed and her cheeks coloured. 'Gorgeous but very young, so I'm not sure he would be up for taking on an older woman with two children and a luggage rack full of baggage. No, I really haven't made up my mind yet. It's just that the last few months have been pretty enlightening, emotionally, and for the first time since Gareth's death I've been feeling alive again.'

'Well, you certainly look good on it, so something is agreeing with you,' Verity nodded.

'Thank you, darling.' Carla did not want to elaborate further. She loved Verity but she did not tend to confide in her, as, sadly, she did not trust her to be discreet. Over the years she had learned that it was best to tell Verity only what she would not mind other people knowing, especially when it came to affairs of the heart.

They sat in companionable silence for a while, watching the children playing. Stefan and Stuart were sitting under the tree while the two younger children could be seen in the tree house. Jo's high voice rang out above all the others and she seemed to be giving Bryn some very specific instructions on how to precariously climb out of the window of the little house. Carla kept her eye on him but didn't intervene, relieved to see him reach the ground without broken limbs or grazed knees. Gareth would have been pleased at her restraint, she thought: he had always said she was too protective of the boys and should let them learn from their mistakes.

'I miss him you know,' said Verity, as if reading her thoughts.

Carla gave her a puzzled frown.

Verity suddenly looked at Carla very purposefully. 'Gareth,' she said. 'I miss him, Carla. I haven't been able to say this because I knew your pain was too fresh, but I think I can now.'

Carla wondered what was coming and if she was ready to hear it, although she wasn't too concerned because she didn't think there could be anything that could hurt her any more than she already had been. She could also see that Verity needed to talk about whatever it was and discussing personal matters was never easy for her. 'Tell me,' she encouraged, simply and not unkindly.

'Carla, I was so envious of you: you were so in love, so successful in your job, so alive; I felt like a grey shadow next to you. And you had Gareth. I think I was secretly in love with him. Is that awful: to be in love with your best friend's husband? Do you hate me?' Verity was now sitting up in her chair, bare feet flat on the floor; she looked like a frightened teenager.

Carla was fully aware of Verity's crush on Gareth. She was not the only woman over the years to become infatuated with the handsome head-turner with the laughing eyes who was her husband, and Carla had become used to it. She also sensed a latent frustration in Verity: that of wanting more in her life but not knowing how to find it.

She leaned forward, resting her elbows on her knees and clasping her mug of tea between her hands. 'Verity, can I ask you something personal?'

'Go on,' Verity nodded.

'How much of how you feel is really to do with Gareth? Or is it more to do with your relationship with Paul?'

It was a question Verity had not considered, looking, as she consistently did, outside of her marriage for someone to fill the emptiness she felt inside: first Gareth, and, after his death, Terry Goodban, the teacher at the children's school. As she thought about it in that way, it dawned on her that her marriage was actually a sham and she'd been pretending – to herself most of all – that everything was fine, when she and Paul were really just going through the motions. Were they doing it for the sake of the children? she wondered. Maybe Stuart's problems were not because he was nervous about going to his new secondary school in September, which was what she had thought when his school work began slipping and he became a quiet, sullen little boy. Was he, in fact, reacting to hers and Paul's unhappy relationship?

Carla sat waiting quietly while Verity pondered the thought-provoking question she had put to her. She could tell Verity had not thought of this possibility before and, at the same time, knew she would be honest in her answer because there was very little, if any, artifice in Verity.

'Carla, my marriage is dead,' she finally sighed. 'There, I've said it: it's stone cold dead. I've tried to revive things with Paul, you know, sexually, but he doesn't want to know.' She paused and looked into the distance, unconsciously twisting her wedding ring. 'Have I become that unattractive?'

'Of course not.'

'Because that's how I feel. Here I am in my thirties and I feel middle-aged. Apart from the children, my life is meaningless and empty and I can't believe that this is all there is!' Verity now had tears of frustration spilling down her cheeks.

Carla didn't move to comfort her, considering it was probably better for this raw emotion to be unlocked. 'Verity, darling, you're a beautiful, sensual woman who, for whatever reason, just hasn't had the chance to unleash the passionate woman within. Paul is a sensitive, creative man who may well be feeling exactly the same way as you do. Maybe you need to try giving yourselves permission to be painfully honest. Start looking at your relationship as a project – as if it's a house that needs restoring. That way you'll find out if you have something that's worth lovingly restoring or a wreck that needs pulling down. One thing is for sure, though, you cannot spend the rest of your life trying to find love in another relationship when you haven't fully investigated the one that you have. Then make a decision based on what you both find. Above all, though, don't sentence yourself to a half-life.'

Verity's tears had stopped and she was looking uncertain. 'You could be right, but I'm not sure I have enough confidence in myself to be able to make the right decision.'

'It's not something that will solve itself straight away – it may do, but I doubt it. But you're like a closed book at the moment – there ain't no love gonna get in there!' Carla joked with a grin. 'Seriously, though,' she continued, 'life is about choices: we make some good ones and some bad ones. At the time we make them, they're the right ones to make – we don't go around knowingly making wrong decisions, do we? We don't know the future and if things change down the line, making a decision seem wrong in hindsight, it's pointless to think less of ourselves for something we had no control over. One decision you can make with absolute confidence, right now, is to choose not to carry on living this unhappy life that's just not fair on any of you.'

'Oh Carla, you're amazing! How do you keep everything so together after everything that's happened to you?'

'But that's the thing, Verity: it's *because* of all the things that have happened to me that I've been forced to change, and that's sometimes easier than actively making the choice to live life differently.'

Driving home across the city that evening with the boys bickering away in the back of the car, Carla thought about Verity and her heart went out to her. The frustration of a broken relationship that may or may not be salvageable must be a miserable situation in which to be living. At least she had been certain of the love between herself and Gareth, even though he was gone from her now. Thinking about it, she realised that since his death, she had learnt more about love, relationships, sex and passion from him and the influences around him, than she had when he was alive. Life has a strange sense of humour, she thought.

She was up early the next morning and flicked the TV on to see the weather forecast. When it held to its promise earlier in the week, that Saturday in the south east was to be hot and sunny, she gave her hands a little clap of glee and grinned at herself in the mirror over the fireplace.

There was a lot to do. It was seven o'clock and Adam was arriving in half an hour to set up the chairs and tables, and sort out the lights for later in the day; they also had to go to the supermarket to buy all the food and drink; and, as a special treat, Carla had bought a large plastic pool, due to be delivered and put up around eleven o'clock. The boys were extremely excited about its imminent arrival. Everyone was expected around two so there should be plenty of time to get everything ready.

Bryn came bounding down the stairs dressed in yesterday's shorts and T-shirt, which were visibly dirty from his antics in the tree house in Verity's garden; he also had some artistic badges of dried lasagne on one of the sleeves. Carla sighed but thought they would do for the time being, and who really cared, anyway – Bryn certainly didn't. She marvelled at herself: the old Carla would have marshalled him upstairs to change. She quite liked this new self.

Through the lounge window, she spotted Adam cycling up on to the drive wearing a light blue polo shirt and beige, knee length shorts; the familiar flip flops had been replaced with trainers. With his rucksack on his back he looked every inch the eighteen year old – and good enough to eat. Carla breathed in and shook her head, unable to get over the physical effect he had on her. She opened the door to him and before she could say anything he grasped her and pulled her to him, kissing her passionately.

'Well, that was some greeting, Mr Barnes!' she laughed breathlessly when he eventually let her go.

'Just getting it in now, 'cos I expect it will be hands off for most of the day.'

'Really?' she cooed, gracing him with her best 'come to bed' look. 'You may need to use your imagination then,' she added over her shoulder as she turned and wiggled her jean clad bottom up the hall towards the kitchen. 'Come on, you're nice and early so we can have breakfast before we get on with things.'

'Can I have you for breakfast?' he said as he caught up with her, sliding his arms around her from behind and nuzzling her ear.

She loved to feel his hard, young body against hers. She pushed her bottom into his groin and he pushed back.

'I want to make love to you – right now!' he whispered urgently.

Carla closed her eyes, resisting the temptation to turn and give herself to him. Turning, instead, to look at him, she stuck the tip of her tongue out on to her bottom lip and traced her finger from his chin, down his chest and then drew her four fingers along the length of his growing erection. In response to his gasp of pleasure, she winked saucily and moved away from him to get food out of the fridge.

He laughed and sat down at the breakfast bar, deciding that sitting was the best option, since he could hear the boys heading towards the kitchen. He busied himself with pouring their orange juice into brightly coloured plastic beakers. Bryn's eyes lit up when he saw him and he ran over to give him a hug, which was becoming a regular occurrence. Stefan, being more restrained, shook Adam's outstretched hand.

'Adam, we're getting a swimming pool today!' shouted Bryn excitedly.

'So I hear. Lucky I brought my swimming trunks with me, isn't it?'

'Yes. Mum, Adam's coming in our pool when it gets here!'

Carla was imagining Adam in his trunks.

'Mum, did you hear?'

'Yes, Bryn darling, Adam's going to swim with you. That'll be fun, won't it?' She looked at Adam, who was grinning at her, clearly knowing exactly what she was thinking.

After breakfast, he took the boys outside to help him get everything ready: they had to set up the barbeque, wash down the chairs and tables, which had literally been in the shed for years, and put up four sets of lights around the deck and the trees. Carla wanted the garden to look magical that evening.

When everything was done, apart from the last set of lights that was to go up at the bottom of the garden and needed another extension, they all piled into the car and drove to the supermarket. Carla felt odd and a little uncomfortable going round the supermarket with Adam pushing the trolley, and wondered if people looked at them and tried to work out the relationship between them. But then she relaxed and got on with the task in hand when she realised that it was unlikely that anyone was really interested as they were too engrossed in their own lives.

They were back just in time to unload bags of meat, salad and rolls, boxes of beer, wine and soft drinks from the car before the van arrived with the eagerly awaited swimming pool. Bryn was beside himself with excitement as the parts were unpacked from the boxes and Adam and the delivery driver put it up together. Stefan was in charge of reeling the hose out ready for filling it, and Adam got on with putting the little set of steps together while the boys held the hose over the edge to fill it up once it was in situ. The sun was blazing and the boys – all three of them – were looking forward to getting into the pool but were told it would take about an hour to fill, so they had to be patient.

Carla, meanwhile, having changed into a light cotton dress and braided her dark hair to keep cool, was in the kitchen preparing the salad and cutting the rolls, ready to put them on trays, foil wrapped to keep them fresh. Adam came in wearing just his shorts, having, as usual, discarded his T-shirt, and followed Carla into the cool utility room where she was stacking the trays of rolls.

She turned to find him leaning against the door frame watching her and she went to him to run her hands over the contours of his chest, bending her head just slightly and licking his nipple, then very gently nibbling it whilst at the same time running her hands around his naked waist. He sighed and caressed her upper arms with his fingertips until she looked up and they kissed. She took his lips between hers and softly sucked on them whilst moving slightly to one side and running her fingers along his stomach, just above the waistband of his shorts.

They jumped apart at the sound of shouts from the garden. They could hear that someone had come round through the side gate and would be in the kitchen is seconds. Grabbing a tea towel to look as if she was doing something, Carla went back into the kitchen; Adam left the utility room and went in the opposite direction, nipping into the hall and up the stairs and innocently reappearing minutes later to go and find something to do in the garden. Feeling deliciously naughty, Carla went out to greet her first guests, Trudy and Trevor. She laughed a great big open laugh when she saw them.

'Oh, thank god it's you!' she laughed.

Trudy laughed back. 'Why am I getting the feeling you were up to no good?'

'Hi Carla, nice to see you again.' Trevor leaned forward and kissed her cheek.

'Sober this time, Trevor, which I'm not sure I was the last time I saw you. Ah, here's Adam. Adam this is Trevor, Trudy's partner, and you've met Trudy haven't you?'

Adam put down the drinks he was carrying and shook Trevor's hand warmly.

Trudy pulled Carla to one side. 'Holy fuck, he's h-o- frickin-t, Carla!' Trudy's eyes were wide.

Carla got right in her face and opened her eyes just as wide. 'Really, Trudy! I hadn't frickin noticed!'

Both women chortled with high spirits as they went into the kitchen, arm in arm. 'Come on,' chuckled Carla, 'let's get you and your man a drink.'

Adam, lying on the grass and enjoying himself, looked around the garden: Mel was coming later, but everyone else was there, including Carla's office staff. The children were screaming with laughter in the newly filled pool and much water was making its way over the side and into the grass. Adam was keeping an eye on them; even though it was a leisure pool, he understood the dangers of water and kids. Banjo was running around like the mad dog that he was, out in the midday sun.

'Come on, Adam! You have to come in!' Stefan had to shout as he had a couple of his rugby friends round and the noise level was bordering on deafening.

'Okay, champ – be there in a little while.' He was hoping the water would warm up a bit.

He was having fun playing a game with Carla: the idea was to touch each other as much as possible without anyone seeing, and it was a real turn on. The problem was he would have to make sure she was nowhere near him when he took his shorts off to get into the pool – his manhood seemed to have a will of its own these days.

Earlier in the day, just before the majority of the guests had arrived, he and Carla had been taking the glasses from the cupboard in the utility room out into the kitchen; they had grinned at each other as they passed in the doorway and their eyes met. Adam had been able to hear Trudy joyously marvelling to the boys about the newly acquired pool, and Banjo had been barking with delight at so many new people to play with. Adam had impulsively pulled Carla back out of sight of the kitchen window and the open back door, and turned her round so that she was facing the washing machine; there was something he suspected and he had wanted to see if

275

he was right. Reaching down he had inched her cotton dress up over her knees, thighs and then higher, massaging her bare legs as he went. He had not been disappointed to discover that, under her dress, she was wearing nothing. He had massaged her buttocks and as she had begun to moan and sway to his touch, he had pulled her dress back down, kissed the base of her neck, left her there and gone back outside, knowing he had left her hot and sticky. He loved the fun of it and the slight danger – it was extremely sexy.

With the boys now urging him to get into the pool, he looked towards the house and could see that Carla was in the kitchen with her friends, Trudy and Verity. He wondered what they were talking about and would have loved to be a fly on the wall; he had always enjoyed being with a group of women when they were chatting. Mel had said it was his feminine side coming out and she had teased him about it, but she always let him come along if he wanted to.

The sun was beating down and he was very hot as there was no shade near the pool; he decided it was as good a time as any to strip off, so he jumped up, shed his shorts and walked around to the steps of the pool. His trunks were quite brief – the same ones he wore when he went swimming with Mel. For some reason he felt conspicuous, which he didn't when he was in the pool with Mel, and assumed it was because everyone was dressed similarly there. In actual fact, although he was blissfully unaware, it was because there were now at least three pairs of eyes trained on him.

'Good grief!' Trudy exclaimed. 'Will you look at that, girls! Boys with bodies like that should not be allowed around women like me. Quick! Take my blood pressure! How can anyone have a body like that at eighteen?'

Carla looked at the man she would be sleeping with that night and licked her lips in anticipation.

Verity didn't notice; she was too busy looking herself. 'Oh my!' she gasped. 'Carla, do you think he would come and be my gardener, too?'

Carla laughed. 'Why don't you ask him, Verity?'

'Do you know, I think I might! Would you mind?'

'No, why would I? Go for it!'

The icy temperature of the water almost made Adam's eyes pop out of his head and he was being liberally splashed by the kids, so he dived under, feeling as if the breath was slammed from his body as the cold hit him. He soon recovered though, and proceeded to join in the fun with the youngsters, while Verity continued to stare down the garden as he splashed and played. The shrieking rose to a crescendo and more water spilled over the side, helped by Trevor who had also stripped off and whose dark, hairy body was bobbing around in the water with Adam's.

Paul stood under the umbrella on the patio talking to Carla's mother. Verity looked from him to the strong, masculine presence in the pool. She had given a lot of thought to what Carla had said the previous evening and she had decided she was going to make changes, whatever they might be, which she wasn't yet sure about. Something had stirred inside her when she saw Adam take off his shorts, evoking images of herself touching his chest and running her hands all over his tanned, young body. She wondered if Carla had similar thoughts and if she, like Verity herself, saw something in him that reminded her of Gareth. It was not something she felt comfortable enough to ask though.

As if to order, Adam pulled himself up and out of the water and stood dripping on the grass, laughing at Trevor who was now the butt of the kids' splashes. Adam had strong upper thighs and firm buttocks from all the rugby training and he knew that he was giving the girls in the kitchen a bit of an eyeful. With that in mind, he grabbed a towel and slowly dried himself, bending over to pay particular attention to his lower legs. Carla knew exactly what he was doing and was enjoying the view as much as the other two.

'Oh heavens! He makes my jaw go slack,' said Trudy dreamily.

Verity just stared, her drink half-way to her lips.

Later on, as the sun started to make its way west, Carla joined Adam in cooking the barbeque. Drink had begun to flow more freely along with laughter and raucous behaviour of the harmless kind. Joyce and Tom were sitting with Carla's mother and Trudy, and they had got through quite a few jugs of sangria between them.

Adam looked over at his parents and drew Carla's attention to them. 'They're really different now,' he said.

'In what way?' Carla asked, curious to know what had prompted the comment.

'Well, they talk more, laugh more. Dad used to be so sullen all the time and I just thought that was his personality, but since it all came out about him not being my real dad he's been much happier. It's odd.'

'Not really, Ads. Your dad had totally accepted you as a son from the minute you were born – probably before – and all the time you were unaware of the situation he might have been worried that a day would come, after you'd been told, when you might decide to go off on some crusade to find your biological father; he was probably terrified of losing you. The dreaded day of you being told came and you openly showed him that he was your dad through and through – the only dad you want. So now he can relax and fully enjoy his family.'

'That's great, if that's how it is. Look at them sitting there having fun and Dad holding Mum's hand – I've never seen that before. Either things are changing or I'm just noticing more.'

Carla stopped her bustling around for a moment and smiled softly at the newly happy couple. 'Come on,' she urged, 'let's get this food on to plates and get them fed. The kids want to treat the adults to being waited on, so will you gather them round to get started, please, sweetheart?'

Trudy sidled up alongside Carla. 'So is lover boy waiting or being waited on?' she whispered with a nudge and a wink.

'I'll let you know which tomorrow morning,' Carla whispered back, giggling.

'Is your mum having the kids?' asked Trudy with a wide grin.

Carla nodded and gave Trudy one of her saucy *oh yes* looks.

While the children sat around wrapped in towels eating hot dogs and bags of crisps, Adam had gone upstairs to Carla's room to change out of his trunks, only to find out he had not brought pants with him. Grinning to himself that he would have to go 'commando', he pulled his shorts on, taking particular care zipping up the fly.

Although his skin was smarting from the sun, plunging in and out of the cold water had made him feel good, but he'd wanted to get back into more clothes because Verity was paying him too much attention, even leering a little, due the number of glasses of wine she had drunk, he assumed. Hopefully, eating something would have sorted her out a bit. He didn't altogether blame her for her behaviour because that husband of hers seemed very odd: he had caught him looking his way once too often and wondered if he disapproved of him being there, or something; whatever his problem was, he made Adam uncomfortable – they both did. He remembered that when he first met Verity she had been crying, so obviously something was very wrong there.

As he made his way down the stairs, he couldn't believe it and was none too happy when he met Verity coming up, both of them reaching the wide step at the turn in the stairs at the same time.

'Oh, hello,' said Verity, still obviously very tipsy. 'You've changed out of your trunks.'

'Er ... yes.' She was looking at him in that leering way again and he felt really awkward being alone with her. He backed up against the wall to let her pass, but she wasn't interested in doing that.

'You're very good friends with Carla, aren't you Adam?' she said, moving closer to him. 'Do you just do her garden or are there other services that you offer?'

She had such a silly expression on her face, made worse by the smudged makeup under her eyes, that Adam felt slightly sickened by her attempt to be flirtatious. He tried to have some compassion for her, but it was difficult, feeling cornered, as he did.

'The reason I ask is 'cos I'd like you to come and "garden" for me.' She emphasised the quotation marks with her fingers, to make sure Adam understood her meaning, after which she became bolder and placed both of her hands on his chest.

Adam tensed, wondering how to extricate himself from this predicament. He didn't want to be rude and manhandle her out of the way.

'Adam,' she breathed into his face, running her fingers over his chest hair, 'would you come to my house, one day, and we can talk about how you can garden for me?' Her hands were making their way towards his abdomen and she gently tugged at the line of hair that travelled from his navel and disappeared below the waist band of his shorts. 'You're a very sex-u-al man, Adam.'

Her drawn out use of the word made him cringe and he decided it was time to take control. He moved her hands carefully away from his chest. 'Come on, let's get back to party,' he said, squeezing past her. Considering her inebriated state, Verity very nimbly managed to follow close on his heels and arrive at the bottom of the stairs with him.

Laughing, she grabbed his hand, pulled him into the lounge and kicked the door to, leaning back against it so that it shut with a resounding and ominous click, causing Adam to feel that his fate was sealed. He began to feel vulnerable and totally out of his depth. It was obvious Verity had issues but he was not prepared for this onslaught. He reached behind her to open the door and she pushed herself against his body, seeking his mouth with hers. She was quite tall and their lips briefly touched before he managed to jerk to one side to avoid her, after which he pushed her away but she moved in front of the door again, deliberately barring his way.

Laughing again and swaying a little unsteadily, she licked her lips and murmured, 'You taste salty, Adam. What else have you got that tastes like that?'

'Stop this, Verity!' he said firmly.

She looked at him like a petulant child. 'Why? You "please" Carla, don't you? So why can't you do the same for me? You obviously have a penchant for older women.' She had some difficulty with the word 'penchant' – it was noticeably slurred.

Now he was becoming angry, both with himself and Verity. How had he allowed himself to wind up in this position? More to the point: how the hell was he going to get out of it? 'Verity, I'm not a male prostitute. I'm Carla's friend and I do maintenance work on the house and garden for her; my mother does her cleaning, and I'm Stefan's rugby coach. She doesn't hire me for sex.'

'Do you have sex, though?'

Adam was outraged. 'None of your bloody business! And this has gone far enough!'

He tried for the door again and she took advantage of his proximity to put her hands on his chest again; he stepped back, she followed and just at that moment, the door burst open and Paul was standing there, looking at Adam with sheer venom in his eyes. Carla was standing behind him, taking in the situation and ready to act on Adam's behalf. She put her hand on Paul's arm in an attempt to come into the room with him but he angrily shook her off.

Everything was happening very fast: both Adam and Verity had been startled by the door suddenly opening, and, at the sight of Paul, Verity had instantly withdrawn her hands from Adam's chest. For a brief second, he had assumed Paul would have seen that and was taken aback by his murderous glare. His eyes were bloodshot and bulbous with rage; a fine layer of sweat covered his top lip – more to do with alcohol than the heat of the day. Stepping into the room, he stood just inches away from the young man. They were of equal height but Adam had not been drinking. Despite this advantage, he was intimidated, backing away with his hands help up defensively.

'You don't understand,' he protested.

'Oh, trust me, I understand perfectly! Who the hell do you think you are, strutting around the place half-naked, flexing your muscles? You like having women falling at your feet, don't you? It's a challenge, isn't it? Something to laugh about with your mates in the pub. Everything about you smacks of cheap bravado. You're nothing, do you hear? You really are *just a pretty face*!' He paused, noticing the young man begin to bristle and sensing strong fists beginning to clench. He knew he was no physical match for this young pup. He turned on his heel and made for the door. As he did so, he threw a last comment over his shoulder: 'I should have finished you off in that alley.'

Adam and Carla stood in stunned silence as Paul grabbed Verity by the arm and pushed her out of the room ahead of him and towards the open kitchen door, barking to the children to get round to the car *'right now!'*.

'Paul!' called Carla, running to the front door. 'He shouldn't be driving!' she exclaimed anxiously as he started the engine and drove off.

'Someone would have had to deck him to stop him, Carla,' said Adam, leading her back into the lounge. His head was buzzing with adrenalin and he dropped on to the sofa to calm down. 'Did he say what I thought he said?'

Carla sat down beside him and put a comforting arm round his shoulders. She was as shocked as he was. 'Yes, he did! God, Adam, he just let slip that it was him who attacked you!'

'Why would *he* attack me? I don't know him – never even met him before today.'

'Because of me, I think,' said Carla with rising horror. 'He made a pass at me months ago and said a lot of things that made the whole thing feel really weird. I even thought at the time that he sounded a bit obsessed. He hasn't tried anything since. I can't believe what he's done!'

'The man's a nutter! And that wife of his ...'

'They were both pretty drunk – not that that's any excuse. God, I'm so sorry, Adam! We have to tell the police! Poor Verity ... and the children! Oh Adam, this is all so horrible.'

'It can wait until tomorrow. There's no point in doing anything now,' Adam reasoned, now much calmer than Carla, who was getting more worked up by the second, 'and I don't want those two to spoil our night together. Your other guests will be wondering what's going on too, if we don't get back out to them, and there are the boys to think about, so let's just go out, make some excuse and carry on with the party.'

Carla looked at him with concern in her eyes. 'Is that what you want?' she asked

'Absolutely! Let's forget it all for now.'

'Well ... okay.'

She smiled at him and his heart skipped a beat. What a smile! As he followed her out of the door, he caressed her buttocks. 'Never a dull moment!' he whispered in her ear, pulling her against him, intending her to feel his heat through her cotton dress, as he nuzzled her neck. 'I want to be inside you,' he murmured, 'and later, when I am inside you, I'm going to so enjoy making you feel like a woman.'

Carla could still feel the heat of him as she moved among the remaining guests in the garden. Stefan and Bryn had come dashing over the minute Adam had reappeared and he was marshalling them off for another rough and tumble. Despite what had just happened, or because of it, she was determined that, later, she would open new doors for him and their night would be one of sensual passion and deeper than ever levels of intimacy.

As she checked that everyone was comfortable and had food and drink, she was grateful that none of the guests had come into the house during the fracas with Paul. No one seemed aware that anything had happened or that the family had left, and Carla decided that if anyone did ask about them, she would make the excuse that one of them wasn't feeling well.

She was so worried about Verity: her ailing marriage would be shattered by what was to come. Even if there was any option but to report Paul to the police, Verity had heard what he said and the whole sorry mess about his fixation would have to come out. She still couldn't quite believe that he had been serious about attacking Adam in the alley, wanting to think his statement had been some kind of bravado. But she couldn't convince herself. She had avoided Paul since the evening when he had come on to her. It had been far from a flattering experience: she had been unnerved by it because it had all felt somehow sinister. Now she knew why.

She looked at Adam's laughing young face as he played swing ball with the boys, his lithe body rippling as he moved. She recognised that she had decisions to make and responsibilities to bear, because he just wasn't old enough or experienced enough to be able to cope with the kinds of experiences being thrown at him as a result of their relationship. It would seem it had even been dangerous for him to be involved with her, which meant it was already past the time when they must consider very carefully what their future, if any, might be. For the rest of this day and the coming night, though, they would put all decisions on hold and just enjoy the time, while perhaps making some singularly precious memories.

It was six thirty by the time Mel had finished work, popped home to change and driven over to Carla's house, which she had not been to before but she knew the area well. She parked behind Joyce's car and checked her face in the rear view mirror. Why did she feel nervous? She was just joining her adopted family at a party – something she had done many times. That thought did nothing to quash her nerves, and she knew the reason for them had everything to do with seeing Carla and Adam together. Getting dressed to go out would normally be a quick wash, jeans and a T-shirt, and then a bit of eyeliner. Tonight, however, she had just about emptied her wardrobe looking for something in which she felt good, and had taken time to carefully apply more makeup than usual. Even she had been surprised to see the exotic result looking back at her from the mirror: being a bit of a tomboy, she didn't own much in the way of dresses and skirts, so she had chosen a pair of black evening trousers and an electric blue halter top to wear, which accentuated her dark skin and broad shoulders; her makeup added the perfect finish.

Taking a deep breath, Mel got out of her Ford Fiesta and walked up the tarmac drive towards the side gate, noticing Adam's bicycle leaning against the fence and hearing laughter coming from the back garden. Ignoring the butterflies in her stomach, she lifted the latch and walked in.

It took Adam a second or two to recognise the gorgeous creature who had just come into the garden, and he was so startled when he realised it was Mel that he took a swing ball directly to the temple, immediately clutched his head and crashed to his knees in intense pain, momentarily losing consciousness. He came to, to find he was stretched out on the grass looking up at Carla and Mel; his mother, who had got to him first, was cradling his head in her lap.

'Shit! What happened?' he exclaimed, wrestling his way out of Joyce's grasp and sitting up, aware of everyone staring at him.

'The ball hit you,' his mother explained. 'Just give yourself a minute,' she added as he tried to get up.

Stefan looked horrified and frightened, and was being hugged by his grandmother. 'Sorry, Adam,' he muttered nervously.

'Nice shot, champ,' said Adam. 'What do I always say about paying attention at all times? I obviously wasn't – and see what happens?'

'You okay, Ads?' asked Mel, peering at him anxiously.

'Yep. Fine!' He was so embarrassed that he had been knocked out by a swing ball.

'Adam, love, you have to be careful after what happened ... you know what I mean.'

Adam knew she was referring to the attack. 'Yes, I know, Mum. I'm fine!'

He looked up at Carla and Mel who were standing side by side looking at him intently, both with the same level of concern. He wasn't sure if it was because of the bang on the head, but he felt momentarily confused and didn't know what to say.

'Come on you!' ordered Carla, offering him a hand up. 'Let's go inside and put a cold flannel on that head, just in case there's any swelling.'

He put his arm round her as they walked up the garden towards the kitchen, watched by Mel. She turned away and caught Joyce looking at her. Was that pity on her face? She hoped not.

'You look lovely, Mel. We don't often see you all dressed up.'

Mel smiled weakly, already regretting being there.

Joyce picked up on her discomfort. 'Come and meet Trudy and Trevor while Tom gets you a drink.'

Mel wanted to go and see if Adam was all right but felt she would be stepping on toes, so she stayed put and attempted to engage in conversation.

'You've had quite a day of it, one way and another,' Carla commented as she bathed Adam's head in the upstairs bathroom. 'I'm so sorry, sweetheart.'

'You have nothing to be sorry about,' he said, pulling her hips towards him. He enjoyed her playing nurse, but he imagined her tending to her boys in much the same way when they were hurt – a thought he *didn't* enjoy – so he massaged her hips and then moved his hands round to her buttocks to give his thoughts something else to work on.

'Mel looks lovely this evening.'

Why did she say that? wondered Adam, looking her straight in the eye, hoping he could tell what she was thinking but he couldn't. The subject of Mel felt awkward between them and he wanted to deny noticing what she looked like, but that would have been ridiculous so he answered in the most open and mature way he could think of. 'Yeah, she looks great!'

Carla stopped what she was doing and looked down at him sitting on the side of the bath. She sighed and smiled, touching his cheek and sweeping the hair off his forehead.

'Don't!' he snapped, jerking his head away.

'Don't what?' she asked, taking a bewildered step back.

'Treat me like one of the boys!'

'What *are* you talking about?'

'Just then – the way you touched me and looked at me: you looked at me like I was a kid, Carla.'

Carla didn't reply but very deliberately put the flannel down on the basin and turned her eyes on him. At first, he thought she was angry with him, but then he noticed the look in those eyes and his heart began to pound. Taking his hand she pulled him to his feet, her eyes burning with the desire they had both been nurturing all day. She lightly traced her fingers across his chest, just as Verity had done, only this time Adam closed his eyes and partly opened his mouth. Carla noticed and slowly ran her finger over his lips before pushing it between his lips and moving it very slightly in and out of his mouth. He smiled. He knew.

'Adam,' she murmured, sliding her fingers down to his abdomen, 'there is nothing remotely motherly about what I'm about to do to you.' She gave him a light kiss and stepped away to close and lock the bathroom door. Turning back to him, she said, 'Take your clothes off. I'm going to fuck you.'

Adam raised his eyebrows at her turn of phrase and undid his shorts, looking at her and enjoying the moment as he allowed them to fall to the floor, leaving him naked.

She took direct hold of his erection and he gasped in surprise. 'No underwear? Tsk tsk,' she admonished, slowly moving his foreskin back and forth. 'Part your legs,' she breathed, kneeling in front of him to run her hands up and down his inner thighs while licking the glistening tip. 'Mmmmm, nice!'

Adam felt his knees go weak and he moaned as her warm hands cupped his sack and gently gripped. Taking him into her mouth, she continued the massaging and then slid him back and forth, building speed as his hands grasped the sides of her head, urging her on, until she pulled away and stood up.

'Sit on the edge of the bath,' she said, pulling her skirt up to just above her knees. 'Feel me,' she added, her voice full of longing.

Extremely aroused – the build up throughout the day now literally coming to a head – Adam slid his hand up her inner thigh and found her triangle of heat. She parted her legs to allow him easier access and he pushed his fingers through the hot folds of her most intimate area, causing her to moan and move against his fingers.

'Bring me to the edge, my darling.'

As he found her pleasure and massaged, slow at first and then quickening with her breathing, she reached down and rubbed her thumb over the tip of his penis. Adam could feel he was wet there and he nearly exploded in her hand. She lifted her thumb, seductively rubbed it across her lips and then slipped it into her already partially open mouth before grasping him and moving in time with his movements on her clitoris. The sound and feel of her arousal was bringing Adam to his climax, which Carla sensed.

'Hold me,' she panted, lifting her dress above her waist. 'I need to feel you inside me.'

With her arms clamped firmly around his neck, she put a leg either side of him, so that her feet rested in the bath, and lowered her wetness on to him. Once he was inside her she gazed directly into his eyes and Adam knew it wouldn't be long; the angle meant that he was in very deeply and Carla's grip around his neck tightened as he steadied her with his hands on her bare buttocks.

'Now, my sweet Adam, I'm going to fuck you!'

She rode up and down on him; he felt her grinding her pubic bone against him and his breath came fast and heavy as the blood coursed around his body.

'Adam, I'm coming! I'm coming!'

He felt her whole body tense and she bucked a few more times before stopping and clamping his head to her shoulder so that he could hardly breathe. Her grunting as her orgasm hit was the final straw for Adam and he felt his head go light as the pent up energy of their day's foreplay shot out of him, causing him to cry out in ecstasy.

They continued to move together as the waves slowed down, Adam holding her close as if never wanting to let her go. She felt his emotion and understood; in that moment she felt acute sadness.

Some moments later, she sat down with Joyce and assured her that Adam was fine and just having a lie down with a flannel on his head; she felt like a guilty teenager, telling stories. She then turned her attention to Mel, who was tucking into chicken and salad and laughing with Tom; he had a gentle, fatherly familiarity with her. 'Is that all right for you, Mel? It must be a bit dried up by now.'

'No, it's delicious, thanks Carla. I'm starving. I haven't eaten all day.'

The children were starting to get tired now, after the sun and excitement of the day, and everyone was just sitting around, relaxing in each other's company, when Adam returned to the garden, looking pink cheeked after his 'rest'; he could well have been asleep for a while. He offered to make tea and Mel watched him as he progressed around the guests taking orders.

'You all right, babe?' she asked, frowning up at him when he reached her.

Adam nodded and grinned at her. 'It was your fault, you know: you walked in and put me off my stroke.'

'Oh well, yes, it would be my fault!' she laughed. 'You can make me a milky coffee for that.'

'Yes ma'am!'

Mel looked at Joyce and raised her eyebrows as he took off in the direction of the kitchen. Joyce returned the look and then glanced over to Carla, who was taking it all in; she just smiled.

Later that evening Adam switched on the garden lights and the relaxed ambience continued. Adam, Mel and his parents had struck up a game of cards, something they did regularly according to Joyce, and the remaining guests, consisting of Trudy, Trevor, Jonathon and Barry, sat around the table on the deck, chatting and laughing. Carla's mother had taken the boys home to her house for the night – not that they had wanted to leave, but the promise of Nana's chocolate cake and lemonade had done the trick.

Carla went into the kitchen to clear away and put yet another load into the dishwasher, glancing every now and again out of the window. The darkness had brought a slight chill with it and she noticed that Adam had put his sweatshirt round Mel's shoulders while the family laughed and teased each other as hands of cards were thrown in and games lost. Adam's face as he focused on his cards and tried to work out what his opponents had was a picture, making her heart skip, especially as she remembered their passion just a few hours earlier and now looked forward to the night they would have to themselves: precious hours when their very different lives would collide in mutual bliss.

Adam's family were the last to leave.

Mel hugged Adam but didn't offer him a lift home or question why he was staying; she didn't need to. "Bye Ads.'

'See ya.'

She smiled at him as he stood barefoot with his hands in his pockets beside Carla, waiting to wave her off. She knew him almost as well as she knew herself; he was so much more than a brother but still just that little bit out of reach. She sighed and waved as she pulled away from the kerb, refusing to think about what they would be doing that night. It was none of her business, she told herself as she switched on the car radio, shook her head free of Adam and started to plan the week ahead.

With all the guests now gone, Carla and Adam turned and walked back into the house, their eyes meeting, filled with the promise of each other. The immediate, exquisite tension between them was so sweet they ignored the last of the clearing up, locked the back door, switched off the lights and went hand in hand up the stairs.

'Let's shower together,' Carla suggested softly as they reached her bedroom. 'I'd like to watch you take your clothes off.'

Adam enjoyed feeling her eyes on him as he lifted his arms and slipped off his vest top. With no underwear to prevent it, his shorts fell to the floor and he stepped out of them, naked, relaxed and intensely alive.

'Now you,' he said, relishing the fact that they could go at their own pace, free of any likelihood of interruption.

Carla simply unzipped her dress and eased it over her naked hips, letting it fall to the floor. Adam moved close and put his strong arms around her. She sighed, breathing in his scent and running her hands up and down his back. Feeling his arousal begin, she drew him into the bathroom and switched on the shower. They stood under the hot, steamy water and just touched and stroked each other, tenderly and lovingly with no urgency. Adam then hugged Carla from behind, running his hands over her breasts and stomach, moving himself up and down against her buttocks while she squirted gel into her hands, ready to wash him. She turned in his arms and soaped his body while he closed his eyes and enjoyed the sensation of her hands all over him.

They were both tired so they quickly dried each other and after both cleaning their teeth with Carla's toothbrush, got into the comfort of Carla's big, waiting bed and lay facing each other in the soft light of the bedside lamp. The early start combined with the heat and events of the day proved just too much for Adam: sleep quickly claimed him. Carla lay awake looking at his face for a long time, indulging in the luxury of being able to do that. From somewhere deep inside her, something was telling her to feast her eyes and fully experience the emotion, as there were few moments in life as tender as this.

* * * * *

EPILOGUE

As he emerged from sleep and his brain kick-started into wakefulness, Adam lay thinking about what the day ahead held for him. It dawned on him that it was Saturday; however, he did have clients coming in at ten and noon, so he would soon have to get up and into the shower. His eyes lazily roamed the cream walls with duck egg blue panels and came to rest on the two faces laughing out at him from the giant portrait on the opposite side of the room: Sebastian and Charlotte, aged five and three respectively. The picture had been taken the summer before on a day out in Broadstairs. It had been a great day, he remembered – simple, no fuss, an impromptu visit to build sand castles and eat ice cream. Funny, he thought, how spur-of-the-moment days often turned out the best, simple pleasures outshining meticulously planned picnics, theme parks or front row seats at the Christmas Panto.

He turned his head and looked at the mother of his children beside him. She was facing him, snoring softly, her mouth slightly open, one arm stretched up in front of her on the pillow, and a shaft of morning sun, coming through a chink in the curtains, was falling across her face. He felt warm and content, until a sly snake of a thought slithered its way into his mind: *it may not be for ever* it hissed and he physically brushed it away from his face, as if it were a trailing cobweb.

Why does the human brain do that? he pondered; the minute we feel we have things just how we want them, a bleak, dark thought comes along to rock the boat. Maybe that's how the subconscious insists we make the most of every day.

He rolled over and slid out of bed. As he stood up and stretched, he caught a glimpse of himself in the full length mirror on the wardrobe door and patted his stomach, turning sideways to take a good look. Yep! Not too bad! He was not particularly vain but he knew he had a good body. Well into his twenty eighth year, he had kept his taut, muscular frame by continuing to play rugby and making regular visits to the gym. He observed his rather impressive morning glory erection and, laughing silently to himself, crept out to the bathroom for a much needed pee.

'Daddy?'

'Shhh! Mummy's still asleep, Seb.'

'Daddy?' came a whisper just as loud. 'Is it getting up time?'

Adam groaned. He liked a little time to himself first thing in the morning, but then he liked being a dad far more, so he grabbed his dressing gown off its hook and made his way along the landing to see Seb's cheeky little face peeping out of his bedroom.

'Come on then, Seb – quietly though,' he whispered. 'Don't wake the others.'

Downstairs, he left Seb in front of the TV while he went into the kitchen to make tea. When the kettle clicked off, he poured water over the teabags in two mugs, let them brew for a minute and then removed one of the teabags to pop it into a little plastic mug, pouring water over the top.

Seb was watching *Peppa Pig* when his dad brought in his tea. 'Thank you, Daddy,' he said without taking his eyes off the screen.

'Okay, champ. Don't spill it.'

'No, I won't.'

Adam doubted that but left him to it, making his way upstairs with the other two mugs and slowly pushing open the bedroom door. She was still fast asleep but had turned over to lie flat on her stomach – her favourite position. Putting both mugs on the bedside table he briefly considered getting back into bed for a quick cuddle. He looked at the clock: there was only just time for a shower followed by a bowl of cocoa pops. With a sigh, he turned to go to the bathroom but noticed movement in the bed and slowly lifted the quilt off his wife's body. She mumbled an objection and fumbled to get the quilt back over her nakedness. He had seen his chance though, and before she could cover up again he leapt on top of her and straddled the backs of her knees, planting a loving kiss on the little round tattoo that he loved so much.

Parking was so much easier in the city on Saturdays, but Adam still liked to cycle in as it burned some calories and meant he could go right to the office door. He opened up and put the coffee on, then picked up the post still waiting to be dealt with from the previous day; he also had some case notes to write up.

The front door banged around nine and he recognised the sounds of his receptionist, Verity, putting her keys and bag on her desk. When he went out to greet her, he raised his eyebrows appreciatively and she gave him a twirl.

'What do you think Mr Barnes?'

'Very smart indeed Ms Stanford. Special occasion?'

'Actually, yes, Stuart's taking me out to lunch with his new girlfriend and her recently divorced father.'

'Verity! That sounds like a blind date to me!'

'Exactly! Although after the success of the last few I'm not sure I'm cut out for dating.'

'Where's Jo? Is she going with you?'

'No, she's up with her father this weekend; they're taking little Joshua to London Zoo. She'll love it, although I do wonder if Paul sometimes uses her as an unpaid child minder. '

Adam chose not to respond.

'I know! I know!' she sighed. 'I'm being mean! The little lad is her brother, after all.'

Adam gave her a peck on the cheek. 'He's paid his debt to society, Verity.'

'I know. Losing his freedom, his family and his career was punishment enough. I suppose I begrudge him his new family whenever I'm reminded of it.'

Adam grinned mischievously. 'Maybe your special someone is nearer than you think ... maybe you'll meet him tonight!'

'I'm not holding my breath,' retorted Verity with a wry smirk.

'Well, you look lovely, anyway. Now, who have we got coming in today?'

Verity looked at the big office diary that was kept in the drawer of her desk. 'Mr and Mrs Speedwell at ten – their second visit – and a Mr Thompson at noon; he's coming on his own.'

'Oh, that sounds ominous,' he said as he made his way back into his office to read through his notes before the first appointment. 'Coffee's in the pot, Verity,' he called as he shut the door behind him.

His ten o'clock appointment arrived on time and after a few minutes of being in the couple's company he could see that things had certainly improved: they were no longer the grey faced people who had come into his consulting room the previous month. At the end of their allotted time he walked them back out into reception. 'Just one more appointment for Mr and Mrs Speedwell please, Verity – in four weeks.'

'Certainly Mr Barnes.' Just as Verity took the diary out the phone rang. Excusing herself, she picked up the receiver. 'Barnes and Trelawny. How can I help you?' Verity beamed when she heard who was on the other end. 'Oh Carla! How lovely to hear your voice! Yes, yes, he's here. I'll just put you through.'

Adam said his goodbyes to his clients and went into his office to pick up the receiver. 'Thanks, Verity. Hello, beautiful! How is LA? Hang on, isn't it the middle of the night there?'

'Oh, Ads, yes, but I couldn't sleep and I'm having one of my I-miss-cold- damp-England moments. Tell me all the news.'

Adam updated his business partner and close friend on how Barnes and Trelawny, Specialists in Relationship Management, was continuing to develop. Carla was pleased with the progress and told of equally solid success in Barnes and Trelawny USA. They spoke for a further ten minutes and then Verity put her head around the door to say that Mr Thompson had arrived.

'Off you go, Ads. Give my love to Mel and the kids. Love you.'

'Love you too, Carla. Tell those sons of yours to look after you.'

''Bye, sweetheart.'

Adam took a moment to reflect on the memorable time ten years before, when they had come into each other's lives. Their love had not only changed their lives but the lives of so many people around them. It had broken his heart the day after the party when Carla had said she was letting him go. He had sobbed like a baby. She had held him and cried with him, but she had stayed resolute and strong.

'The best gift I can give you, right now, is your freedom. Yes, we could carry on like this, having great sex, but I can't give you what you'll ultimately want and need, my beautiful Adam. I love you dearly, but I'll only ever be completely in love with one man, and he's waiting for me in another place. You need to be someone's number one, my Adam, not my second best.'

Mel had been there to pick up the pieces. Mel was always there to pick up the pieces. She had taken the lead and gently loved him until his broken heart had mended. Now, as he looked at the picture of his family that he kept on his desk, he felt blessed – so very blessed.

He had continued to work for Carla and they had developed a friendship that was deeply important to both of them; it had resulted in them starting the business five years later, after Adam had gone to college and then university to study psychology.

He welcomed a harassed-looking, unhappy and extremely nervous Mr Thompson into his consulting room. After offering him coffee and being refused, Adam sat down on the sofa opposite him. 'How can I help you, Mr Thompson?'

The man fidgeted and looked at the ceiling self-consciously. 'Well, Mr Barnes, I don't really know how to say this, but I think I've forgotten how to make my wife happy.'

Adam's smile reached his twinkling, cornflower blue eyes and graced the man opposite him.

'Then you've come to the right place,' he assured him.

'Yes, I believe so. You certainly come highly recommended, Mr Barnes. Nevertheless, now I've met you, I hope you don't mind me saying that you seem very young to be a relationship counsellor.'

Adam laughed and nodded . 'You're not the first to say that, Mr Thompson. What you don't know, of course, is that I had a very good teacher.'

* * * * * *

For more information or to contact Jill Tipping, please visit:

www.jilltipping.co.uk